ONE
LAST
SUMMER

ALSO BY KATE SPENCER

In a New York Minute

ONE LAST SUMMER

Kate Spencer

FOREVER

New York Boston

Copyright © 2024 by Kate Spencer

Cover design and illustration by Holly Ovenden.
Cover copyright © 2024 by Hachette Book Group, Inc.

Hachette Book Group supports the right to free expression and the value of copyright. The purpose of copyright is to encourage writers and artists to produce the creative works that enrich our culture.

The scanning, uploading, and distribution of this book without permission is a theft of the author's intellectual property. If you would like permission to use material from the book (other than for review purposes), please contact permissions@hbgusa.com. Thank you for your support of the author's rights.

Forever
Hachette Book Group
1290 Avenue of the Americas, New York, NY 10104
read-forever.com
@readforeverpub

First Edition: June 2024

Forever is an imprint of Grand Central Publishing.
The Forever name and logo are registered trademarks of Hachette Book Group, Inc.

The publisher is not responsible for websites (or their content) that are not owned by the publisher.

The Hachette Speakers Bureau provides a wide range of authors for speaking events. To find out more, go to hachettespeakersbureau.com or email HachetteSpeakers@hbgusa.com.

Forever books may be purchased in bulk for business, educational, or promotional use. For information, please contact your local bookseller or the Hachette Book Group Special Markets Department at special.markets@hbgusa.com.

Library of Congress Cataloging-in-Publication Data

Names: Spencer, Kate, 1979- author.
Title: One last summer / Kate Spencer.
Description: First edition. | New York : Forever, 2024.
Identifiers: LCCN 2023054971 | ISBN 9781538737668 (hardcover) | ISBN 9781538737675 (e-book)
Subjects: LCGFT: Romance fiction. | Novels.
Classification: LCC PS3619.P4653 O54 2024 | DDC 813/.6--dc23/eng/20231204
LC record available at https://lccn.loc.gov/2023054971

ISBNs: 9781538737668 (hardcover), 9781538737651 (ebook)

Printed in Canada

MRQ

Printing 1, 2024

For my dad, who has always loved and accepted me just as I am
(1 percent amazing, 99 percent a pain in the butt).
And in memory of my mom, always and forever.

ONE
LAST
SUMMER

1

THE TEXT MESSAGES from my assistant, Lydia, came through back-to-back at exactly 7:24 p.m., announced by two beeps chirping from my phone, like baby birds fighting over a worm from their mother.

OMG. Clara!!!

Charles is ENGAGED.

????????? I replied, smashing the question mark key until the tip of my index finger ached. This was the universal text message bat signal for Ex-Boyfriend Panic, and I was now deep in it.

Just the sight of Charles's name sent my sweat glands immediately into overdrive. It didn't help that I was already an anxious mess over the disaster on the computer screen in front of me. If there was ever a moment for my drugstore antiperspirant to show off its promise of forty-eight-hour "protection," this was it.

After waiting through the longest minute of my life, I finally shot up from my desk with an exasperated huff and rocketed out of my little corporate cave, plowing straight into a wall of sensible, pale-blue collared shirts tucked into equally sensible khaki pants. I'd landed behind the sales team, and right smack in the middle of the Summer Friday happy hour I was definitely supposed to be attending.

In the center of it all was Amaya Conrad, our company founder and CEO, dinging the edge of her iPhone against a plastic cup of champagne. She'd never met a toast she didn't love to give, especially when it was about all the money Four Points was raking in. And this quarter, Four Points' earnings had "been lit," according to a recent company-wide email she'd sent.

Lydia had scrunched her nose in horror when she'd read it. According to her, forty-somethings using Gen Z slang was "cringy." Lucky for me I was only thirty-five, so she cut me some slack when I did the same.

"I'm so thrilled to celebrate our biggest quarter yet!" Amaya shouted through a cupped hand as she simultaneously kicked off her Valentino rock-stud pumps with the gusto only a buzzed person could muster.

She practically tossed her drink to her assistant, Abe, who had taken up his usual spot, hovering dutifully just a few inches off to her side. Then, with a grunt, she pushed herself up to stand on a chair. Stepping onto his pristine white desk, she steadied herself with the edge of his computer screen before grabbing her cup back, chugging whatever was left, and pumping her fists in the air.

Oh, yeah. Definitely drunk.

I glanced down at my text messages—still nothing—and then back at Amaya, who was pontificating about the many ways in which Four Points was "the freaking G.O.A.T. of creative marketing here in Boston. We are the Tom Brady of branding. You could literally call us Tom Branding!" Oh, man. Someone was going to be chasing ibuprofen with Gatorade tomorrow morning.

I gave my phone another impatient glance. "Come on," I murmured under my breath, which elicited a stern look from…Mark? Mike? Our sales team was made up entirely of straight dudes with M names, and they all seemed to blur together into an amorphous blob of button-down shirts or fleece vests, depending on the season.

Engaged to who? I tapped out as my heart ping-ponged around my chest.

Blocking Charles across the internet had done wonders for my post-breakup mental health. But it had also severely restricted my favorite hobby of late-night internet sleuthing and falling down social media rabbit holes. I had no idea what he'd been up to since he'd unceremoniously dumped me in the middle of the Public Gardens last year with the casual disgust of a person discovering a week-old cup of coffee in their car console and emptying it out in the street.

Not being able to stalk Charles online hadn't stopped me from obsessively wondering, of course. Crafting elaborate fantasies of my ex miserable and regretting his decision was a skill I'd honed over this past year: Charles, devastated when he couldn't remember our Netflix password (it's B@@bs69, which was obviously hilarious but never made him laugh). Charles, restless and grumpy waiting for his drink at the Starbucks counter, crumbling when they called out an order for someone with my name.

None of these concocted tales included Charles falling in love with another human, much less proposing marriage. But it was fine. And I was fine! Totally fine. He was my ex; he could get engaged to whomever he liked.

After all, I was also off doing my own thing. I'd bought a new vacuum this year, one of those futuristic handheld thingies that cost a small fortune but can suck up an entire spilled bag of Dorito crumbs in, like, three seconds flat.

When I hadn't been self-soothing with late-night internet shopping, I'd been channeling my energy into work, like the looming proposal that was currently causing me acid reflux, for Boston's very hip, woman-owned brewery, Alewife.

Our pitch—selling them on why we should brand and launch their new Summer Ale—was in exactly two weeks. Current status: a total fucking mess, and my chest tightened at the thought of it, the same kind of heart-racing, jaw-clenching anxiety that had become my constant companion.

I'd be fixing it tonight, all night if I had to.

I was absolutely, completely fine.

Amaya's voice cut through the din of jumpy thoughts in my head.

"You all are killing it out there." Her face crumpled ever so slightly, like a parent about to weep at their kid's high school graduation. "I'm so proud, and so deeply honored to know each and every one of you."

I clapped along, following the lead of the Mikes and Marks in front of me. My phone buzzed in my hand, setting off a jolt of adrenaline that electrified every muscle in my body.

Finally!

But the new message at the top of my screen wasn't from Lydia at all.

There, instead, was my oldest camp friend, Sam Cohen; she'd sent a photo of her face—framed by her gorgeous, dark ringlets—peeking out from under a white cap on her head. Her cheeks were rounder, with circles under those familiar, wise eyes, and she was pointing a finger at the logo on her hat, a dark green pine tree, complete with an exaggerated pout.

It was a photo designed to make me feel guilty, and it definitely worked. I'd missed our last five reunions at Pine Lake Camp, and tomorrow our old crew of camp friends was making the annual trek up to the woods of northern New Hampshire without me, yet again.

This had been the year I swore I'd finally get back up there, workload be damned. I'd even ordered a sleeping bag online from L.L. Bean and then took a nap in it on the couch surrounded by piles of notes I'd taken researching New England breweries. But then the Alewife pitch took over my life, and there was no way I could head off to New Hampshire with it unfinished. So I'd bailed on Pine Lake again this year, certain that my friends would understand why.

I tapped out a crying emoji face to Sam in reply just as Lydia's text came through.

Not tagged, Lydia wrote. Cute though. Looks like he did it on a swan boat. Want me to screenshot it?

The words registered with shock, like someone holding an ice cube to the back of my neck.

Those ancient red boats, with their beautiful carved swans on each side, circled around a murky pond in the middle of the Public Garden. I'd lived in the city for over a decade and never once ridden them, because, well, who on earth actually did any of the cash-grabby, touristy things in their own city? Surely no New Yorker ever walked across the Brooklyn Bridge. I'd never once been to Paul Revere's House, and that was, like, less than a mile from my apartment.

But the swan boats had meant something to Charles, who'd grown up just steps away in the South End and had loved riding them as a kid. And so for his thirty-sixth birthday, I'd indulged him, planning a date night that started with a boat ride and ended with a picnic in the park. An emergency meeting at work upended our five p.m. meet-up plans, and I raced over a little after seven with a bottle of wine and a mouthful of apologies. But I was too late—to save our date or our relationship.

"I've done some thinking," Charles had said.

"Huh?" He'd caught me off guard, right in the middle of digging through my tote bag for a tissue to wipe the sweat off my forehead that had accumulated after power-walking ten blocks.

"I don't know if I'm in love with you anymore." His delivery was matter-of-fact, like he was reciting data points off a presentation rather than ending our eight years together.

"Because of me missing the fucking swan boats?" I'd yelled back, almost knocking out a nearby goldendoodle with the Pinot Noir in my hand.

"No, it's not that. It's not you. You're the best." He'd stepped forward and rested both his hands on my shoulders, giving them a gentle squeeze as I blinked back in disbelief. "You do everything right. I just don't think that's what I want anymore."

At least after all that, I'd found a tissue.

Sam sent through a broken heart emoji, recentering my thoughts onto camp for a moment. When had I last seen her? She'd been in Boston a few years ago with her now ex-wife, Regan, for a wedding. Maybe then. But I couldn't remember the last time we'd really talked, besides the occasional text. Our friendship had fallen by the wayside over the years, life's collateral damage, pushed aside in favor of sticking to the path I'd so meticulously laid out ahead of me. I really owed her a phone call and some dedicated catch-up time, but there was no way to do that now.

Miss you! I typed back, as Amaya let out a high-pitched "wooooo!" and suddenly my attention was back in the room. Drunk Amaya didn't come out very often, but when she did, she was even more intense than the sober version, which was saying a lot.

"Four Points' mission is more than just selling products and producing events. It's about creating a pathway to people's emotions, and hearts," Amaya gushed, beaming from above. "But we can't do this work unless we take care of our own emotions too."

Amaya's belief in her own brilliance was more enviable than annoying, but it also meant she rarely backed down once an idea took hold, whether it was a creative brand theme or a company-wide meditation class, which she'd implemented last fall.

This combo of laser focus and uber-confidence was how she'd built

Four Points into the kind of company that had won the local marketing trade mag's Agency of the Year award for three years straight. But it also made her, occasionally, slightly terrifying. Like right now, for example.

"Burnout is real," she lamented, her tone now boss-serious. "And it not only can destroy us individually, but it can wreck a company's success if it's not addressed head-on."

Someone gently bumped my arm with their shoulder, and I turned to find Lydia squeezed in next to me as Amaya's voice carried from overhead.

"I know this firsthand, which is why my yearly silent meditation retreat in Sedona is so vital to me as a person, and as your boss." She beamed down at us, our very own, slightly tipsy motivational speaker. "And so I'm proud to share with you today that we are implementing our new 'Four Points, Five Days' micro-sabbatical program, for folks to take breaks when needed. This will be in addition to the four weeks of vacation time everyone already currently gets."

One of the Mikes/Marks grunted out a "wow," and there was a smattering of applause from around the room. Someone on the other side of the gathering hollered out, "Slay!" and Amaya beamed.

"Yes." She nodded proudly. "This *does* slay."

Next to me, Lydia pressed a clenched fist to her mouth, trying to suppress a laugh.

"You can ask for a micro-sabbatical for yourself, of course," Amaya continued, "but this program is unique because your supervisor or your direct report can also suggest you take one. It's just one way we can look out for each other here."

Delilah, the designer working with me on the Alewife pitch, hooted excitedly nearby as the room erupted in boisterous, booze-fueled applause. I tried to stay focused, and in the room, but the news about

Charles had rattled me, and my thoughts spiraled back in time to our final conversation.

"Clara, look, I know we make sense together, like on paper," he'd said to me in a steady, patronizing voice. "But come on. There's no spark between us anymore. There's nothing sexy about spending most of our time together watching reruns of *Friends* and occasionally having sex. We're like roommates. I don't want to feel like I'm dating my sister, or, like, one of my fraternity brothers."

"Are you fucking kidding me right now?" I'd shouted through the foggy lens of tears, so loud a couple pushing a baby in a stroller had fully stopped in their tracks to gawk at us. "Your sister?"

But he had just shrugged and wrapped me in a tight, clinical hug.

"I really want you to be happy, Clara. Like, truly happy. Not just what you think happy should look like."

He'd said this with a firm nod before wandering off to sleep at his parents' house, leaving me to stumble home, blotchy-faced and weepy, polishing off that bottle of wine alone.

Now here, almost a year later, my shoulders twitched as the uncomfortable memory echoed through me. Nothing had hurt as much as that comment, not even the breakup itself. Something about it had felt too revealing, like he'd suddenly figured out something about me that I didn't yet understand.

The next morning I'd marched into the office with swollen eyes and a raging hangover, and informed Amaya that I wanted to take on a heavier workload as project manager, to see if I could gain some experience that could level me up to vice president even. She'd been vaguely alluding to a promotion in the months since, and I'd kept hustling, assuming it was just within reach.

One of the finance bros next to me gave me a friendly elbow jostle, and I popped my head up just in time to see Amaya windmilling her arms as she said with gusto, "—the person who has been here almost as long as I have. Let's give her a round of applause, shall we?"

I'd completely spaced out, and the roaring applause shook me out of the past and back into the room. I knew instantly who she was talking about, and the eager, curious faces of seventy-five of my colleagues—all frozen in my direction—confirmed it.

She was talking about me.

2

PULL YOURSELF TOGETHER, *Clara!* cried the alarm bells going off in my head. *It's happening! She's about to promote you in front of the entire office.*

The realization was so thrilling that my fake smile transformed into something genuine, proud even. I quickly puffed up my chest and tucked a loose strand of hair—the same stick-straight, bark-brown strand that would inevitably fall right in front of my eye in approximately thirty seconds—behind my ear.

All eyes were angled in my direction, and the two most important ones in the room were gazing down at me with such affection that I instantly felt guilty for totally tuning out what she'd been saying before.

"From intern to assistant to almost every other job in between, she's worked her way up to project manager, where she's juggling some of our biggest accounts. Clara, we all see how hard you bust your ass here at Four Points. How many of us have left to go home for the night, only to see the lights still on in Clara's office?"

There was a murmur of agreement from the crowd.

"Girl, you are an example to all of us." Grabbing her glass back from Abe, Amaya pointed it in my direction as she pressed her other hand against her chest, creasing the creamy silk blouse that looked both entirely effortless and perfectly put together.

"Thank you," I said with a polite nod. It was an attempt to be humble in front of a crowd, but inside I was full-on glowing. I'd dangled the fantasy of this promotion in front of my own face like a carrot, and it had been the only thing keeping me slogging along in the wake of this bleak, depressing year.

Charles can have his swan boat engagement, I thought. *I have this.*

"An example," she drew the words out slowly, seriously, "of burnout."

"Wait, sorry. What?" My chin practically dropped off my face in shock as I rewound her speech in my head, desperately trying to process exactly what was happening.

"She wants you to take a micro-sabbatical," Lydia hissed in my ear. "Like a vacation."

"Clara Millen, your Four Points, Five Days micro-sabbatical starts now," she said, bending forward, hands on her knees to look at me, as my colleagues laser-beamed their eyes onto my face. "Because you need it more than anyone else here."

Every drop of moisture exited my mouth until all that was left were dust and some teeth. All the grinding, and late nights, the years I'd spent following her instructions to a T, and the last twelve months of foaming-at-the-mouth devotion to my job and she was...

...diagnosing me with burnout, like she'd run me through some sort of internet quiz? Which, I recalled with a flush of shame, was something I had actually taken a couple of months ago thanks to an Instagram ad and which had, indeed, suggested that I might be kinda fried at work.

"But the Alewife pitch," was all I managed to squeak out as my hair slid—as predicted—right back into my face.

"Can wait," she said, chipper. "I want you to focus on *you* first."

Landing a major account like Alewife had been on my goal list for years, and I was mere days away from being able to put a giant check mark next to it. What the hell was happening?

"She was supposed to go to New Hampshire this week!" Lydia blurted out next to me, and Amaya's face lit up.

"Perfect!" she replied with a clap of her hands, tossing her empty cup on the floor below her.

"But I can't actually take a whole week off right now," I protested, trying desperately to keep a calm look on my face, even though inside, panic reigned. Sure, the pitch wasn't in the greatest shape, but I'd get it there. I always did.

Amaya thought for a moment, index finger tapping at her painted lips.

"Clara, tell me, in your own words. How are you feeling? Right now."

Exhausted. Confused. Like I wanted to cry and throw up at the same time, and then hide in my bed for approximately forty-eight hours.

"Fine," I countered.

"You know what a synonym for 'fine' is?" she asked.

"Good?" I ventured, my voice pitched and hopeful, like a kid desperately guessing on the final word of a spelling bee.

"No, Clara," she continued. "*Fine*" is code for terrible. When someone says they're fine, what they really mean is they've been working around the clock on something and getting nowhere but stressed out."

"Well, yeah." I let out an uncomfortable laugh, desperate to salvage this conversation. "But that something still needs a lot of work. That's why I can't just take time off next week."

"In order for the pitch to be better, I need *you* to be better," she said, and it was clear from her tone that Zen Amaya had been replaced by take-no-prisoners Amaya.

I swallowed hard, willing the tears that were rushing to the corners of my eyes back where they came from.

"Okay," I said quietly. If I could just keep my face emotionless and steady, then no one would see the mortification that was bubbling up just underneath the surface. But I caught Delilah's face out of the corner of my eye, and the pity etched across her brow was enough to send my shoulders clenching. I pressed my lips tightly together in a futile attempt to quell the panic that was overtaking me.

"This is going to be so good for you, Clara." Amaya summoned me toward her with a wave. "*Healing,* even."

The Mikes and Marks parted as I awkwardly stepped forward until I was face-to-face with her waist. She bent down and wrapped her arms around me.

"Can't this wait until after the pitch?" I pleaded, stiffly leaning in to her embrace.

"Clara, we just announced it in front of the entire office," she said, her voice low. "It's official."

Because I wasn't already humiliated enough, her diamond tennis bracelet snagged in my hair as she pulled away. All I could do was stand there, cheeks flushed, as Abe rushed forward and gingerly yanked us apart.

"See, everyone?" she said, once we were separated. "This is how I want you to support your teams, the people you manage, and your managers. I expect my inbox to be inundated with time-off requests. I can't wait to hear all about your plans. And now, we celebrate!"

The room exploded in giddy applause, and soon everyone was grouping off into their collective work cliques, Rihanna thumping from a nascent desk speaker somewhere.

I rushed back into my office before someone could corner me in conversation about my newly announced vacation and plopped down in my chair, dumbfounded. My eyes settled on my trusty spiral-bound notebook. Aside from Lydia, this thing was my best friend. I'd spent weeks agonizing over the cover color (sea-foam blue) and paper style (dotted) alone.

The notebook was flipped open to my current scribbled to-do list from hours earlier. The words taunted me with their ignorance of what was to come. This morning I'd titled it "Clara's Friday To-Do List: Get It Done And Go Home!!!" which now seemed a bit on the nose after Amaya's proclamation. I plucked my favorite pen off my desk and pressed its round point against the paper with an exasperated, emotional huff.

Directly underneath "Print budget PDF for review," I drew a small square and wrote, "Have life thrown into a tailspin" next to it, practically carving the words into the paper.

And then I checked it off.

3

"HEY, BOSS. I thought you might need this." Lydia hustled into my office clutching a stack of cardboard containers in her arms, tucked under her chin for balance. The savory scent of French fries washed over me like a siren song, and my stomach immediately responded with a greedy growl.

"Here." She passed me one that was overflowing with crisp, matchstick fries, and a greasy, paper-wrapped burger. "Extra pickles."

"Hell yes, thank you." I reached forward eagerly, barely getting the words out before inhaling a handful of fries, so hot they singed the roof of my mouth.

"I hope it's okay that I yelled out about your New Hampshire trip. I swear I was just trying to help," she said, offering me an apologetic look as she flopped down on the modern, steel-gray love seat next to my desk. "You looked shook, like you were about to freak out."

"Oh, I'm not about to freak out," I said, tearing open a packet of ketchup with my teeth.

"Well, that's good—"

"I'm already there. I'm in def-con five, the world's about to explode, and mankind as we know it will be extinct freakout."

"Oh." Lydia's face fell, bright pink lips pursed with worry.

"It's not your fault, Lyd," I said through bites. "You didn't know Amaya was going to make me the poster child for burnout in front of the entire office."

"Yeah, that was wild." She wrinkled her nose, giving me a sympathetic look.

"And you know how much stuff we still have left to do!" I smacked at my notepad with the back of my hand to make my point. "We're so far in the hole on this thing. How am I supposed to fix it if I'm not here? I know for a fact that Amaya secretly checks her email when she's on that ridiculous silent yoga retreat. She's so full of shit."

Lydia rolled her eyes in solidarity. "She has serious main character energy. It's terrifying. But..."

I raised brows at her, impatient. "But what?"

"But, it's not the worst idea she's ever had. I don't think you've taken a full week off since I've been here, and I'm going on three years." She very purposefully avoided my stare and propped her laptop on the edge of my desk, flipping it open to the PowerPoint we'd been working on all week. This morning I'd spent an hour obsessing over a slide featuring an animated pint glass only to delete the entire presentation in a fit of frustrated rage.

"Excuse you." I reached over and lowered the screen so she couldn't ignore me. "I went to South Carolina in March."

"For, like, your great-aunt's funeral," she scoffed.

"Yeah, but I totally saw the beach while I was there," I mumbled, taking another bite of my burger. "And I had dinner with my dad. That counts."

"Look, I don't mean to comment on your tendency to, like, be an extreme millennial, but your work–life boundaries could use some help." Lydia's brown eyes shifted as she studied me, in therapist mode. "Remember when you slept here?"

"It was one time! I fell asleep on the couch. It wasn't, like, planned."

It had actually been three times, but that was neither here nor there.

"Whatever you say," she replied, though her tone said otherwise.

"Let me see the picture of Charles first." I flipped my palm open, demanding her phone. "This night's already a shitshow. I might as well just completely go balls to the wall."

"Seriously?" she asked with a raised brow, and when I didn't reply, she simply shook her head and handed it over.

A few clicks later and there they were, beaming in front of those giant, polished swans. She was cute. Muddy brown, straight hair, not much different from mine. A smattering of freckles across pasty white skin. Nice smile. She fit easily into the crook of Charles's arm, whereas I, at five foot ten, was always a smidge taller than him.

Charles looked completely different: His reddish hair was now shaggy and—I squinted just to be sure—he had a short, clipped beard. But it wasn't just the fact that he'd gone and given himself a makeover; it was something even bigger, more jarring: he looked relaxed. Happy. This was not the tightly wound Charles I knew, who constantly worried about things like hurricane preparedness and forgetting to take out his Invisalign before a meal.

I scrolled down to the next photo in his feed, the two of them red-faced, sweaty, and beaming, rackets in hand.

"Good lord, they play pickleball?" I dug around in my brain for any mention, any inkling of interest, that Charles might have expressed in pickleball. I came up blank.

"I thought everyone over thirty played pickleball," Lydia said.

"I don't play pickleball," I replied.

"Maybe you should," she countered. "Isn't having a hobby, like, a major part of self-care?"

"Right now, my hobby is Charles's Instagram." I swiped the screen gently so as not to accidentally hit the like button on any of his photos. "He's turned into a completely different person in, like, twelve months. Oh my god."

I paused and shot her a shocked look. "There's a photo of him camping, in jean shorts. *Jorts.*"

Lydia—whose wardrobe was almost entirely made up of vintage scores from the By the Pound floor of the Garment District—turned her mouth down in horror. "Well. That's just poor sartorial judgment."

"I know, but"—I spun around in my chair to face her—"he's morphed into this entirely different person, and all I have to show for myself since we broke up is that I'm doing a shit job at work and am so burned out I have to be forced to take time off."

"Don't let Amaya get in your head," Lydia said, grabbing the phone out of my hand.

"Oh, it's way too late for that," I grumbled.

"They went to Tulum!" she cooed, tapping her bejeweled nails on the screen. "God, this looks amazing. Now I want fish tacos."

"You should have told Amaya I wanted to go to Mexico instead of New Hampshire."

The words came out more bitter than intended. It wasn't that I didn't want to spend time with my friends at Pine Lake, a place that conjured up memories like an old song on the car radio. But heading back there meant revisiting cherished relationships I'd neglected, all for a job I apparently sucked at.

"Clara." Lydia crossed her arms in front of her chest, assuming her favorite no-nonsense position. "You're a fucking rock star. Just because you need a little break doesn't mean you're not good at what you do. This place isn't going to collapse without you. Go try to get some sleep."

"What's sleep?" I joked, just as my phone buzzed on my desk.

"Do you even hear yourself?" Lydia snapped back as I wiped my hands with a scrunched-up pile of napkins.

I did hear myself. I sounded defensive, panicked, even. This wasn't me, I reasoned. But when I paused to think about what was me, especially lately, I came up blank, empty—just like the PowerPoint on my screen.

4

"CLARE-BEAR!" SAM'S face was tiny and cloaked in darkness on my phone screen. "I'm just trying one more time to peer-pressure you into coming up to Pine Lake this weekend. I want to wake you up by throwing socks on your face."

The memory of fifteen-year-old Sam chucking her clothes at me as specks of morning sun snuck in through the cabin windows flashed in my mind. It was a good one that shone brightly in an otherwise hard summer. Things had been raw and unsettled at home before I'd left for camp that year, but nothing could have prepared me for the letter I'd gotten one afternoon from my mom, informing me that she'd told my dad she wanted a separation.

Sam had wandered into the bunk shortly after I'd opened it and found me listening to Fiona Apple on my iPod and sobbing into my sweatshirt sleeves. She'd promptly marched me to the camp store, still in tears, and bought me three packs of Reese's Peanut Butter Cups, which we ate side by side, our feet dangling off the edge of the dock that stretched out into the lake.

"You are not going to believe this," I said, panning the phone to show Lydia behind me, who greeted Sam with a wiggle of her fingers. "But my assistant Lydia is going to hold things down here so I can come."

Before I could tell Sam the uncomfortable reason why, she shouted, "Shut up!", her voice crackling through the phone speaker as relief settled across my body. Eventually I'd tell Sam the real reason my plans had changed. But Amaya's public pronouncement was too raw, too fresh to even discuss.

"I will not shut up," I said, forcing what I hoped passed for a cheery smile onto my face. "I think I can make it after all."

"Oh my god, this is the best news. I'll put you on the group chat. Nick and Trey are flying in on a red-eye from Oakland tonight, so I bet you could ride up with them in the morning. And Mack's going to be excited."

Mack's name was almost enough to distract me from the fact that there was a text chain out there for our group of camp friends, and I wasn't on it. My constant absence had pushed me outside of our inner circle, and I felt the taste of shame in the back of my throat.

"Mack will be excited to tease me about old camp stuff and accuse me of being a corporate sellout," I said with a groan. Even though I hadn't seen him in years, I knew exactly what to expect from Mack, who was both obnoxiously "chill" and always up for anything, including ribbing me. He would have a field day with the news of my boss forcing me to take a vacation.

"Oh, please, you've always been on his case, too, with your Color Week captain bullshit. Just because your teams tied and you both couldn't handle not winning. And you still can't. The two of you are cut from the same cloth," Sam teased. "He just refinished the boathouse, by the way."

"That's because he lives in the boathouse," I snapped back, before turning to give Lydia the short version. "He still works at our old camp. He never really left."

"Oooh, is he, like, a sailor or something?" Lydia said, looking over my shoulder.

"Lydia, ask her about their kiss," Sam said before changing the subject. "Hey, you never told me if you got the thing I sent you in the mail."

"I don't think so," I said, squinting in thought, trying to remember exactly what was in the pile of mail that had been accumulating on my kitchen table. "What is it?"

But before Sam could elaborate, Amaya draped herself around the doorway to my office, announcing herself with a dramatic wave of her arm.

"Sam, I gotta go," I said quickly. "I'll text you later once my plans are final."

"Time to vacate, baby!" Amaya punched the air like a cheerleader. Well, a drunk cheerleader. Her flaxen hair, normally taut in a bun at her neck, was now loosely draped over her shoulders, and she was still shoeless.

"I thought my micro-thing started tomorrow?" I said.

"Sabbatical," she corrected. "It's a time for you to get away and"— she inhaled a long breath and then let it go loudly, a smile spreading across her face—"breathe."

"I breathe just fine in Boston," I grumbled. "I like the rotting fish smell of the harbor."

Lydia made a gagging sound from the couch.

"Clara, I'm on your team here," Amaya purred as she stepped closer and rested both hands on my shoulders. "You can't possibly lead a pitch in front of a client when you're this fried."

"Totally." I nodded, because agreeing with her seemed like the easiest way out of this conversation.

"I'll see you in a week," she said with a decisive nod.

As soon as she was out the door, I turned toward Lydia.

"I feel like an idiot," I said, my stomach sinking again. Amaya using me to make a point in front of the rest of our team was one thing.

Somehow, her reiterating it tenderly one-on-one made it that much worse. "Have I just been oblivious to the fact that I am currently in my burnout era?"

"Tell me more about this romantic camp kiss," Lydia said, looking down at her phone. "I need to see a photo."

"Wait. Do you think I'm burnt out? Fried? Seriously, you can tell me." I swiveled myself back around to face her, leaning closer as she squinted her eyes, apologetic.

"A little?"

"Crap." I collapsed back in my chair, which wobbled in all its ergonomic, supportive glory. I spun around in panicked thought, letting out a giant yawn.

"See?" she said pointedly. "I don't think it's crazy that you could be, you know, burnt out. You've had a really hard year."

"Don't you think I would know if I was struggling?" I huffed, turning back to examine my checklist. I hated feeling defensive, but digging into this felt way too exposed. I forced a breath through my lips, trying to slow down my pounding heart.

"Let's just try to get through this and call it a night," I continued more gently.

"Oh, shit, he's cute."

My feet tip-tapped as I turned back around to face Lydia again, only to find her holding her phone within an inch of her face. She flipped it around to show me her screen, and there was Mack, grinning, a wet suit unzipped down his chest, the ocean a blur in the background. He still had that disheveled, sun-kissed, light brown hair, and the same bump in his nose from when he broke it playing in the boys' soccer tournament the summer we were twelve.

I'd long ago just accepted that the sight of him, in person or on a tiny screen, would flick on some sort of switch inside of me. It didn't matter that I'd changed so much since we first met as kids. This one thing had stayed exactly the same.

She looked up and made a perplexed face. "He can't be that bad."

"He's not bad," I replied finally. Mack was a lot of things: cocky, pointedly funny, often obnoxious, and, fine, occasionally kindhearted—with tousled hair that was one beat away from being a tangled mess and soft lips that curled into a mischievous grin at even the slightest hint of a joke. Once, he'd even been a boy I thought I loved, before I understood what love was and wasn't. And now?

"He's just…Mack."

"You're supposed to tell me about the kiss." She wiggled her eyebrows at me.

"Oh my god, it was just stupid teenage drama." I tried to keep my voice light, brushing the conversation aside. She gave me a look that very clearly signaled that she didn't buy it, but she didn't push it either.

"Come on," I said finally, stretching my arms over my head. "Let's give Amaya what she wants and go…sabbatical. That's a verb, right?"

She laughed and tapped at her phone. "Listen to this. The internet is telling me that the word 'sabbatical' comes from the Greek word 'sabatikos' and the Hebrew word 'Sabat,' or Sabbath, which is a day of rest."

"Great, thank you, internet," I said, shoving work files into my tote bag. "I'll rest then."

The only problem was, I wasn't quite sure I knew how.

5

THE TO-GO MARGARITAS had been Lydia's idea, grabbed at the Mexican restaurant around the corner from the office.

"Nothing says rest like tequila!" she toasted before popping her straw through the top of the plastic cup. The drinks sloshed in our hands as we walked across the Congress Street Bridge toward my apartment, navigating the usual sidewalk traffic that made up Boston's crooked cobblestone streets on a Friday night.

"You don't need to walk me home, you know," I said with a raised brow to Lydia, who met my skeptical look with her own, enhancing it with a loud slurp of her drink.

"And you don't need to tell me what to do," she replied, booze-sass mode activated. "Technically you're on a micro-sabbatical right this very second, remember?"

"What a terrible, made-up word." My eyes rolled as I sucked up another ice-cold gulp, the tequila going down easy. "She should have called it a playcation, or something cute that actually makes you want to do it."

"Wow, playcation." Lydia nodded, giving me an approving look. "I like it. See? This time off is already doing you some good."

"Shh, you sound too much like Amaya," I said, and she let out a cackle. "I can still work even if I'm not in the office, you know. You've seen how much we have left to do for Alewife."

"Clara, I know it's hard to believe, but the pitch will survive without you for one week," she said as we crossed the street in front of the Old State House building, lit up in all its ancient, redbrick glory. This time, there was not a trace of sarcasm in her voice.

"Maybe I can convince her to let this sabbatical thing wait until after the pitch," I offered, a reasonable compromise. "I'm going to email her this weekend once she's sobered up."

"You already told Sam you were coming!" Lydia said.

"I'm sure she'd understand," I reasoned. "She knows how important this job is to me."

"I just don't get what's so bad about taking a break." Lydia rarely let things get to her, but tonight her frustration with me was palpable.

I didn't have words sharp enough to describe the sinking feeling that plagued my stomach at night, when it was just me and my thoughts, curled up together in bed. Work was my only distraction, and the thought of being without it to focus on was terrifying. Voicing those fears aloud was even worse.

"I just like being busy," I said instead, and was met with an exasperated sigh as we rounded the corner to my apartment building.

"Oooh," she admired, gazing up at the sleek, black facade, an endless wall of windows. "I can't believe I still haven't seen this place."

"Don't get too excited," I said dryly, waving my fob in front of the keypad. "It's more like a dorm for finance and biotech bros."

I'd chosen this apartment without much thought, and I'd signed the lease while functioning with a post–breakup brain that was operating in survival mode. It was reasonably priced, close enough to work, and had a dishwasher. Worked for me.

Lydia laughed as the glass door swung open, welcoming us into the sterile lobby, with its pristine marble floors and bright neon lighting. "Shit, I see what you mean."

"Right?" I said as she followed me over to the mailroom, where I unlocked my tiny silver box and pulled out a stack of what was surely junk mail.

"Dentist office waiting room chic," she said, analyzing the large, ornate topiary in the corner. "But, like, a fancy dentist."

It was an accurate assessment. This place had the personality of dried dog poop, but it had been easy—elevator building, gym on the top floor, and the apartment came partially furnished. All I'd had to do was move in. But enough time had passed that it felt like it should feel like home. And this was, well, not that.

The elevator chugged its way up to the twenty-fourth floor, and when I finally cracked open the door to my studio, she let out a cautious, "Okay."

I tossed the mail onto the pile that had already taken shape on the tiny kitchen table and watched as she made her way around the room, stopping to pause in front of the windowsill.

"You murdered Richard!" She gasped, pinched the drooping, yellowed leaf of my snake plant—her holiday gift to me this past year—between two fingers, examining it with a grimace. "I have to hand it to you, Clara. This is, like, the hardest houseplant to kill, and yet somehow, you've done it."

"Please don't use that plant to make some sort of metaphor for the state of my life right now," I warned, plopping my drink down on the table and scooting onto a chair.

"That plant had a name, Clara," she corrected. "And I don't need to say anything when Richard says it all, don't you think? Farewell, sweet angel."

I raised my margarita somberly. "May he rest in peace."

She turned and walked toward me with a devious grin. "But seriously, you need to inject some sign of life into this place."

"It's basically just corporate housing," I said quickly. I still mourned the loss of the South End apartment I'd shared with Charles, with its giant bay window that practically sucked in the sunshine, and the sliver of garden in the back that overflowed with lilacs each spring. It had felt like a living, breathing thing. This place felt like a funeral home.

At first it had seemed too permanent to decorate my new apartment, and I'd assumed I wouldn't be here more than a couple of months. But two months turned into four, and then six. I pondered putting some art up on the walls, but every choice left me frozen with indecision. What did I—me, Clara, all on my own—even like? I had no clue. And so I did nothing.

Well, not absolutely nothing. I did kill Richard.

"Yeah, but you're not corporate housing," Lydia crowed, hands on hips. "You are better than this beige carpet and"—she wandered over to my fridge and let out a huff—"one pet adoption flier from six months ago."

"I was thinking about getting a dog," I explained with a shrug. "There's no way, though. I'm too busy. I took it off my list."

"Get the dog!" she said, her voice landing somewhere between amused and exasperated. "Slap some art on these walls! Stain this carpet!"

She jokingly tilted her cup, which was half full of strawberry margarita, toward the floor, and I yelped.

"Don't! I want to get my deposit back."

"I wouldn't actually do it," she said as she yanked out the chair across from me and sat down with a huff. "But can I be real with you?"

I nodded. "Of course."

"You're an amazing boss. I know you'd go to bat for me, the same way you always show up for everyone at work. For Amaya. The same way I know you showed up for Charles too. But you need to start showing up for yourself."

"You sound like one of those posters with the cat hanging from a tree branch," I said, reaching forward and sliding the stack of mail toward me.

"I have no idea what that is," she said.

"Are you kidding me?" I raised my brows at her, horrified.

"Excuse me if I don't get all of your old-person references," she scoffed back. "Seriously, though, Clara. You know how my dad died right at the beginning of my sophomore year in high school?"

I softened my expression, nodding. She'd told me about losing her dad in a car accident in bits and spurts, but I never pushed it, wanting to give her space to share her grief on her own terms.

"Well, after that I threw myself into building my art portfolio. My dad was a photographer, went to art school at RISD, moved to New York City, all that shit. So I thought that's what I should do too. What I was *supposed* to do. And so it was all I did. Obsessively. For over two years I devoted all my time to art so I could follow in his exact footsteps." She threw up her hands, making her point. "And you know what I didn't do?"

I shook my head, not entirely sure where she was going with this.

"I didn't deal with my grief," she continued. "I didn't do anything for myself that truly made me happy. I don't even think I really *wanted* to go to art school. It was just what I felt like I should do, which is probably why RISD rejected me."

"Well, I'm selfishly glad that you ended up at Northeastern, because it means you got to be my intern," I said as I fiddled with the lid of my now-empty cup.

"That's not the point of this story!" she scolded.

"I know, I know, I'm sorry. Continue." I waved her on.

"I want you to get out there and fucking live, that's all!" Lydia smacked her palms on the table emphatically, leaning forward. "I think you've been doing what you've thought you should do for so long that you don't even know what it is you want. And don't make some dumb fucking dad joke about wanting pizza or something right now, to deflect from this conversation."

I let out a snort of a laugh. "Am I that obvious?"

"Most of the time, yes." She slumped back in her chair, like this talk had exhausted her.

"Thank you for sharing that," I said, tilting my gaze to catch her eye. "Seriously."

"But?" she asked, still wary.

"But," I said as I slipped off my sneakers and curled my legs in my chair, "what if I go away for a week and nothing's changed? Or what if I go, and I still screw things up with this Alewife pitch? It's just not what I'm supposed to be doing right now."

I'm supposed to land Alewife, run the account, and snag a promotion, I thought to myself, refocusing. I'd repeated these goals over the last few months like a mantra, written them over and over in my notebook, as if they could save me from that sinking feeling of dread that plagued me when my thoughts drifted to anything other than work.

And sometimes they actually did.

"Were you not just at the same office party I was at?" Lydia cracked, and I avoided what was surely a look of disbelief, turning my focus to the mail pile in front of me.

"Go to New Hampshire! See your friends. Relive your past," she continued, leaning forward to tap me on the hand as I riffled through the stack of catalogs, yanking out the occasional bill. "Get out of here for a little bit. Go run naked through the woods."

"Excuse me?" I paused and looked up, giving her a look. "What the hell kind of camp do you think I went to?"

She shrugged. "I've never been to sleepaway camp. I've only seen *Wet Hot American Summer* and both versions of *The Parent Trap*."

"And you make fun of me for being a millennial," I scoffed.

"What?!" She raised her hands defensively. "I stand by the Lindsay Lohan remake. It's better than the original."

"Well, I'm not sure streaking through a forest naked is going to fix my issues." I pressed my lips together, holding back a laugh.

"Says you," she snapped, never one to back down from a fiercely held opinion about something ridiculous. "Do you have anything to drink in here?"

She gave her chair a scoot back, hopping up with an expectant clap of her hands.

"I think there's some wine in the..." I trailed off, my mouth dropping open at the sight of the letter I was about to toss in the junk pile. "Holy shit."

That was enough to send Lydia backtracking. "What?" she asked, leaning a hand on the table as she peered over my shoulder.

"This is what Sam was talking about," I said, tracing a thumb across my name, neatly printed across the front of the envelope. "Oh my god. I'd totally forgotten we did this."

Sam had sent it to my old address on Tremont, scribbled in her messy cursive. But my name, written above it in those precise, familiar block letters—I'd recognize that handwriting anywhere.

It was my own.

6

THE LETTER HAD finally found me, and the sight of it sent my heart pounding, the rush of once-foggy memories suddenly clear in my head.

"Did what?" Lydia asked, puzzled. "Did you guys all secretly bury a body somewhere decades ago but the person survived and is now writing you all letters?"

"The wine is in the cabinet next to the fridge," I said, smacking at her with the envelope. "And no, I'm not a murderer, yet, unless you wanna try me."

"I've seen you attempt to kill a cockroach," she said with a snort. "I'm not too worried."

I turned the envelope over in my hands, studying its slightly worn shape with awe. "We wrote these letters to our future selves on our last night of camp. Sam said she'd mail them to us twenty years later, because that seemed so ancient and grown up to us then. I had no idea she actually kept them."

Glasses clinked behind me as Lydia made her way around my kitchen. "How teen movie of you guys," she cooed. "I love it. By the way, I'm adding bananas to your grocery list. Because I'm eating this one sad banana you have in here."

"What should I do?" I asked, flipping the unassuming envelope over in my shaky hands. It felt like a brick in my palms, even though it probably weighed as much as a feather.

"What do you mean, 'what should you do'?" Lydia said through a mouthful of banana, placing a tumbler of red wine down in front of me. "Open it!"

"Fine." Squeezing my eyes closed for a quick second, I caught a glimmer of the carefree girl I'd been at the start of that summer. Fifteen and fearless, until the grim realities of adulthood arrived in the form of that letter from my mom.

"Wait! Wait. I need to use the bathroom," Lydia said. I waved her toward the door next to my bedroom.

"I'll be quick!" she said as she scurried across the room.

I'd then thrown myself into everything I did during those last few weeks of camp; as if I could somehow change what awaited me at home by being the strongest swimmer, the best Color Week captain, the most perfect, put-together version of myself. By kissing Mack, the boy I'd adored for years.

And god, how it had hurt—an acute pain so sharp I could still feel it in my heart—to realize how naive I'd been. My dad had already moved out of our house by the time I got home that summer. My mom started dating my stepdad months later. They finalized the divorce just before my high school graduation, where they sat rows apart, not speaking.

By then my dad had transferred to Hartford for work, which meant I only saw him on the weekends, and Mom had sold the house and moved us into an apartment in Providence. I spent my last summers of high school scooping ice cream at White Mountain Creamery and saving for college.

My entire world—and everyone in it—had completely turned upside down in just under one calendar year. I'd made a promise to myself back then to never let anything catch me off guard like that again. And now here I was, blindsided by a micro-sabbatical and this unexpected piece of mail sitting in front of me, waiting to be torn open.

Inside was a piece of lined notebook paper, folded precisely in thirds. I held it gingerly in my hands, a priceless heirloom, before pressing it flat against the table, carefully smoothing out the twenty-year-old creases with my fingertips. A portrait of my teenage life unfolded in front of me, painted in thick, blue ballpoint-pen ink. I fluttered a huge sigh through my lips, my shoulders tense with suspense.

"I am *dying* to know what this thing says," Lydia said, plopping back down across from me. "If you feel like sharing, of course."

I gave a quick nod and then shifted my eyes downward, facing my past.

"'*Dear thirty-five-year-old Clara, Hello from your younger self,*'" I read, a shiver of nerves tiptoeing up my back. "Wait, hold on. I need a drink before I do this."

I paused and took a giant, needy gulp of wine.

"Okay, here goes." A tremor pulsed through me, my hands shaking ever so slightly. "'*It's finally here: the last night of your last summer at Pine Lake, your absolute favorite place in the world. It's 10:38 p.m. and we've snuck out to write these letters to ourselves here at the Water Front. Tomorrow you head back to Providence, which is the last place I—we?—feel like being. The thought of going home makes me want to barf.*'"

I paused and looked up at Lydia. "This was the summer my folks split up."

"Oh god, Clara." She winced, her eyes sympathetic. "That must have been so hard."

I let out a shaky breath, the memory rushing through me like a heat wave, clammy and hot. I'd cried so hard the day they picked me up from camp that my eyes were practically swollen after.

"*But tonight,*" I continued, "*for one last night, I'm here, at camp, writing these letters with the people who mean the most to me in the world. Eloise has gone off to write alone in our bunk, but Nick is here next to me on the dock, crying of course, and Sam is scribbling something in her notebook that is surely profound because you know how Sam is. Our little poet.*"

I looked up at Lydia, who was still watching me with kind eyes. "This was my group of best friends," I explained. "Eloise was, like, ultra-serious and intense about everything, and Nick was the funniest person alive and the best actor at camp. And Sam was, well. The same. She hasn't changed much. The smartest one. Wiser than the rest of us. An old soul."

"When was the last time you saw them all?" she asked.

"It's been a while," I said, my eyes circling back to the printed names. "Five years-ish."

I looked back down at the paper and groaned. Of course.

"What?" She leaned closer, her eyes lighting up with curiosity.

"It's time for the Mack portion of the letter," I said, dreading whatever was to come.

"Yes," Lydia hissed, enthralled. "Boathouse boy."

"I'm already cringing. '*Mack is here too, farther down at the end of the dock, but I've been ignoring him all week. Did I want to end my last night avoiding the person I've had a crush on since I was ten? No. But I also didn't expect us to kiss and then for him to not talk to me for days, so screw him. And the worst part, after all this stupidity—of us being Color Week captains, and the kiss, and then him completely blowing me off—is that I still can't bring myself to hate him. Also, can I just say—I can't believe Steve and Marla expect us to share the Color Week Captain medal?! He can stick it up his ass, as far as I'm concerned.*'"

"Oh my god, Mack, what a piece of shit player!" Lydia screeched.

"The worst," I said, surprising myself with how hurt I still felt over something that happened so long ago. Our kiss had been an eruption, burning everything in its wake. And then his silent treatment had followed, a harsh blast of ice.

"And because our teams tied during Color Week competition and we were both captains, they made us share this stupid winner medal with each other. We've literally never once talked about how we kissed, but we still send that medal back and forth to each other."

"Wait, *still*?" Lydia's mouth dropped open. "It's been twenty years! You and hot boat boy have been long-distance flirting over a medal for *two decades*?"

"Oh, stop." I could feel my cheeks heating and took another sip of wine for cover. "It's just a way to annoy each other."

"Mmm-hmmm." She was looking at me through narrowed eyes. "And where is it now?"

"I sent it to him up at Pine Lake when I moved out of my place with Charles," I explained. "And I didn't give him my new address, so I assume he still has it."

The medal was like a yearly reminder of our make-out session, and it got under my skin more than it should have.

"He probably sleeps with it under his pillow," Lydia joked.

"When Sam got married, to her ex?" I continued. "He wore it to their fucking wedding. Then he left it at the front desk of the hotel we were all staying it. He paid them to give it to me when I checked out."

My mind immediately pulled me back to memories of that night in Brooklyn all those years ago. Charles and I had just started dating, but work had kept him from joining me at Sam's wedding, and Mack's gaze had lingered on me the entire night, like he was constantly waiting to see what my reaction would be to that dumb medal dangling from his neck. So I'd done what I always did when I really wanted to piss him off: I ignored him.

"Okay, I'm going to need you to keep reading." Lydia tapped her finger impatiently on the table.

I nodded. *"'But Sam made the very important point that we are feminists, and so I'm not going to let one immature guy get me down. Especially not MACK.'"*

I paused to turn the paper over as Lydia squealed with delight.

"Oh my god, little feminist Clara!" She stuck out her bottom lip in a pout, hand at her heart. "I love her."

"'Sam told us to write to our older selves and remind them of who we are now, who we want to be, and how we want our lives to go. So if she does remember to send this to you in twenty years, I want to make sure I do exactly that. I've decided—and this is very me, I know—to make a list of the things I want to do by the time I'm thirty-five.'

"Oh god, I can't read this." I pushed the paper across to Lydia, grimacing. "This is mortifying."

"It's adorable," she said firmly, grabbing the letter out of my hands. "I love that you were making checklists for yourself all the way back then."

She straightened out her shoulders with an exaggerated "ahem" and kept reading.

"'Please check off each one that you've completed, and if you haven't done them yet: what the hell are you waiting for?' Are you ready for this, Clara? Your teenage self is bossing you around from the past."

I pressed my palms against my temples and nodded, overheating with embarrassment. This all felt too revealing, like snooping through a diary. Except that was almost always a betrayal of trust. This was something that the teenage me had wanted me to see.

"Okay, so, number one," Lydia said. *"'Do something meaningful with your life. Don't waste it.'* So sweet, teen Clara!"

"Ugh. It's so clichéd." I groaned. "Please just keep going so we can get this over with."

"Oh my god!" She squealed, her face lighting up. "Listen to this. *'Two. Get a dog.'* It's a sign."

"Well, clearly I need to get on that," I muttered with a wave toward the flier on the fridge.

"'Three, surround yourself with people you love, who love you.' Done." Lydia pointed at herself.

"'Four, do something that scares you. Daily. Take risks, goddamnit! (Jump off the high dive, you chicken.) Five. Take a lot of LOVERS (lol). Or at least have one passionate love affair.'"

I audibly snorted as the memories rushed back in an instant. "Eloise brought a bunch of historical romance books to camp that summer. I was on a kick."

"You actually wrote *'LOL'* there. But still, good advice." She chuckled. *"'Six, Chop your hair off. Come on, do it once! Or at least cut it short! (I almost did it this summer but I bailed, so now I'm holding us to it.) Seven. Experience real joy. Eight. Be kind to yourself!'* With an exclamation point," Lydia added, giving me her brightest smile. *"'Nine. Have a shitload of fun. Ten. Be a great friend.'"*

I looked up and watched as her eyes scanned the paper. "Is that it?" I asked. Please, god, let that be it.

She nodded. "Yeah, then you just say, *'That's all from me. I can't wait to find out who I am as an adult. Remember—I love you. Xo, Me/You/Clara.'* See? It's not that bad!"

Lydia pushed the letter back toward me.

"I sound so naively optimistic," I murmured, staring down at my words. "Like I was in total denial about all the shit going on at home."

"I'm sure it was a lot for you to process," Lydia said.

"Also, why are there no actual, concrete goals here?" I traced my finger over my instructions. "You know, like, save for a down payment, or run a marathon."

"Ew, that's boring adult shit you'd write now. This"—she leaned forward and tapped a finger down on the letter—"is a sign. A DM from the Universe. A checklist for your soul. Teen Clara wants you to go to New Hampshire. Take a risk, goddamnit."

Disagreement perched on my lips, ready to remind her again that we had a huge, life-changing pitch staring us down. But instead, I kept my mouth shut and ran my fingers along the blue lines of the notebook paper, trying to remember how I'd felt when writing these words. So much had changed since then, but a piece of me still lived on this page, and she'd wanted so much from her life. From me.

Could I even check a single box off Teen Clara's list? Work could be considered meaningful. Right? And I did love working with Lydia, so maybe I could give myself a check there as well. I loved my parents in theory, I guess, even if they did both drive me a little nuts. But I didn't have a group of friends around me who cared for me unconditionally as I'd had back then. I tried to think back to the last time I felt truly joyful and drew a blank.

I'd had the same dull, shoulder-length, layerless haircut since I was thirteen years old.

Jesus. Maybe this letter *was* a sign.

"So, what, you think I should just say fuck it, and actually go up to camp for the week?" I asked, and for the first time, I felt a genuine pull to do just that.

"Yes!" She threw up her hands again, completely exasperated with me. "I've been telling you this all night. Go take a week. You owe it to your fifteen-year-old self. And your *current* self."

"I guess I do feel a little fried." I took another sip of wine, weighing the idea. "I could even live up to teenage me and check off the rest of this list. Except for the hair chop part, obviously."

"I'm not sure this is a do-it-all-in-five-days sort of list, Clara," she mused. "This is, like, big life stuff."

"Excuse me, if there's one thing I'm good at it's killing a to-do list," I said adamantly, and she held up her hands in defeat.

"Okay, okay, that is true."

"I mean, look." I shrugged. "I can at least try. I'll go on my playcation—"

"See!" Lydia clapped her hands together. "That really works!"

"I'll follow this list, check everything off, come back to Boston, and kill the pitch," I reasoned. "Show Amaya that I'm still just as good at this as I've always been. Better, even. And maybe if Alewife goes well, I'll finally think about getting a dog."

And joy, I thought to myself as I folded the letter back up and tucked it inside its envelope. Pure, unadulterated, ecstatic joy. Laughing so loud that you don't care who hears you, running so fast it feels like your legs will never stop. The sensation of your heart cracking open with so much happiness you almost break into tears. That one word was so simple, and yet it contained an entire world of emotions in just three letters.

"And a lover," she said, lips curling. "Who has a boathouse."

"Don't get ahead of yourself," I said, though my body warmed at her words. I still thought back to that kiss with Mack at the strangest of times. Late at night, sure, but also in the middle of grabbing a burrito for dinner after work. One minute I'd be asking for extra guac, and then suddenly I was pressed up against the rough bark of that tree, Mack's mouth hot on mine.

"Whatever you say, boss," she said with a shake of her head. "Now, let's go get you packed."

"I haven't done laundry all week." I chewed at the edge of my index finger, suddenly unnerved at the thought of traveling at the drop of a hat. "Normally I'd have planned all my outfits and packed already."

"Aw, look at you living on the edge already!" Lydia cooed, hand pressed against her chest.

"I like a packing list," I grumbled, anxious at the thought of doing all of this so last-minute. "Is that so bad?"

"Of course not! But isn't it exciting that you're already doing something that scares you?" she said, grabbing the letter off the table and waving it in my face. "I'm so proud."

"Very funny." I brushed her off and moved to my closet to dig around for my duffel bag.

I hated being unprepared, and I could feel the tension building in my body as I prepared to face the unknown. But I felt something else, too, something that felt faintly like optimism. It hummed along the surface of my skin, a familiar buzz that reminded me of who I'd been that summer: sparkling and hopeful, invigorated by possibility.

Maybe it was time to get her back.

7

"BABE." NICK LEVELED an exasperated look at Trey, who had gamely offered to drive my car so I could work. "You have the cruise control set at sixty-two in a sixty-five-mile-an-hour zone. Maybe you should kick it up a mile or two so we get there before sunset?"

Nick's tone was light, but he had a point; it felt like we'd been driving for ages.

Not that I wasn't grateful; despite not hearing from me for months—or good lord, was it years?—Nick had responded **Obvs!** within minutes of me texting him to ask if they'd want to drive together up to Pine Lake, followed by a row of hearts from Trey. They'd been able to cancel their rental car, and I'd picked them up at the airport, nervous but excited to see them both again.

Nick's openheartedness was classic him, as classic as the banter he and Trey had perfected over the years, a singsong soundtrack that wasn't unpleasant, even as I tapped through my email trying to forward Lydia everything she could possibly need before we got to Pine Lake.

My sleep last night had been restless at best, one of those weird nights where you linger in that delirious purgatory between asleep and awake. I was exhausted but wired, and a dull, thumping panic throbbed behind my eyelids.

I'd spent the better part of the drive so far chewing the side of my mouth raw as I scrolled through endless email debates about creative direction and brand vision for Alewife. Amaya had shot down every idea we'd had so far, and now I was on my way to the land of limited internet access with less than two weeks to go before we had to present our pitch. Correction: only one week for me to get it right after this stupid micro-sabbatical. A wave of nervous nausea hit high tide in my stomach.

"Shhh, just do your crossword and let me drive." Trey swatted at his boyfriend, his intricate tattoos flexing on his golden-brown skin, as Nick ducked playfully.

"Look, I just don't want your Australian brain to get confused. Roads are hard for you." Nick's lips curled into a wicked smile as he baited Trey.

"I'm seriously about to pull over and leave you on the side of the highway." Trey turned quickly to give Nick a ridiculously dramatic, brooding glare, and his lush, dark brows and thick black hair made him look like some sort of Austen-inspired grump-hunk.

Years ago, back when my group of friends was working at Pine Lake as counselors, Trey had rolled in from Down Under to teach waterskiing on a work visa, and he'd wooed the entire camp instantly with his down-to-earth charm and universally appealing biceps.

But Nick had been the one to win Trey's heart, which surprised no one.

"I forgot how cute the two of you are together," I teased, giving up on my emails for a moment to watch them.

Nick lodged a pointed glance at Trey before turning back to me, tugging at one of his chin-length black locs, which were not new, but new to me. I'd only ever seen them in photos online.

"Be honest, you're only coming this weekend to see the two of us."

"Oh, one hundred percent," I agreed sarcastically, hoping he wouldn't dig around for the real reason. I'd given no explanation for my about-face, other than my schedule magically changing at the last minute. The humiliation of my boss sending me on a forced vacation because I was utter shit at work wasn't something I'd figured out how to share. Not yet.

"Charles and I never had adorable fights," I muttered.

"I'm sorry that didn't work out," Trey said, his accent making even the most mundane words sound charming. "He always seemed like a decent dude."

"Yeah, he was." I smiled diplomatically. "He *is*. It just didn't work out. We grew apart, wanted different things."

This had been my rote answer for the past year, and it had worked in most social situations when people asked about him. The real answer was far more complicated and nuanced, something I still couldn't quite put into words. When I tried—only in my head, of course—it amounted to something like, *I think he was right. I loved the idea of him, and the stability I thought the relationship gave me, more than I actually loved him.* But I'd never said anything close to this aloud, to anyone.

"That makes a lot of sense," he said, nodding. I noticed Nick peek ever so slightly toward Trey, who caught his eye for a moment before turning back to the road ahead. "Well, wait until you see Eloise with her boyfriend. We met them up in Sonoma for a night a few months ago, and it was..." He shook his head like he still couldn't believe what he'd seen.

"It was what?" I pushed, as Nick chuckled, making me feel even more like I was missing out on something. Eloise was the kind of person who had seemed forty years old at fourteen, so composed and collected it was hard to imagine her as anything else. She was wildly different from the rest of our group, serious and stoic to our silly, but that only made her fit in more, like a cork on a bottle of wine.

Nick turned in his seat. "Imagine two people in the honeymoon phase of a relationship and then multiply that times a hundred."

"So much kissing," Trey added with an amused shake of his head.

"Wow," I replied. I didn't know what to make of this loved-up version of Eloise other than it was an oversized example of everything I'd missed out on by not keeping in touch.

Unsure of what else to say, I gazed back down at my phone, hitting send on another email forward to Lydia.

"Clara Millen." When I looked back up, I found Nick staring at me expectantly, like he was waiting for his coffee in the middle of Starbucks' morning rush hour.

"Yes, Nick Reyes?"

"Are you...*working*?" The face Nick made back at me was so purely him—his arched brows and quirked, giant smile—that it was like looking directly into the past. Even though he was sitting directly in front of me, the sight of him made me nostalgic.

"No," I lied, tossing my phone onto the seat next to me, on top of my notebook and the file of Alewife documents I'd dumped out of my tote bag the second I'd slid into the back seat.

"You finally get your ass up to camp after six long years—" Nick continued, chiding me again.

"Five!" I cut him off, giving him a hurt look. "It's only been *five*."

"Oh, as if that's any better."

"You're right, you're right. I'm sorry." I waved my hand. "Continue."

He cleared his throat dramatically. "You finally get your cute ass—"

"Oh, why, thank you."

"—up to camp after five long years, during which you ditched your dearest friends—"

"I didn't have a choice! I had to—"

"Work. We know. Your first love."

"Okay, that's a bit much," I said, crossing my arms defiantly. "My first love is cheese."

Nick leveled a look at me, and we both burst out laughing. It felt amazing to slip right back into our friendship, like an old, worn bathrobe that was still warm and cozy after all these years.

But there was just the tiniest bit of hurt buried in his comment, and I added it to my mental drawer of shame, where I'd stored Sam's reveal about the group text, and Teen Clara's hopeful expectations for her life that I'd so far failed to meet.

"You have promised to give yourself over to this friend-union this week, work be damned," he reminded me.

"I promise. Just let me hit send on this email and then I'm all yours."

"Pinky swear?" Nick held out a finger, and I latched mine around it, giving our joined hands a shake.

"Pinky swear," I said firmly, though there was a part of me that felt like a liar. I wasn't sure how to completely check out of work, even though I was being forced to do just that.

Be kind to yourself, I thought, and glanced down at the pile of papers next to me, where I'd tucked my letter, hidden between spreadsheets and outlines. But that felt easier said than done, the demand of an idealistic, naive teenager trying to cope with the emotional tornado on her horizon.

Satisfied with our agreement, Nick turned back around in his seat. As promised, I tapped out one more email and then put my phone down. NPR filled in the lull between our chitchat, as Massachusetts turned into New Hampshire, which flew by the window in a mix of every shade of green imaginable.

"The way life should be!" Trey announced as we crossed the border.

"Honey, that's Maine's motto," Nick reminded him with a pat on the shoulder. "New Hampshire is 'Live Free or Die.'"

"Christ, of course it is," Trey muttered. "I forgot about their absurd no motorcycle helmet law."

New Hampshire was so often overlooked, overshadowed by the lush rolling hills and earnestly cool vibe of Vermont to its left and the breathtaking beauty and storied seaside villages of Maine on the right. It was the middle child of New England states: kind of weird, occasionally out of step, often forgotten. And yes, they did not require motorcyclists to wear helmets, because of the whole live-free-or-die ethos, which was deeply rooted in every nook and cranny of the place.

But to me it was magical; New Hampshire had an old soul. It was simple and complex, stoic and serene, and I felt utterly like myself when I was here.

"I don't know," I mumbled, admiring the beauty through the window as Mount Monadnock appeared on the horizon. "This is definitely the way life should be, if you ask me."

Eventually I dozed off in the back seat, my head jolting forward every time Trey slowed the car to a stop. I slept hard and deep, and finally willed my eyes open about an hour later, just as we approached the three white buildings that made up the town of Peridot's tiny square.

"Nothing's changed," I muttered, shifting my head back and forth to ease up the cricks in my neck. The village wasn't frozen in time; there was wear and tear on everything, faded paint holding on for dear life, and a gazebo that looked like it was ready to retire. Rather, Peridot survived despite the passing of time, the town hall, library, and tiny church still standing there, almost defiant in the face of time racing past.

"Nothing ever changes here," Nick corrected, his voice reverent. "Remember Margo, who ran the dining hall? Her family still owns the General Store."

He pointed to the small dusty red building in the center of town, with its rickety porch that seemed more lopsided than I remembered, the sign of a life well lived. The New Hampshire state flag hung off the banister, and next to it was a banner that read "Live Free Or Die, But You Gotta Pay For Your Dinner."

Trey flicked on the left blinker and steered the car onto the bumpy dirt road out of town, the final stretch of our trip. Instinctively, we all rolled down our windows at the same time, the fresh, summer air pushing its way into the car, which smelled of the now-stale Dunkin coffee we'd grabbed just after leaving Boston.

Trey slowed down to five miles an hour, the only way to savor the approach to camp. I swear all of our shoulders lowered a full inch. Just past a small gray-shingled cabin on the left was the lake, which appeared through the emerald-tipped pines in all its deep blue, sparkling glory. I let out a pleased sigh, and Nick leaned his head out the window, a blissful look on his face.

"We welcome you to Pine Lake Camp, we're mighty glad you're here," Nick started singing. "We'll send you in reverberating with a mighty cheer. Come on, Clara!"

I pressed my lips together and shook my head no, self-conscious. But Nick just waved me on expectantly. He and Amaya should swap notes in getting people to do what they want.

"We'll sing you in, we'll sing you out," I sang begrudgingly, my voice getting just a little bit louder with each word. "And we'll raise a mighty shout!"

It felt ridiculous, yelling these familiar words as the air swept my hair up against my face. But my tepid smile quickly bloomed into a grin, and god, it felt good to be giddy about something again.

"Hail, hail, the gang's all here at Pine Lake Camp!" I sang with newfound abandon. And for the first time since Amaya pushed me out of the Four Points office and into the woods, I felt downright ecstatic to be here. Joyful, even. Fifteen-year-old Clara would almost certainly approve.

I was so caught up in the moment that it took me a beat to register that something was wrong after Trey blurted, "What the hell?"

"Whoa," Nick said, all the sunny brightness that normally occupied his voice gone.

"What?" I asked, thoroughly confused, still high on singing.

Trey pointed toward Nick's window, and when I looked to the right, I saw the giant wooden sign that read PINE LAKE CAMP standing proudly at the entrance, like always. Its stark, bright white background had long since faded in the sun, but the name, printed in deep forest-green, was still as clear as ever. Next to it stood Steve and Marla waving at us, the sun glistening off their speckled gray hair.

And just behind them, Mack.

But this wasn't what had thrown Nick and Trey off. It was the sign next to them staked into the ground, small, square, with sharp blue lettering.

SOLD.

8

"HOLY SHIT," NICK muttered from the passenger seat.

"They finally decided to do it." Trey's voice was almost reverent. "I never thought I'd see the day."

Nick squeezed his boyfriend's arm while keeping his gaze out the window. "Babe, pull over," he demanded, his chipper voice now stern and insistent.

I wasn't quite sure what to say. I knew this place intimately, like a lover's body. But I'd also avoided it, let life keep me away, prioritized other things, and pushed returning to camp and seeing all my friends to the bottom of my to-do list. I'd just always assumed Pine Lake would be here, waiting for me when I needed it.

The feeling stirring inside of me felt distinctly like sorrow. But I hadn't been to Pine Lake in so long; I wasn't quite sure I was even allowed to be upset about Steve and Marla selling the place. A long list of shoulds ticked through my head, the first one being that I should have come back here long before now.

Following Nick and Trey out of the car, I raised a hand to my brow to shield my eyes from the sun, which was still shockingly bright in the late afternoon, even with sunglasses on.

"We figured if we stood here long enough, eventually you kids would show up," Steve joked as we walked toward him, a calm smile on his face, hands on his hips. He looked skinnier and just a bit more crooked than the last time I saw him, his trimmed black hair now fully gray.

He had the weathered, rough complexion of a white person who had spent 90 percent of his life outside in the sun. His exterior was all hard edges—a crooked nose broken skiing in his twenties, thick, furrowed brows that almost always appeared knitted in thought. His quiet demeanor could often be misinterpreted as sternness, but he operated from a place of kindness. He'd figured out how to keep Pine Lake in business while offering up more financial aid than other camps in the area, making it possible for kids like me to attend.

Marla, on the other hand, was soft inside and out, her dark brown, apple-shaped face youthful and bright despite the hint of lines that creased her skin. In all the years I'd known her, I'd only ever seen her gray hair pinned back in a twist, and she was always good for a hug when a camper was homesick. But Marla had a hunch to her posture now, and she also looked thinner than I remembered. Still, she was eyeing us with that familiar, gentle face, as if she was ecstatic to see us.

"Oh my god, you're seriously selling camp?" Nick spat out the words even before eking out a hello. He was the first to reach Steve and Marla, and he leaned in to hug them as Trey and I hovered behind him.

"Hi to you too, Nicholas," Steve said playfully as he pulled away. "Trey!"

Steve wrapped him in a one-armed hug, just as Marla stepped forward and pulled me into an embrace. She barely came up to my cheek, and her hug was warm and comforting in a way I didn't know I was craving until I was wrapped up in it.

Marla had always looked out for me as a kid, something I never fully grasped until I was an adult and able to rewind through moments of my life with a grown-up's perspective. She must have intuitively sensed that my life at home was lonely and strained, my parents distant with each other and only slightly more present with me.

"We're so glad you're here," Marla said, and gave me a smile I knew was genuine. "We've missed all you kids, of course. But it's been so long since you've been able to make it up here, Clara! What a lovely surprise."

"I'm downright shocked," came a voice to my right.

It was Mack, of course. Even though I hadn't laid eyes on him in ages, I was certain he was biting his bottom lip in a smirk, which caused his right eye to shut almost completely. He always did this when he wanted to prove a point or get his way.

Marla gave me one last squeeze before releasing me, and I turned to find him there, lips pursed and eye crinkled just so. And around his neck hung a familiar talisman: the circular wooden medal, Color Week Winner 2004 scrawled on it in black ink, looped through a red ribbon that had faded to salmon pink over time.

He'd worn it, of course, to do what he did best—needle me. And so I returned the favor and pretended I didn't notice.

"Millen," he said as he showed off his charming, mischievous grin, with that little gap between his two front teeth. The one that said, *I'm innocent! But you know I'm really not*, in all its slightly arrogant, crooked glory. "I never thought we'd see you back here."

"Hey," I said, giving him a smile and a quick once-over as I smoothed out the rumples in my linen sundress. His hair looked like it had been permanently styled by one too many windy rides out in the camp waterskiing boat, slightly shaggy and tousled still.

"Work stuff changed at the last minute," I said with a quick shrug of my shoulders. "So here I am."

"Are you sure you didn't come dressed for the office?" He leaned forward and ran a finger over the edge of the strap of my dress, and even though he barely touched my skin, my stomach still fluttered, warm and wanting. "You know we get messy here."

"I'm aware," I said, narrowing my eyes slightly and swatting his hand away. "It hasn't been that long, thanks."

"Good," he said, tan arms crossing in front of his faded, threadbare Pine Lake Camp T-shirt that looked almost as old as Steve. "I was worried you'd forgotten your roots."

"That's so weird," I said, reaching out to tap on the evergreen logo on his shirt, reminding him that I still knew how to play this little game between us. "Because it looks like you haven't changed at all, including out of the clothes we wore when we were kids."

"Oh, sick burn, Millen!" He scrunched up his face in exaggerated pain, before pulling me in for a quick hug. His arms were warm against my bare shoulders, and yet inexplicably I felt goose bumps prickle up at his touch.

"I really am glad you're here, you know," he said, his lips grazing dangerously close to that sensitive spot just below my earlobe.

For a second the teasing in his voice was gone, and I could hear traces of the other Mack I knew, the gentle, earnest one who'd nervously kissed me back when we were fifteen.

"Admit it, you're excited to see me," he said as he pulled away, and then that dumb, perfect grin returned. He shook his head, hair flying in every direction, before he ran a hand through it, looking back at me.

"Oh, very," I replied, sarcasm hanging on every syllable. To torment him a little more, I averted my gaze to dig around for a hair tie in my bag as if it was the most important task of my life.

"I almost forgot," he said with a smack to his forehead. "I've had this for too long. Time to share."

He lifted the medal from around his neck and placed it over my head, straightening it out with a gentle tug. "Perfect."

My eyes desperately wanted to roll to the back of my head and never return, but I just gave him a blasé smile. "I'll have it back to you shortly."

"Oh, no, take your time, Millen, please."

Our snarky back-and-forth was interrupted when Steve came over and gave me a gentle squeeze on the shoulder. "Hey, kid. It's been too long."

"I know, I'm sorry it took me forever to get up here. And to think, I was going to try to buy this place!"

He chuckled at this, a low rumble, and then cleared his throat and shuffled back a few steps to look at our group.

"So," Steve started with an awkward nod. "You saw the sign."

Next to me Mack started humming the Ace of Base song loud enough for everyone to hear. I turned to give him a "not now, you dipshit" glare, and he met my face with a wink, almost like he knew what I was about to do even before I did it.

"I would have thought our dear old friend Mackenzie Sullivan would have said something," Nick said, sounding hurt.

"Hey, I just found out this week!" Mack raised his hands in the air defensively. "I've been dealing with some shit with my parents and their business. I've been distracted."

This caught my attention. Mack's family ran a successful music licensing business out in Los Angeles. He'd always been upfront about the trust fund they'd set him up with, and how he refused to touch it. Nick once told me Mack had never even taken a dime from them after he graduated college, which definitely earned my respect. Not that I'd tell him that.

"And we wanted to tell you ourselves. We didn't realize the real estate agent was going to stake that into the ground this morning," Marla explained, pointing at the sign. "We just finalized our plan a couple of days ago," she added.

"So, what, you're selling it to someone random?" I asked, trying to keep my voice light, even though I was suddenly agitated, all the shoulds of my life bubbling to the surface. That heavy feeling of time lost, with nothing to show for it, circled back through my body, gripping my shoulders.

"Glamp Camp. They're a company based out of Denver; they have a bunch of glamping resorts all over the country. Our friends who used to run Green Mountain Camp in Vermont sold to them a couple of years ago."

"*Glamping?*" Trey said without trying to hide the horrified skepticism in his voice.

"Oh, it's not that bad," Marla said with a chuckle. "You know, nice big tents with bathrooms attached, linen sheets, that sort of thing. They want to put in a pool, offer massages. You kids should come spend a weekend here when they open!"

Our bodies weren't even touching, but I could somehow feel Mack stiffen next to me, and a quick glance revealed a worried crinkle at the edge of his eyes, his lips twitching briefly into a frown before turning back upward. But there was no playful edge to his smile now. We were both silent, no doubt each of us living out our own terrible version of *Pine Lake Camp 2.0: The Glamping Years* in our minds.

Thankfully, Nick was there with the save, like always.

"Yeah, I just always assumed you guys had a plan for…this." Nick gestured up the road toward camp. "And for it to stay Pine Lake forever."

"Our plan was to keep doing this until we got tired," Steve said, a softness to his voice, which still rang with the long r sound of a Maine accent. "And we're tired."

"We can't quite keep up like we used to," Marla added, wrapping an arm around Steve's waist. "And we've got plans to travel. I want to see South America. And then we might relocate. I'm sick of the cold."

"I can't imagine why," Mack said, and then turned toward us. "We got, like, two feet of snow here in April," he explained.

"That definitely helped move the conversation along." Steve nodded. "And that they offered all cash."

Considering the cost of lakefront real estate, it was a logical assumption that someone would swoop in and grab the place. I shuddered at the thought of Pine Lake Camp getting divided up into plots, the beautiful old buildings razed to the ground to make room for fancy yurts and a pool.

Nick sucked in air through clenched teeth. "Well. I guess we better make this one last week extra special, then."

I dug my teeth into my thumbnail, a nervous habit I'd picked up somewhere in childhood. One week. This was the only time I had left at Pine Lake, period. I had to make it count.

"Why don't you all head to the bunks and get settled in? Sam's up there with Eloise and her new beau." Marla gestured toward the pickup parked along the road. "We're heading down to Portsmouth for the night to visit some friends, but as usual you're in good hands with Mack."

She wrapped her arm around his shoulder and tugged him close to her, his tense face shifting into something boyish and sweet.

"Forgive me for asking, but it's been a while," I said, digging into my bag for my phone. "Can you give me the wireless code? I still have to check in with work while I'm here."

"No working!" Nick reminded me with a poke to the ribs.

"Check-ins," I said, jabbing back. "Short, quick check-ins."

"I'll give it to you," Mack said, reaching out to tap my forearm. "I have it written down in the boathouse. Come grab it after you get unpacked."

"Thanks," I mumbled. I could have sworn Marla shot Steve a confused look, but I was too flustered to give it much thought.

Annoying Mack was easy to handle. But kind Mack always left me oddly at a loss for words.

And somehow that bothered me more.

9

"YOU HAVE TO hand it to them, it's a pretty badass way to break the news," Trey said as he steered my Prius along the bumpy dirt road. "Just dropped the sign in the ground. Boom. Sold. We're out."

Trey flung his fingers out in front of him, mimicking an explosion. Nick snorted and shook his head. For once, he was speechless.

Mack was next to me in the back seat, his long limbs going every which way. Worn jeans cuffed at the ankles, a pair of beaten-up, slip-on navy Vans. He still looked like a cool kid from Southern California, and it dawned on me as I surveyed him that he'd always been like this, stylish without ever even realizing it.

I shifted my gaze back out the window, taking in all the small changes to the place. My eyes centered in on a patch of land that had been divided into rows, each of which overflowed in a beautiful bounty of green. A fence ran around the perimeter, painted all different shades of the rainbow, and at the entrance, a tiny farm stand.

"Is that a vegetable garden?" I asked as we got closer, the small wooden baskets of zucchini and tomatoes now coming into view. "Where the tetherball courts used to be?"

"It is; good memory, Millen," Mack replied. "Do you want me to go stake some balls out there so you can play next to the corn?"

"Only if you want me to throw one of the balls at your head," I snapped back.

"That's number one on my list of things for us to do together while you're here," he said, reaching a hand across the middle seat and ruffling my hair, not missing a beat.

"Mack planted that whole garden himself, Clara," Nick chimed in from the front. "He's like Pine Lake's Johnny Appleseed."

"My pet project from a couple of summers ago," Mack said nonchalantly. "I worked on it with a bunch of senior kids."

"Wow," I said. Even I could begrudgingly admit that this was, well, very cool.

"Yeah," he continued. "The campers grow everything, and what we don't use for meals, we give away to the community at the stand."

"Mack's being humble," Trey said. "Didn't someone write an article about it, and you? And how you brought the locals and Pine Lake closer together?"

"Just the town paper, not, like, the *Boston Globe*." Mack waved Trey off, but it was obvious from the way his eyes glinted as he spoke that he was clearly proud of what he'd created. "But, yeah, I love working with the kids on the farm stand. I was going to keep it going this fall and try to bring schoolkids in to run it."

"I bet they'd love that," I said, marveling at the beauty of this once-empty slice of land that now bloomed full of life.

"Yeah," he sighed, more wistful than I was used to seeing him. "Plans changed, though."

Here it was again, that earnest side of Mack that disarmed me.

"What?" he said with a raised brow when he caught me staring.

"Nothing, you're just sitting on a bunch of work stuff that I need," I said, pointing to the manila folder peeking out underneath the edge of his thigh. Inside was fifteen-year-old Clara's note, and I breathed a sigh of relief when he shifted and slid it toward me. The last thing I needed was Mack using my ten teenage action items to torment me. He'd probably try to cut my hair off in my sleep. And the lover thing? I'd never hear the end of it.

"Maybe this is Mack's way of helping you take a break," Nick said matter-of-factly as he leaned over the console to talk to us in the back seat. "Clara swore a sacred vow that she'd try not to work this week."

Mack gave a shrug, his hair flopping down across his forehead. "I should probably keep sitting on your stuff then. For the cause."

"Yeah, I'm sure my boss would love hearing that all my files got ruined because of some guy's ass," I huffed, clutching the folder tight in my lap. We rolled past the soccer field and the art barn, which was still covered outside in splatter paint, and almost surely overflowing with camper arts and crafts projects.

Three figures stood in front of Sunrise, the juniors bunk our group always made our home base during weeks like this. It sat in the middle of a row of identical cabins, painted a bright white with forest-green shutters. "Whoa," I said, marveling at their shiny new colors. "Didn't the cabins used to be gray?"

"Lotta big changes up here, Millen," Mack said slyly.

Nick twisted around in his seat. "Mack convinced Marla and Steve to paint them a few years ago."

"They look good," I said, as the shapes in front of us began to take a clearer, human form. So clear that I could see as we approached that one of the people was very, very pregnant.

Holy shit.

"Sam!" I practically fell out of the car as Trey shifted into park. Tripping on my sandals, I raced to get to my oldest camp friend, who stood, hands pressed against her lower back, talking to Eloise and the tall, lanky man next to her.

Sam turned her head, awash in its usual crown of black curls, and shrieked. "Clare-bear!"

She opened her arms wide, which I knew was intended to end in a hug. Instead, I stopped a couple feet in front of her, gawking.

"Look, I don't ever like to comment on people's bodies, but I might have to make an exception here. You're—"

"Yup." She nodded, a smile wide across her face. "Big time."

Eloise sauntered up next to her, her orange-red hair tucked under a baseball cap—her fair skin could burn even on the cloudiest of days—and braided tightly down her back. It shone like the last moment of a sunset, that explosion of color that occurred just before the sun slipped past the horizon. True to form, she was decked out in all black, her leggings and tank top somehow looking like formal wear on her.

"She's peed like five times and we've only been here an hour," Eloise said, leaning in to give me a peck on the cheek, and then tugging me in tight for a hug, which was more emotion than I was used to getting from her.

"That seems reasonable," I said, still shocked. "Also hi."

"Hi," Eloise purred back, dragging out the word as she squeezed me, a departure from her usual curt staccato. If I didn't know any better, I'd assumed she was stoned, but Eloise rarely let any substance other than pure, type-A energy, and the occasional cocktail, control her. She could be both effortless and calculated, which had been a formidable combination on the soccer field and in swim meets back in the day.

I inhaled the faint scent of some sort of luxurious hair care product as we embraced, that intoxicating mix of chemicals intertwined with florals. Her eyes trailed down my neck as she pulled away, her lip crooking up just a bit. "Nice necklace."

"Mack was waiting at the entrance of camp to give it to me," I said with a shake of my head as I yanked the stupid thing off and shoved it into my tote bag.

"Of course he was," she replied, brows tweaked knowingly. Eloise was a stock analyst, a Wall Street job I didn't quite understand, other than it meant she was paid to see things from all angles and then attempt to tell the future of a company's financial prowess.

She grabbed the man next to her by his elbow, tugging him close. "Clar, this is Linus. My partner."

Eloise's normally controlled, clipped delivery dripped with affection, the closest I'd ever seen her come to swooning. Nick and Trey weren't lying. Eloise was smitten.

"Nice to meet you, Clara," he said with a firm grip of my hand.

Linus was handsome, with close-cropped black hair, olive skin, and delicate, wire-frame glasses.

Sam leaned into my shoulder. "He brought a solar-powered lantern," she murmured in my ear. "He thought we'd be in tents. He's sweet."

"She seems different," I mused as we watched Eloise and Linus saunter hand in hand over to the rest of our group.

He was decked out in a loose white button-down and army green hiking pants—the kind that you could unzip at the knee and turn into shorts. I distinctly remembered my seventy-one-year-old dad wearing a very similar pair last summer, and the fact that Linus was almost definitely half his age and wearing them unironically made me like him instantly.

"She is," Sam agreed, nodding. "She's in love."

"I heard, but I didn't quite believe it until I saw it with my own eyes." I shook my head, overwhelmed. "I'll process that in a second, but first can we discuss you?"

Arms wide, I finally gave Sam a proper hug. She was so short my chin practically rested on her head, and I squeezed her as hard as I could without squashing her beautifully round belly.

"Were you going to wait to have the kid before you told us?" I asked, looking down again to make sure what I was seeing was real.

"Well, you're the last person to find out, actually," she said, and her eyes shifted slightly. "I tried to tell everyone in person or over the phone. I've been waiting for you to text me back so we could set up that FaceTime chat."

My stomach sank. All around me were signs that my friends' lives had chugged on together, with me on the periphery. They shared a closeness that I'd once been part of, but now I was the outsider, the last to learn about all the ways their lives were growing and changing while mine had seemingly stalled out.

And I had no one to blame but myself.

10

"OH, FUCK, SAM. I am so sorry." My entire face was on fire, one hundred degrees warmer than the rest of my body. "Things have been crazy, and I just totally spaced."

Because, of course, Sam had texted months ago that she wanted to talk. **Clare-bear, I have things to tell you!**

I'd replied, telling her I'd respond soon with some free days when we could hop on the phone. And I'd meant it at the time—as soon as I could come up for air, I'd get back to her to set up our chat. But then the days ticked on. Meetings bled into other meetings, late nights went later than expected.

It had crossed my mind occasionally that I owed her a call, but my brain always moved on to the next thing, and the thought of catching up with Sam fluttered away back into the ether.

These were all excuses, of course. And none of them made this situation any better.

"I'm so sorry," I said again. "I really flaked."

"Well, hey, now I get to tell you in person." She gave me a big smile, and I hoped that meant we were okay, though it didn't erase the sick feeling coursing through my body.

I hadn't texted an old, dear friend back, even though it was clear they had news to share, because I was too busy. But *was* I, really? Sure, work was a lot, but I'd had time to scroll TikTok for hours on end, just waiting for my brain to shut off. What kind of person chooses mind-numbing videos of strangers over talking to their very oldest friend?

I pushed all the uncomfortable thoughts aside and focused on Sam. A person I loved, I reminded myself, quoting from teen Clara's list of intentions. "I have many questions for you."

She pressed a hand to her lower back and shifted on her feet. "I figured," she chuckled. "Sperm donor, thirty-seven weeks, yes, it's fine for me to drive still, yes, I have to pee all the time, no, I don't have any weird cravings, but the thought of touching raw chicken makes me want to die."

She stuck her tongue out, gagging slightly.

"Okay, know-it-all, those were some of my questions," I said, trying to let go of the awkwardness I felt. It had always been so natural, being here with her, with our friends. But now I was clunky, out of practice.

"Um, did you already unpack?" I asked.

"Yeah, I put my stuff in Sunrise." Sam nodded. If she sensed my uneasiness, she didn't let on. "Eloise and Linus have decided to have their own bunk." She raised her eyebrows as she shared this big news.

"Their own bunk?" I looked back over to where they stood, hands still linked. "Wow. Breaking tradition."

The one time Charles had tagged along with me to Pine Lake for a week, early on when we were dating, we bunked with my friends in Sunrise like I'd always done. What did it say about me, and my past relationship, that instead of seeking out some privacy with my boyfriend, I'd made us sleep in bunk beds alongside my best friends?

Sam leaned into me, speaking quietly. "They're very, very extra. You'll see."

She took off slowly toward the rest of our friends, and I stood back for a moment, taking them all in before turning to face the lake. Eloise was in love, Sam was on the verge of motherhood, and this place that had brought us all together so many years ago was now about to be lost to us for good. Even Charles was off on some new path, growing out his hair and posting sweaty photos of himself for all the world to see.

I fought the urge to panic. Deep breaths. I just needed to get through this week, and I had a plan to do it too, mapped out on a piece of notebook paper half a lifetime ago. I'd find some joy, bask in the beauty of this place and these people, and then head back down to Boston recharged and ready to run shit.

"Hey." A low, deep voice vibrated against my skin like a tiny tremor. "I hope you brought a bathing suit."

I only had to turn my head a fraction of an inch to see Mack's self-satisfied face, eyes smoldering and eager for my reaction. Instead, I held it back, denying him the satisfaction.

"Obviously, why?" I played it cool as I tried to resettle myself into this old game of ours: back and forth, tit for tat, always finding ways to best each other. I didn't want to let on that I felt a little rusty.

"Let's have a race this week. You and me." He tugged at the front of his T-shirt like some sort of teenage jock. "Freestyle. I gotta find ways to remind you who the better Color Week captain is."

Good lord. Here I was marveling at everyone leaping into the next phases of life and, of course, look who hadn't changed at all.

"Nice try, Mack," I muttered, even as my cheeks burned. Suddenly I felt fifteen again, annoyed and thrilled by him all at once.

"Aw, come on, Millen, don't tell me you're scared." He took a step closer, then another. Now he was just inches away, and my eyes drifted to his chest rising and falling beneath his threadbare T-shirt, the outline of his shoulders broad and strong. "That's not the girl I remember."

He blinked once, studying me intently, like he could find the old Clara inside me, lurking just beneath the surface of my skin.

"I'm not scared of losing to you," I said defiantly, lifting my chin as I thought of the words scribbled on that paper stuffed inside my bag: *Do something that scares you.*

Certainly, this wasn't what young Clara had in mind. Nothing about racing against Mack scared me; I could kick his ass any day, past or present. So why did something about his words feel utterly terrifying?

He took off jogging toward the waterfront, whipping his head around to look at me with an enormous grin. "You and me, Millen! Rematch!"

"We're not fifteen anymore!" I yelled after him. It was barely a zinger, and he let me know how little it affected him by flinging his arm up in the air, shooting his middle finger up at me without breaking stride.

"I know, that's why I think I can win!" he shouted back.

I stood quietly and watched him go, too distracted to come up with some sharp retort, too focused on what was dawning on me as I watched him tear through the grass, those tan legs carrying him with a speed I could never match.

I'd only been in his presence for a few minutes, but I was already reminded how just a single comment from his mouth could throw a wrench in my best-laid plans. I wasn't here to get swept up in our old back-and-forth.

I heard him shout my name in the distance, but this time, I didn't react. Instead, I headed back toward Sunrise to rejoin my friends and get on with our day. Mack might have been able to knock me off course when we were kids, but I wasn't an easy mark anymore.

11

"SLOW DOWN, YOU'RE coming in and out." Lydia's voice crackled through my phone and then got drowned out by loud cheers erupting around her. "The Red Sox just scored, so people are going nuts."

"Sorry, sorry," I said, tromping through the grass down to the waterfront in my ratty old Northeastern sweats. "It's just kind of important."

"You called at the perfect time," she said, and the noise around her calmed. "How's the list going? Check anything off yet?"

"Not a thing," I said, tucking my free hand into my pocket to make sure the letter was still there.

"You come home next Saturday, right?" she asked.

"Yes," I said, fingering the pointy edge of the folded paper.

"Well, hurry up, the clock is ticking. Better start having a shitload of fun."

"Very funny," I grumbled, pausing a few feet away from my friends, lingering on the outskirts of their circle of camping chairs centered around the fire pit. "Listen, I just wanted to see if anything new came out of the Creative meeting today."

"Clara!" Lydia scolded. "I definitely don't remember 'check in with work when you're not supposed to be working' being something teenage Clara wanted you to do."

"I know, I know, I'm only going to ask about this one meeting." Our team had a three-hour brainstorm on the calendar for today, complete with catering, which was Amaya's attempt at being generous while still forcing people to work on a weekend.

"Not unless you count Delilah trying to sell us on the idea of creating tiny mascots named Barley and Hops, and recounting the time she did a keg stand while tailgating at a Harry Styles concert as 'anything new.'"

I let out a groan. "Ugh. We're fucked, aren't we?"

"Hold on a sec, boss." Lydia's voice was muffled, and I paced as I waited for her. Mack stood at the edge of the flames, which spotlit him against the shadows of dusk creeping across the sky. He looked perfectly content, an easy smile on his face as he held a beer in one hand and used the other to poke at the sparking logs with a giant stick.

I shuffled a few steps closer as he lifted the bottle to his lips, the Alewife logo unmistakable in the bright light of the fire. Jesus Christ. Work had followed me here whether I wanted it to or not.

Mack shifted to say something to Nick and caught my eye, the edges of his lips curling up ever so slightly. He gave a small nod as if to say "come here," and suddenly I was fifteen again, walking back to the junior bunks after campfire with Mack, only to feel his hand slide into mine, tugging me behind a tree.

"I should have sabotaged your laptop before you left," Lydia said, her voice, still choppy from the terrible phone service, jolting me back to the present. "Listen, try not to worry while you're up there. It's a brewery, for fuck's sake. We'll figure it out."

The swoosh of a toilet flushing echoed in the background.

"Are you peeing with me on the phone?" I asked, laughing, still watching Mack.

"Hey, you called me and said it was urgent!" she protested. "Now, can you please go relax? We have two weeks to figure this out."

"Thirteen days," I corrected.

"Please don't 'well, actually' me about this," she said, chuckling.

"Sorry, it's just been a weird day. Marla and Steve—who own this place—sold it, and we all just found out."

"Oof," Lydia grunted.

I cleared my throat, lowering my voice as I backed up a bit so no one could hear me.

"One more thing."

"Yeah?"

"My friend Sam—the one we talked to yesterday—she's pregnant."

"That's cool!" Lydia said enthusiastically.

"No, like, almost about to pop pregnant. She wanted to tell me in person over FaceTime months ago, and I forgot to find a time for us to talk. So she never told me. Until today."

Lydia sucked in a breath on the other end of the line. "Yikes."

"I know," I groaned. "I need to figure out how to make it up to her."

"You're a good friend, Clara. You literally created a calendar for the office to track every person's birthday at work. And you've somehow coordinated regular cupcake deliveries off of that schedule. That was extra labor you definitely did not need to do."

I laughed at her assessment. "Sam's birthday isn't 'til November, though."

"I'm not saying you need to go get cupcakes. Just focus on being present up there with her this week," she said. "Do things that help you reconnect."

A firefly flashed its light off in the distance, signaling the arrival of nighttime, and I took it as a sign. "You're right. You're the best, Lyd."

"So are you, boss. Now go get drunk or hike or whatever it is you're supposed to be doing this week. Those are on your list, right?"

"No," I said. "But I'm about to have a beer and—you'll love this—Mack drinks Alewife."

She said something that sounded like a garbled, "Of course he does." And then the line went dead.

"Hello?" I said. "Lydia?" But the call was dropped, cursed by the lack of cell towers here in northern New Hampshire. Defeated, I stuffed my phone back in my pocket and turned my attention to my friends, admiring the scene in front of me. Nick pontificating, holding his drink like a microphone. Trey's mouth open, mid-laugh, as Sam watched over everyone, perched like a sage in a camping chair. Eloise and Linus hovering by the picnic table, her arms wrapped around his waist, while Mack lingered over the fire attentively, in the center of it all.

The water behind them carried their voices around the lake, echoes of chatter and laughter, the most comforting sound. There was nothing special about this moment, other than how much I had missed times like this: all of us together, talking forever about absolutely nothing.

"Hey," I said, finally joining my friends on the small sliver of sand. "I'm all unpacked. I took the single bed next to Sam."

I turned toward Nick and Trey, who grabbed a bottle from the six-pack at his feet, twisted off the top, and passed it to me. "You guys seriously want to share a bunk bed? Why don't we push two beds together for you, make up the old camp king?"

This was how I'd always remembered their bed set up at our friend reunions before, and I'd been surprised to see their stuff neatly stacked on a top and bottom bunk instead.

Trey shook his head. "My snoring has been driving Nick nuts," he explained. "Hopefully I won't keep all of you awake."

"I can always go sleep with Eloise and Linus," I quipped, intending it as a joke.

But Nick just nodded adamantly. "Honestly? I'm considering it."

Trey swung around to look at him, a sharp crease between his brows. He sat there for a second, as if he was deciding on exactly what to say. Nick watched him expectantly, almost like a challenge, and I realized there was a silent conversation going on between the two of them that had nothing at all to do with my stupid crack.

Eventually, Trey hopped up and headed in the direction of the picnic table, which was covered in pizza boxes and ripped-open bags of chips. Nick simply let out a sigh and turned back to the fire, where Mack was crouched on his heels, crumpling newspaper into tiny balls and shoving it under the stack of logs.

"Reliving your rope burn glory days, Mack?" I needed to deflate whatever tension this was that had invaded our fire circle, and ribbing Mack was an easy solution. And I couldn't resist reminding him that I had kicked his ass in the rope burn in our final Color Week competition.

He swiveled around with a bemused look on his face, his knees hitting the ground as he caught my eye. But just as I settled confidently back into my seat, he lifted the hem of his T-shirt to his brow, wiping away the sweat on his forehead and offering up a look at his stomach, which was just as sun-kissed as the rest of him. The muscles of his abs shifted as he moved, and when he bent forward again I caught a glimpse of the edge of gray boxers, and a trail of hair, and I was off-kilter once again.

"Oh boy, here we go," Nick cackled, rubbing his hands together. "I love that you just rolled in here after years away, Clara, and you're already giving Mack crap about Color Week."

"I'm just remembering how hard he worked to get the fire lit under the Blue Team's rope, and, I dunno, how easy I found it." I glanced down in an attempt to nonchalantly study my fingernails, anything but look back at Mack's dewy skin, his shimmering eyes.

"Ohhhhhh!" Sam taunted, hooting at me through cupped hands. "I give that dis a seven out of ten."

I shimmied my shoulders, forcing myself to loosen up, and then did my best impression of a runner prepping for a race, stretching an arm in front of my chest. "I'm just getting started."

"And here I thought your shit-talk would be rusty." Mack threw back another sip of his beer from where he now sat on the ground, elbows propped up on his knees, and then raised the bottle toward me, a nod of respect.

"Some things just get finer with age," I said, mimicking his toast before taking a small swig, the sharp iciness of the beer a delicious relief.

He pointed at his chest, his brows suggestively high, and my gaze landed on his eyes, amber and green flecks in the firelight, the color of sea glass. Had his lashes always been this long?

"Well, welcome back, Clara." He gave a sweeping gesture. "Dinner's on the picnic table, and there's more beer and seltzer in the cooler. And I'll be sure to find some new ways to remind you that our team kicked your team's ass."

"Can't we just settle this like adults?" I leaned forward in my chair, enjoying the banter much more than I should. "The World Series doesn't end in a tie. Let's just say my team won, and that I was the better captain, and move on. Ties don't exist in the real world."

"Aw, but I'd tie with you anytime, Millen," he said, that cocky, pleased-with-himself smile appearing, half lit up, half covered in shadows of darkness.

"Oh, really? Is that why you were walking around here wearing a medal that has been around since before the invention of the iPhone, goading me into a swim race?" I challenged, fiddling with a strand of hair between two fingers.

"There's nothing I love more than two adults fighting over something that happened a billion years ago," Eloise chimed in, swirling the wine in her plastic cup, which was the same shockingly bright red as her hair, before bringing it to her lips with an eye roll in my direction. I learned long ago not to take it personally; she rolled her eyes so often that it was practically a reflex.

"Just making up for lost time, El," Mack said, his eyes back on me. I decided to give the pizza table my undivided attention, and walked over to the food, slapping two greasy, no longer hot slices onto a paper plate.

Eloise was now perched on Linus's knee, her body pressed against his chest, arm wrapped around his neck. Mindlessly, she started running her fingers along the nape of his neck, and he moved his hands on her hips in an echoing rhythm. Jesus.

I dragged my chair over next to Sam and scooted it until I was practically sitting in her lap, so I wouldn't have a front-row seat to their foreplay.

"Favorite camp memory," Sam said, pointing at me. "Go."

"Oh, crap, um. Winning the senior girls' swim race during my last summer." The words came out garbled, my mouth full of pizza. "Sorry, Eloise."

I'd kicked her butt by a few seconds, and later that night she'd cried over her loss. Tonight she just waved me off and went back to canoodling with Linus. I'd worked so hard that summer, showing up to swim laps after each day's activities were done. That feeling of winning by the skin of my teeth had been downright euphoric, a high that had numbed my worries for a day or two until the reality of my parents' split settled back into my brain.

"Oh! Wait, I've got another one," I said as a memory flashed brightly in my head. "The night we raided the kitchen for cookies and almost got caught by Marla. I think we were twelve."

"By we, you mean *you* led the way, and our entire bunk followed." Sam shifted in her chair, her hand holding her bump. "You were always leading us into precarious situations."

"That was back before I knew better." The words came out sadder than I intended. "I also gave the entire bunk lice that year."

"Like I said." Sam swatted my knee. "Precarious situations."

She pointed at Nick. "Nicholas. Go."

"Capture the Flag my first summer, when that kid with the blue hair—"

"Wilson Frank," Eloise interrupted.

"Yes, Wilson! When everyone forgot he was stuck in the other team's jail and left him there forever, and when we finally figured out we needed to rescue him he had his pants down and was peeing behind the goalpost because he was too committed to the game to leave and go to the bathroom."

Eloise let out a huge laugh, leaning forward on Linus's lap. "Oh my god, yes. That was the first time I'd ever seen another person's genitalia. That gets my vote."

"He was so embarrassed!" Nick could barely get the words out, he was laughing so hard.

"He's an attorney now," Sam said, looking down at her phone. "According to LinkedIn."

Finally catching his breath, Nick added, "And every play and musical I ever did here. I never had the confidence to do theater before coming to camp. And now it's my whole life."

"You should have seen the production of *Newsies* he directed last year," Trey said proudly. "The kids were amazing."

Nick offered him a wistful look in return as a quiet lull fell over our group, the fire crackling in the wake of our silence.

"Mack?" Sam asked, shifting in her chair to get comfortable. "I mean I know you work here, so you have a wealth of moments to choose from."

"*Worked*, you mean. Pretty sure I'm about to be unemployed and moving back in with my parents." Mack's mood shifted for a moment as he dragged a hand through his hair, his smile now a tight line.

A dull throb pulsed in my chest, an actual, honest-to-god ache, as I thought of Mack this afternoon, lighting up at the sight of his garden, the spark in his voice as he'd talked about his dashed plans for next year.

It was obvious that he loved it here. Pine Lake was Marla and Steve's, of course, but Mack's touch was all over this place. It was a loss I hadn't fully considered until this very moment.

He studied the ground in thought, tracing a circle in the sand with his index finger. Then he looked up with an earnest smile. "This."

"Oh my god, you're so full of shit," Sam moaned, digging a marshmallow out of the bag in her lap and lobbing it at his head.

"Hey, what?!" Mack ducked defensively, and the marshmallow landed with a plunk in the fire. "I'm serious! I look forward to this week all year. And I'm glad we're all here for the last one."

His eyes darted toward me, just for a second, but it was long enough to fill me with fifty different dirty thoughts, all of which involved his mouth pressed against various parts of my body.

Mack's teeth grazing the soft skin of my forearm, or his lips pressed against my thigh.

It wasn't the first time my mind had traveled to the Land of Naked Mack Thoughts. But now, with him just a few feet away from me, the fact that they could actually happen in real life felt both terrifying and thrilling, like the moment you get buckled into a roller coaster before it rockets up that first hill.

It was the same thing I'd felt the first time we'd met as kids, when we'd kissed at fifteen, and every time he draped that medal over my neck again and again with satisfied glee. When it came to drawing me in, like a moth to a flame, Mack always won.

12

"HERE, HERE," NICK agreed as he hopped up to smack Mack on the back affectionately. I snapped back to reality, nodding eagerly along to what Nick was saying, just in case someone noticed I'd drifted off into X-rated fantasy land.

"Plus," Mack added, "you're way more fun to hang out with than teenagers. Don't tell my fifteen-year-old self that, though."

"Oh my god, was your letter as painfully earnest as mine?" Nick asked.

"Yeah, man, I had a *lot* of feelings." Mack made a horrified face, and though I laughed along with everyone else, I was secretly dying to know what he'd written in his letter.

"Mine was just a list of everything I'd accomplished," Eloise said, head bobbing as Linus massaged her shoulders. "Not to brag, but there were quite a few things."

"Sam, you're a real hero for saving those." Nick clapped in her direction as she took the tiniest bow.

"I only had to move them across the country like two times and remember not to throw them out for twenty years," she joked, digging back into the marshmallow bag to pop one in her mouth.

"Well, it was worth it, thank you," Nick said. "Even if I did have to relive my decision to write my letter as a poem."

"Aw, Nick!" I cooed.

"The drama," he replied with a shake of his head.

"Every teenager is dramatic," Eloise said. "They're all hormonal and depressed and emotional. It would be weird if you weren't."

"I wasn't," Linus said, his chin nestled on Eloise's shoulder. "I started my first business in the tenth grade."

"Everyone but you, honey," she said sweetly, twisting around to give him a kiss on the cheek.

"Oh my god, I have the best idea." Nick gasped, eyes wide with his sudden stroke of genius. "We need to read them to each other, out loud."

My stomach dropped at the suggestion. I'd let Lydia read it, sure, but her degree in Clara Millen history only went back a couple of years. Everyone sitting around this campfire knew me then, and the thought of revealing my teenage self's hopes and dreams, only to contrast them with the current mess of my life, was terrifying.

"Clara, did you ever get yours?" Sam asked, and before I could really put a plan into action, I felt myself shaking my head.

"It must have gone to my old address," I said with a shrug and a smile, as if my insides weren't quaking with nerves. It wasn't a lie, not exactly, but the words tasted sour and wrong in my mouth.

"Well, mine's back home in Brooklyn," Eloise said. "Otherwise I'd definitely be reminding you of how many blue ribbons I got that year."

The collective quiet that fell over the group told me that Nick's idea had hit a mutually agreed upon dead end, and my shoulders sagged with relief.

"Maybe they won't go through with it," Nick said finally, and we all knew who—and what—he was talking about.

"Oh, honey," Sam said sympathetically. "We all want that, but they already have."

"Eventually everything good has to come to an end," Mack said quietly, in a stoic tone I'd never heard him use before. "It's time to move on."

I looked at him across the flames, but he was staring off toward the lake. His elbows were on his knees, hands clasped, and I traced the muscular shape of his arms with my gaze, strengthened from days spent hefting kayaks out of the water and dragging boats ashore. His hands were almost certainly rough and calloused, and my skin prickled at the thought of what they'd feel like pressed against me. I gave my head a little shake, clearing out the lusty thoughts.

"Jesus, Mack, enough with the nihilism," Nick scolded. "It doesn't go well with your boyish good looks."

Mack chuckled at this and tossed a stick in the fire. "Welcome to my dark side, buddy."

"Enough of that," Nick scolded. "Positive vibes only!"

My eyes drifted over to Trey, and for a moment he looked utterly annoyed with Nick, scowling like he found every word coming out of his mouth insufferable. But then I blinked, the smoke wafting in my direction and stinging my eyes, and when I opened them again Trey was back to his even-keeled, content self.

"Y'all, we need to do something to send this place off," Nick continued, peeling the label off the edge of his beer bottle. "Something big. Fun. *Stupid fun.* Anyone?"

He glanced around at us expectantly.

"What if we just became campers again for a few days," I said, an idea forming out of the bits and pieces of memories in the back of my mind.

He pushed his glasses up his nose and leaned forward. "I'm listening."

"Okay, well, I don't want to speak out of turn because I know I've been MIA these last few years," I said, treading carefully. "So maybe things have changed. But normally when we've been up here in the past we just kind of hang out."

"Um, speak for yourself," Sam said. "Last year I tried to jog around the lake and had to call Mack to come pick me up after half a mile."

"It was really hot," he added, with a knowing nod toward Sam.

"I'm not saying we shouldn't still hang out, but what if we also did, I dunno, camp stuff. One final week of creating the best Pine Lake memories we can possibly make."

Stuff that would be fun, joyful, and maybe even scary, I reasoned to myself. Things that would get me closer to what I'd set out to accomplish this week, and further away from moments like this, when there was nothing to distract me from Mack.

"Oh, boy," Eloise muttered, curling in closer to Linus, who was watching me with a curious look on his face.

"Come on, El, it's not that crazy," I said, rising out of my chair. "We're already sitting around a campfire tonight. That counts. Capture the Flag would be super easy with this many people."

"Yes!" Nick gasped with excitement. "I have been craving some good old-fashioned Capture the Flag chaos. Linus, you have that silent but deadly energy thing going on. I want you on my team."

"Um." Linus looked deeply unsure of himself but nodded. "Sure."

I twiddled my fingers, my brain now going a mile a minute. "We could kick each other's asses and complain about how old our bones feel. Losers buy the winners lunch."

"Well, shit, I'm out," Sam declared, pointing at her belly with a laugh.

"That's okay. We'll need fans to watch," Trey chimed in. "And refs."

"Yes! I love it." I pointed at him, and for a moment I thought of

Amaya, teetering on Abe's desk, staring at me. *See?* I thought. *I'm doing exactly what you wanted.*

"Ooh my god, we could do a dessert party!" I spitballed, remembering the magic of the annual late-night dining hall kitchen "raid" for the winning Color Week team.

"Oooh, yes," Sam said, eyes lighting up.

"I'm sure there's leftover ice cream from the one we had this summer," mused Mack. "We just need to dig through the freezers in the dining hall."

"Truth or dare!" Eloise shouted from her perch on Linus's lap. "In...the dining hall?"

"Sure." I chuckled.

"It's multitasking," she added.

Something clicked on inside me; I was shifting into project manager mode. This was everything I'd once loved about my job, the spontaneous creativity and hive-mind energy, brilliant ideas birthed out of thin air.

"So we're cramming every Pine Lake Camp tradition into, like, five days?" Mack asked, and I couldn't tell if he thought this plan was ridiculous or brilliant.

"Exactly." I squared my shoulders, giving him a firm nod. I was going with brilliant, no matter what he thought.

"Wow, look at you," Sam said, giving me a playful once-over. "Getting right back into the swing of things."

"We could do friendship bracelets in the art barn," I continued. There was no stopping me now. "Oh! And we have to do wish boats in the lake on our last night!"

"I'm not following," Linus said, pushing his glasses up his nose. "I've barely understood, like, half of what you've said. It's like you're talking in code. Wish boats?"

"You'll get used to it," Trey joked. "And the boats are cool. We write wishes on the bottom of little pieces of wood and then toss them in the lake."

"Excuse me, sir," I countered, the horror in my voice exaggerated for effect. "Wish boats are way more magical than that."

"Yeah, there are candles, for Christ's sake," Sam said, an impish grin on her face. "Which you light and fit into the top of the wooden boat. And the legend is that if your boat reaches the other side of the lake with the flame still going, your wish will come true."

"One year I wished for a flip phone and then my parents got me one for my birthday," Nick said. "So it's definitely real."

"Yeah, I mean, I just did this a few weeks ago with campers," Mack said with an earnest nod of his head. "And I wished for Clara to get her ass up here again, and here she is."

"Oh, will you shut the fuck up?" I hissed as he stuck his tongue out with a laugh.

"Fine," he said, his eyes staying put on my face. "What about Color Week then? It's the most important tradition here."

He pointed a finger at his chest, and then tilted it toward me, brows raised, like it was a challenge.

"No way." I pressed my lips together tightly, giving my head a deliberate shake. "Color Week has approximately fifty billion different activities. Are we going to do them all with, like, seven people?"

"Fine, we can pick one thing from Color Week," he goaded, leaning forward, elbows on knees. "The relay. Let's have a rematch."

"Oh my god, you and your fucking rematches!" I snipped, though I begrudgingly liked the idea. The relay was the final competition of Color Week, a hodgepodge of ridiculous challenges. It was absurd and silly but also legitimately hard, which made it sort of perfect for our final week at Pine Lake.

"How else am I going to get you to hang out with me?" he asked, and the playful tone of his voice sent me spiraling back to the visions I'd had earlier. A new thought sizzled in my brain; this time it involved his mouth against my ear, teasing me in an entirely different way.

"Fine!" I said finally, throwing my hands up. "You help me plan it, and we'll do the relay."

"Done and done, Millen," Mack said with a pleased nod.

Sam pushed herself up to stand with a groan, pressing her hands into the sides of her waist.

"I love you all, but I'm exhausted. It's past ten. I'm going to head up to bed."

"Wait, so when do we start?" asked Eloise.

"Why not tomorrow?" I said with a shrug. "All we need for Capture the Flag are the flags."

"We have, like, a billion handkerchiefs," Mack said. "I helped Marla pack up a bunch last week. They're in the storage room off the office."

"Perfect," I said with a confident nod of my chin. "Noon tomorrow."

"Literally the hottest time of the day," griped Trey.

"Yes, but everyone can sleep in, pound coffee, and then sweat it all out and nap after," I said, plopping back down in my chair, satisfied with how easily I'd set our week into motion. Maybe I wasn't the best at experiencing joy—yet!—but I sure did know how to make shit happen.

If only the Alewife pitch had fallen into place that easily.

I dug my phone out of my pocket, attempting a quick scroll of my inbox to see if anyone had sent over any updates. But even with one bar of cell service, my emails wouldn't load.

"Fuck," I muttered under my breath. I wasn't used to being cut off like this, and unlike Sam, I felt wired and wide awake, like I was ready to start the day, not end it.

"Everything okay?" Mack was suddenly standing in front of me, hovering. His hair fell in his face, forming a soft halo around features that had sharpened since I last saw him.

"I need that Wi-Fi info from you." I waved my unusable phone in his face. "I have spotty cell service, and I need to be able to monitor what's going down at my office. Can't you do that thing where you share the password from your phone?"

"Yeah, sure. But my phone's in the boathouse." He took a couple of steps back. "Just swim out to the diving dock with me first."

He lifted his T-shirt over his head and flung it on the back of a chair. *Do not look at his chest, do not look at his chest,* I thought as I immediately looked right at his chest, broad and smooth in all the right places.

"Do it, do it, do it," Sam chanted as Trey and Nick picked up empty bottles, tossing them into the recycling bin that lived by the dock.

"Oh my god, Mack." I shook my head, silently willing my eyeballs to focus on his face. "I don't want to swim now. It's late."

"Come on, Millen, what happened to making memories during our last week together?" He reached a finger out, poking me playfully on the shoulder. "You don't think you could win that senior girls' race now? Eloise? Thoughts? Fighting words?"

"I think she'll kick your ass!" Eloise said as she pushed herself off Linus's lap, joining in the cleanup efforts.

"See?" I channeled whatever affection was bubbling up for Mack into a pointed glare as I tossed my paper plate into the trash and walked toward him. "Even my former competitor agrees with me."

"I'd be interested in seeing who wins," said Linus diplomatically.

"One point for me; thank you, Linus." Mack dragged a hand through his hair as he took a few steps backward toward the water.

"I'm just in very comfortable sweatpants that I don't feel like taking off right now," I insisted, following him. "I could beat you, easily."

"Wow, you really have gotten soft," Mack taunted as he unbuttoned his jeans, kicking them off at the ankle as my eyes immediately followed, betraying my good intentions again. "I guess that's what happens when the city girl can't drive the three hours to get up here once a year."

"You really think you're going to get me to swim by calling me a 'city girl'?" Irritation warmed in me like a fever. "Okay, camp counselor."

"Come on, Millen, do it for the Wi-Fi password at least." He stretched a long arm overhead, moving with such effortless, calm ease. "And I'm the waterfront director, and winter caretaker, not a counselor. Get it right next time."

Mack was practically naked now, watching me as I stood there flustered. I don't think I'd ever used the word "languid" in a sentence before, but I remembered it from SAT prep in high school, and it was exactly how I'd describe Mack at this moment, standing there in nothing but a pair of black boxer briefs. The air around me felt fuzzy and warm, even though we were down by the water's edge, away from the fire.

I hadn't slept with anyone since Charles and I had split, and clearly the presence of a half-naked man was making my libido misfire.

"Okay, sure. Fine," I said with a huff, though there was a part of me craving the frigid water, in the hope that it might stamp out this crackling heat that kept rising inside of me. "One race, just to shut you up."

I was annoyed at his ridiculous challenge, and I rolled my eyes one more time just to let him know. But there was another part of me that felt eager and alive, open to possibility. Like a wish boat, about to be set out on the lake.

Maybe everything I wanted was really out there, just waiting for me on the other side.

13

"OH, IT'S ON, Millen." He gave me an eager smile, rubbing his hands together and jogging in place to get warm as I tossed my sweatshirt into the clothing heap growing by my feet. I had nothing on but an old wireless bra and some dingy pink underpants faded to gray from years of washing. But something in Mack's face twitched, just for an instant, as he glanced at me.

I pointed at him, about to issue some sort of challenge. But before I could he made a dash for the water. And just like that he morphed from relaxed, beach bum, boathouse-living Mack to the cunning competitor that I remembered as a kid, shapeshifting into a blur of black boxer briefs hitting the lake.

"Goddamnit!" I shrieked, scrambling to catch up.

"Come on, Clara!" Sam hollered somewhere behind me.

The water was shallow off the beach, barely past my knees, but that didn't stop me from diving right in. The chill of the lake hit me like a brain freeze after a bite of ice cream, cold and sharp. I didn't care. Instead, I kicked furiously, driven by the urge to win, as if beating Mack right now could somehow make up for all the other parts of my life that I was failing at.

Arms tearing through the water, I was soon behind him, then next to him, and then, somehow, miraculously, reaching a hand onto the faded wood of the diving raft before him.

Seconds after my fingertips grazed the smooth planks, he was there, panting, mouth open, water tracing wet lines down the curves of his cheekbones.

"Jesus Christ, Millen," he huffed. He sounded stuck between annoyed and impressed and gave me a befuddled, awed look.

It was impossible not to smile.

"I told you—no ties." My voice was choppy as I caught my breath, enjoying this opportunity to gloat. "Looks like you're a little rusty. Which is weird because you literally live on this lake year-round, and I—as you pointed out so *kindly*—haven't made the three-hour drive up here in years."

He laughed as he shook the water from his hair, his moves registering somewhere between a supermodel and a golden retriever puppy. I stuck my tongue out at him and then dove toward the ladder on the other side of the floating wooden dock, hoisting myself up onto the platform. It bobbed in the water under my weight, the night air hitting my skin with a slap.

The diving dock was huge, complete with the high-dive tower that I'd been too scared to jump off as a camper. Sitting here under it, I could see why—it seemed even taller and more terrifying than I'd remembered.

I sat down, knees bent, waving at my friends on the shore. They were tiny versions of themselves, shrunk by the distance, but the lake carried the echo of their cheers across the water. Then Mack was next to me, standing, hands on his hips, bent over and out of breath. I tilted my head up toward him, a sassy comment on the edge of my lips, until he caught my eye with a look so sultry all words evaporated on my tongue.

My face was now precariously close to every spot on his body I swore I would stop thinking about. But I couldn't, not when I could practically reach out and nip his hip bone with my teeth. My heart pounded against my rib cage, beating blood into every vein as Mack leaned forward, turning the distance between us into mere millimeters.

He reached a hand toward me, fingers soft against my shoulder, gliding up the back of my neck. My heart was good and gone now, leaving my body, falling into the water, dropping straight to the bottom of this lake. His fingers twisted in my hair—and just as I was sure I'd completely lost my ability to breathe, he stepped back, a rust-colored leaf dangling from the tips of his fingers.

He twirled it for a moment, his eyes still on me, completely unreadable.

Then, without a sound, he walked to the edge of the raft and did a flip-dive into the water. He could go from smoldering to utterly ridic-ulous in an instant, but these two sides of him pulled at me equally. That duality was all Mack, and I'd forgotten the spell it put on me.

But now? Now I remembered, and it took me a moment to regain my composure and rediscover my pulse. Leaping to my feet, I backed up to the far edge of the raft and took off running, as if this jump into the water could prove that he didn't just knock the wind out of me.

"Cannonball!" The words barely made it out of my mouth before my body smacked into the lake. I sunk into the blackness, a brief escape from the heat bubbling between us. When I finally made it to the sur-face, he was already climbing back up onto the platform, hanging on to the ladder as he watched me move through the water. Seconds later he was diving in again, and so I followed.

On and on we went like this, over and over without a word. Slowly, my brain started clearing out, the water sweeping away all my thoughts of Amaya, and Charles, and my bare, depressing apartment. My heart settled back into my chest, that sweet ache of pure, physical exhaustion slowly seeping into my bones.

From a distance, in between jumps and leaps and dives, I watched as our friends waved at us from the shore, gathered their stuff, and stomped out the coals of the fire. Soon they were mere shapes fading into the darkness as they headed up the hill toward the bunks, and it was just Mack and me, out here alone.

After what felt like an hour of propelling our bodies into the water, I clambered back up onto the raft and splayed out flat like a starfish, exhausted. Above me, the moon was tucked behind a shred of clouds, and the only sound was my breathing and the mournful call of a loon, floating somewhere on the lake. It was a haunting, high-pitched wail that was somehow both eerie and beautiful all at once.

The platform dipped as Mack lifted himself back on and scooted across the boards, lying down beside me. I didn't turn to look at him, but I could feel him there, inches away. This was the thing about Mack. He radiated warm energy, a big, blinding beam, like a flashlight with fresh batteries.

The water was cold, but the air wasn't much warmer, and my skin prickled with tiny goose bumps. Still, the pleasure of just lying there, wearied by the water and the emotion of being back in this place that I loved, outweighed my desire for warmth. I exhaled audibly, a sigh laced with pure pleasure, a sensation I'd missed more than I'd realized.

"Admit it, you're glad I made you go swimming," Mack said, giving my hip a gentle poke with his finger. "I think Pine Lake missed you."

His touch lingered for only a fraction of a second, but it ricocheted through me like a bolt of electricity.

"It's amazing how the magic of this place can come right back to you, like riding a bike," I replied, trying to keep my voice steady and my eyes locked on the stars bobbing and twinkling above. "It's in my bones."

"I get it. Sometimes it feels like this place was born inside of me," he murmured, all scratchy and low. "I'm gonna miss it."

"You've been here for so long." I tilted my head far enough to see the outline of his face in my peripheral vision. "That makes sense."

"Yeah, I'm not even quite sure what to do with myself if I'm not working here, you know? It's been my whole life, practically." He bit the corner of his mouth in thought. The sadness in his voice went straight to that soft part of my heart that always opened up a crack whenever he was near.

"Sometimes I feel like I use work to hide," I confessed, and I quickly looked back up at the sky, not quite ready for eye contact. It was the first time I'd said this to anyone other than the therapist I spoke with online from time to time. "It's a distraction from all the stuff I don't know how to deal with. And now I almost can't survive without it."

"Is that why you haven't been up here in forever?" he asked. He could have made some joke about it, called me a city girl again, but he didn't.

"I guess," I admitted, running a finger back and forth along the grained wood beneath us. "That, and there was just always something else happening that felt like it was more important."

"Ouch," he said in a pained voice, sucking air through his teeth.

"That's not what I meant!" I scooted up onto my elbows to look at him.

"Relax, Millen, I'm just fucking with you. I know what you mean."

"Oh, really?" I said, giving him a look that said I didn't believe him.

"Yeah." He rolled onto his side to face me. "It's, like, the things you think you're supposed to do take precedence over the things you actually want to do. And then somehow you don't even want to do the things you cared about anymore because your brain has tricked you into thinking what you should do is more important. Or something. That might not make any sense."

He lay back down and I followed, stretching out long again.

"It does, actually," I agreed. "It makes total sense."

"My parents asked me to go back to LA. They want me to run their business with my brother." There was no humor to his voice now; he sounded flat, lifeless. "They need someone to handle operations, which I can do easily."

I couldn't imagine anything less Mack-like than music licensing. Judging from the way he sounded right now, he couldn't either. And yet, he still smiled. It was resigned, and shadowed by sorrow, but it was a smile nonetheless, and this meek attempt twisted my heart up into a knot.

"It sounds like a 'supposed to' thing, instead of something you want to do." I reached over and gave his forearm a sympathetic squeeze. As my fingers left his skin, his hand was suddenly in mine, pulling me back to him.

This is how it had happened, all those years ago.

The two of us walking along the path toward the cabins after campfire, flashlights in hand. Then, a quick brush of skin, and his hand in mine, pulling me into the shadows until we were face-to-face, up against a tree.

And now—just like when we were younger—it felt like the stars I'd been watching overhead were spinning down to earth.

"Isn't that the way it goes, though?" His voice was a rumble; I could feel it across my skin. "Sometimes it feels like getting older is just letting go of what it is that you really want to do with your life."

"Um, excuse me," I said, running my thumb over his knuckles. My heartbeat thrummed in the palm of my hand, thumping loudly in my ears. "You do not sound like the Mack Sullivan I know."

He let out a quiet laugh. "That's just because you beat me tonight, and I'm a sore loser."

"Oh, well, *that* Mack Sullivan I know," I said, and he jerked his elbow into my side as retaliation, never letting go of my hand.

We stayed like this for a moment, still and staring up at the sky in contemplative quiet.

He shifted next to me, and I followed him with my eyes as he untangled our fingers and propped himself up onto his elbow.

"The last time you were here, you had your boyfriend with you," he said finally, staring down at me.

I waited, expecting some salty, coy retort to slip from his lips. But his face was oddly serious, and it registered that this wasn't a statement—Mack was asking me something.

"We broke up last year," I said, a rush of sound roaring in my ears, despite the quiet of the night. "He ended it."

"Oof," Mack said, lying back down. "I'm sorry."

"It's okay." I tilted my head to look at him, admiring the way his face curved and slanted, the strong shape of his nose, the delicate pout of his bottom lip. "I mean, it's sad. But you know, I think our relationship became a 'supposed to' sort of thing. At least it was for a long time. Or maybe it always was. I dunno."

I pressed my lips together, retreating back into myself. I'd said too much, more than I'd ever said to anyone about Charles and me. Touching Mack had scrambled my ability to think straight, and his soft, serious words disconnected my brain from my body, leaving my heart exposed and raw, and frighteningly open.

"I am really glad you came this year," he said, his eyes still locked with mine. "Even if you did just kick my ass."

"Well, see, that's a want. I wanted to kick your ass, so I did." I let out a low chuckle, but in my head it sounded like someone shrieking after sucking down helium.

"What else," he said, his voice so low it was almost a whisper, "do you want?"

I rolled onto my side, his eyes steady on me as I tucked one hand under my head like a pillow. And then, as if possessed, I reached out and brushed those damn tendrils off his forehead, taking a moment to admire the smooth skin of his cheeks, and the lines that were beginning to form on his brow. There was a softness to him that was new, like he'd eased into his skin while I'd been away.

"Millen?" He said my name like a question, and I nodded, not sure of what I was answering, exactly, but confident that my answer was yes.

This time his hand reached for my face, his thumb running across my bottom lip, our eyes so close that our lashes could almost lock together.

And then it all happened at once, symbiotic; Mack pulling me closer, closer until I was hovering over him, straddling his hips. Me, leaning into him, letting myself fall, hands tangled in his damp hair as his lips, still cold from the lake, just barely pressed against mine.

It had been so long since I'd spontaneously kissed someone that I'd forgotten how something so simple could ignite the most complex sensations in the world. But here my body was, jolted to life.

I flattened my palm against his cheek, as if I couldn't quite believe it was his body I was feeling and I needed to prove it to myself somehow. But yes, there he was: a nip of teeth, a hint of tongue, his chest firm against the damp cotton of my bra. Every cold part of my body was now raging and hot, a roaring fire somehow burning in the middle of a lake.

Have a passionate love affair.

Maybe fifteen-year-old Clara had been on to something.

His other hand stroked the back of my neck, his lips urgent against mine—and then like the smack of our bodies hitting the water, reality snapped back into us, and we pulled away from each other at the exact same time.

I scrambled backward as he watched me, his eyes wolfish, hungry.

"Um." I was full-on panting like a sprinter.

"I'm sorry, I thought—" he started, a slightly bashful look on his face.

"No, don't apologize," I interrupted. "I wanted to do that."

The cocky half-smile returned, but he didn't say anything else. Instead, he shifted forward to stand, and I rushed to mirror him, assuming we were now going to have a very adult conversation about how we'd just reverted into two horny teenagers. But then he gave me that look, one I'd seen a hundred times before, eyes bright, testing me.

"Race you," Mack challenged. Then he dove off the dock, slicing through the water like a knife, so sharp and smooth he barely made a ripple.

14

BACK AT THE beach, Mack grabbed his clothes off the ground and dragged his T-shirt over his wet hair and down his face, using it like a towel.

"Did we just make things weird?" I blurted out as I hoisted myself out of the shallow water, scanning the shore for my clothes. "Jesus Christ, it's so cold my nipples are going to fall off," I muttered before he could answer, rubbing my arms frantically.

Was I trying to make a joke to deflect from what had just happened? Absolutely. But it also felt like it was ten degrees colder here on the beach than it was out on the diving raft, where I'd been wrapped up in a blanket of lust.

"Okay, now you've made it weird." Mack snorted a laugh as he watched me, tossing me his T-shirt. I immediately pressed it against my face, as if I could somehow hide underneath the soft cotton. But it smelled distinctly like him, a mix of burned leaves and damp wood, and the lingering scent of powdery detergent. My body hollowed with want.

I hadn't really planned on having a passionate love affair with Mack—or anyone, for that matter—this week, despite what I'd promised my fifteen-year-old self. But my focus—once so clear in my day-to-day life—was slipping.

I rubbed his shirt down my arms as he gathered his stuff, trying to come up with some sort of plan for how to handle this situation unfolding in front of me.

"Thanks," I said as I tossed the Pine Lake tee back to him, my mind still racing through our conversation, our kiss, to my world before I landed here at camp.

"Of course," he said, draping it around his neck. "Are you okay?"

"Uh-huh," I muttered, hurrying over to the spot where I'd unceremoniously dumped my clothes. But was I? It didn't seem like I was feeling anything that remotely landed me in the category of okay.

And honestly, I couldn't remember the last time I'd felt okay. This whole last year had been a blur. I should have been dating eligible people in Boston, making my way toward a new, better relationship, but I hadn't even tried to meet anyone. I focused instead on killing it at work, except all I'd managed was to burn out, something I was the last person to realize. And now I was on a break I didn't ask for, kissing Mack in a way that even fifteen-year-old me would never believe.

This wasn't where I was meant to be at all, except maybe it was, and all these contradicting thoughts, combined with the thick, churning desire coursing through my body, had my mind spinning.

"Millen?" I heard him call.

"Sorry, it's just been a weird twenty-four hours, and I'm not totally thinking right," I babbled, not looking up as I grabbed my phone and clothes off the ground and balled them up in my arms. "Work is crazy right now, and my boss—"

Mack was already gone, walking back toward the boathouse.

"Hey! Mack!" I hustled after him, wincing as the pebbles underfoot dug into my feet.

"Come on," he said, leaning against the screen door to hold it open for me. "Let me get you the wireless password."

"Are you serious right now?" I shuffled inside and narrowed my eyes at him as he studied me with an amused look on his face, the door closing with a thud behind him. "We just kissed and you're talking about the wireless password?"

"Isn't that why you're here, Clara?" Mack turned to look at me, and the person I'd known almost my whole life was gone. No impish smile or teasing, raised brows. This Mack was somehow smoldering, like his bones were coal, illuminating him from the inside out.

He never called me Clara.

"No," I said firmly. "I'm just here to make sure this"—I waved a hand between us—"isn't weird."

"It's not weird." His voice was steady and firm, which only lit me up more. With his hair slicked back off his face I could see how his eyes crinkled in the corners as he watched me, and he suddenly looked old to me in a way I'd never noticed before.

Even as we grew into our twenties, I always thought of Mack as a boy, the handsome, shaggy-haired kid who got under my skin in every way imaginable. But those years were long gone, and this person in front of me was so clearly a man: his chest broad and filled out, his skin creased and freckled from years in the sun.

"But we just kissed," I said slowly and emphatically like I was explaining it to a small child. "We shouldn't have done that. We're *friends*."

I wasn't sure I meant it, but it seemed like the right thing to say, the wisest plan, the best way not to rock this very unstable boat we were now teetering in.

"Are we? *Friends?*" His eyes bore down like he was challenging me to really, truly, answer that question. I wasn't used to him like this, with no jokes or jabs coming out of his mouth.

"Yes," I said, gulping. "Obviously."

"Well, we did that once before," he said, and he gave me an amused look, like he was enjoying watching me try not to squirm. He was still shirtless, and he crossed his arms as he leaned back against the door, keeping his eyes on me the entire time. "Don't you remember?"

I wrapped my sweatshirt awkwardly across my chest. "Of course I remember. And come to think of it, you've literally never told me why you gave me the silent treatment after."

The kiss we'd shared that night at camp had been very hot, which honestly was something that confused me as I got older and had more experiences to weigh it against. Making out was supposed to get steamier as you aged and learned what made your body ignite.

But that first kiss with Mack had been, well, *something*. And as much as I hated to admit it, I'd been chasing that something for years and never found it again. Until tonight.

And now I was freaking out.

"So what is this then, Millen?" he asked, gesturing a hand between us. "Is it just another thing you wanted to do as part of your big, last camp hurrah plan?"

I opened my mouth to remind him that he'd just ignored my question about his silence all those years ago. But then he tilted his head lower, eyes locked on mine, so close that I could see a hint of stubble on his chin, remembering the sensation of it scraping the edge of my cheek just moments ago. I couldn't have found my words if they were printed on a paper in front of me.

Luckily, I didn't have to. "And then you followed me in here just to let me know that we shouldn't have kissed?" he prodded.

I could feel the entire gravitational pull of the earth through Mack's eyes, so intense that his pupils seemed to disappear altogether.

"I'm just saying, maybe it's not the best idea."

My voice was a raspy whisper, and I stepped backward, bumping into something. Sure, I'd once jokingly advised my adult self to take lovers, have some sort of passionate, sex-filled affair. But pursuing whatever the hell this was with Mack didn't feel like an actual solution to my problems. It felt like the match that could light everything in my world up and then burn it all down.

"Okay." Mack nodded, crossing his arms. "That's fair. Because we're *friends*."

"Because we're friends who drive each other crazy," I clarified, flustered. "Be honest. Haven't you always found me annoying? Isn't that what the whole race thing was about tonight? You proving some sort of point about me?"

"So you're saying you find me annoying," he said, not answering my question. *Again*.

"No, that's not what I said!" I sighed, exasperated. "I just…It's like, we haven't seen each other in person in years and we're already going around in circles like this. It's been like this for as long as we've known each other."

"You make me crazy, Millen." He dragged his hands across his temples and through his hair, gazing up at the ceiling as if he couldn't stand the sight of me.

"Yeah, dude." I threw up my hands. "Same. So let's not make it worse just because we're, I dunno, horny."

He let out a clipped laugh. "So that's what this is? We're…horny?"

I nodded, trying to hold my ground.

"Okay," he said with an exasperated shrug of his shoulders. "We will never kiss again."

It was exactly what I'd said I wanted, and I waited for relief to kick in. But all that was left was a strange, heavy sadness that sat on my chest, as if I'd lost the thread and had no idea how to get it back.

"It's pinelake1933, by the way," he said, his face steady. "All lowercase."

I squeezed my eyes shut and then opened them, the sorrow I'd felt just seconds ago now shifting into something that prickled with embarrassed anger. "The wireless password is pinelake1933."

"Yes," he said, like it was obvious. Because it was. There was no scramble of letters and numbers, no endless symbols. It was just the name of this place, and the year it was founded.

He'd gotten me again.

"Which you have memorized," I said, my voice pitching louder. "So you could have just told me, right when we got here."

"Oh, come on, Millen, you've been gone for five years. I had to mess with you a little bit."

The edge of his mouth crooked up, as if he knew I was fuming with humiliation. No, as if he *liked* it.

"You're a real dick sometimes, you know that?" I hissed, pushing away from the wall and heading toward the door.

"Only when I want to be." He waved a hand toward the door with his usual half-smile, as if he were daring me to leave.

Something had shifted out there on the dock. When we kissed, it felt like we'd traveled through time to another dimension, where our bodies made sense together. But now we were firmly back in the present, where this truly was a bad idea. Or maybe we were still stuck in the past, forever trapped in our who-could-annoy-who-more cycle. Either way, I needed to get out of here.

"Good night, Mack!" I chirped, my voice purposely cool and clipped. "Thanks for the swim! It was a delight."

"Any time, Millen." Through hooded eyes he watched me as I took off through the screen door and into the night, enjoying the sound of it slamming behind me.

And then I tromped through the now-damp grass up to Sunrise, alone.

15

EVEN IN THE dark cover of night, I could still make out some of the larger signatures on the ceiling above me. I'd been lying here for hours now, tucked into my sleeping bag. I'd tried all the things I normally did when I couldn't fall asleep, which was often these days. Counting backward, half-assed attempts at meditation, a breathing exercise I'd learned thanks to a TikTok video Lydia had sent me.

Nothing had done the trick, so I'd resorted to scanning the ceiling and the wooden beams, where the names of past campers, and the years they attended camp, covered the planks overhead. The bright light of the moon stretched across the ceiling, highlighting pieces of the past: Casi, Jessica, Ilana, Christina, 1979, 2012, 1986, 2023, painted in bright colors, and scribbled in Sharpie. Summer after summer, kids scrambled onto top bunks and left their mark, only for them to eventually be written over by somebody else, another person who wanted to hold on to their summers here, to be remembered in some small way.

In the past I'd loved reading these names; it was like flipping through a yearbook from a school you didn't attend. But tonight it was just a reminder of the steady rush of time. This sleepless night might have been ticking on slowly, but all around me, life was speeding by. Just the thought of all the uncertainty that lay ahead had my heart racing, and I flopped over onto my stomach, willing myself to calm.

But there was no peace to be found as my mind bounced between remembering the tenderness of Mack's touch on the diving raft, and the twisted pleasure he seemed to take in tormenting me with the wireless password. And then, a parade of negative thoughts about myself flooded in, right next to the ones about Mack. My mind felt like a bar on a Friday night during happy hour, crowded and full of frantic shouting, where no one can hear a thing.

Reaching down to the floor, I yanked my phone out of the charger and opened a web browser, typing "signs you have burnout" into the search bar. I scrolled down through the results, article after article after article. Words like "exhausted" and "drained" floated by on the screen. Finally, I tapped one titled "5 Signs You're Burnt Out and How to Beat It!"

A stock photo of an attractive woman in a bright red business suit clutching her forehead took up half the page. "If you're depressed at the office, struggling with sleep, missing out on work–life balance, and cycling through negative thoughts about yourself, you may be dealing with burnout. But don't worry, besties! We've got the blueprint for breaking free from burnout to help you live your best life yet!"

I grimaced and quickly closed the article.

Maybe I didn't want to think about the signs of burnout, after all. Besides, I had a plan to fix things, and now—with my eyes nowhere near drooping closed—was as good a time as any to get to work on it.

I dug my headlamp out from under my pillow, sliding it over my messy bun and tightening the strap around my brow. My therapist had once told me to move locations when I had insomnia; apparently some studies showed that just the change of setting could help our bodies recalibrate and get back into the right mindset for sleep. I might as well try it, even though I'd found it wasn't always foolproof.

I grabbed a few things to keep me busy—my notebook, camp

letter, and a pen—and tiptoed toward the door of the cabin, opening it slowly, inch by inch, so as not to make a sound. Despite what Trey had said earlier, there was no snoring coming from his side of the room, just the repetitive whir of white noise blasting from Nick's phone, plugged into the wall.

Outside, I settled into the wooden swing that hung on one end of the cabin, suspended by thick metal chains. I gave myself a tiny push with my feet, setting it rocking back and forth gently. I thought back to what Sam had mentioned, that Mack had installed swings at all the cabins, yet another small touch that showed how much he loved this place.

Thanks to the moonlight, I could make out the outline of the boat-house, and I wondered if Mack was having a sleepless night too. But then I remembered who I was dealing with. He'd probably crawled into bed with a smile on his face and fallen asleep to sweet dreams of taunting me with that stupid medal.

I fiddled with the pen in my hand, tempted to start a new list with one item on it: Stop thinking about Mack.

I'd probably go to my grave still trying to check that one off.

Instead, I unfolded my old letter and placed it next to me on the swing. My headlamp lit up the paper on my lap like a spotlight. My list from work, written just yesterday, stared back at me. I flipped the page on that part of my life. It was time to start fresh.

I thought for a moment, and then wrote: **Clara's Camp List: Must Be Completed In Order to Save Job.**

Good enough, especially on no sleep.

Lydia always teased me about my to-do list titles, but writing them out like this organized my brain and helped me to see the end goal. And this one was clear: Get through this week, and head back to the office a better, brighter, shinier version of myself. I imagined Amaya stumbling off of Abe's desk in awe as I sashayed into the office with my proverbial shit together.

I glanced over at my letter, covered in my tidy teenage handwriting. There was no way I was getting a dog or cutting my hair this week, so those were automatically out.

Starting at the top, I copied over every goal I'd declared for myself on that final night of camp in clear, deliberate penmanship, with a large, empty box next to each one. The bigger, the better, I thought.

Underneath each action item, a bullet point followed by a brainstorm, just like I was sitting across from Amaya, prepping for a new business call with a client.

1. Do something meaningful with your life. Don't waste it.

- What counts as meaningful, anyway? My job???

2. Surround yourself with people you love, who love you.

- Maybe already done? I'm here! Check!

3. Do something that scares you. Daily. Take risks, goddamnit! (Jump off the high dive, you scaredy-cat).

- Anything but that stupid high dive. Sorry, old self.

4. Experience real joy.

- More wants. Less shoulds.

5. Be kind to yourself.

- Meh. I'll try.

6. Have a shitload of fun.

- Camp games! Color Week! Wish boats! Do all the stuff I loved once.

7. Be a great friend.

- Fix things with Sam.

8. Take a lot of LOVERS! Or at least have one passionate love affair.

Directly below it, I penned, *Mack.* Then I crossed it out. Then I wrote *Mack?*

Why had I included this on my list back then? I vaguely recalled the word "lover" being an inside joke that summer between me and Eloise, as we devoured her fat stack of romance novels. And I'd jotted "LOL" next to it as if to discount it further.

But I'd also written this letter right after my first true moment of raw lust, tangled up with Mack for a minute in the woods. I knew that somewhere, there was truth in this demand. So I tried to channel the Clara I'd been back then, and what she would have wanted from a lover.

Sex, I'd decided. Definitely, sex.

And that was almost certainly not happening after the very weird and intense encounter with Mack.

But we'd kissed, so that counted as something.

I turned the page again, trying to push out the memory of him with a new list.

ACTIVITIES TO ACCOMPLISH ABOVE GOALS

- Capture the Flag
- Friendship Bracelet–Making Party
- Color Week Relay
- Dessert Party
- Truth or Dare (for Eloise)
- Wish Boats

All things I'd loved as a camper, all totally easy to replicate this week. Pressing my hand gently on the page, I tore it along the edge and folded it up into a tiny square, no bigger than a matchbook.

It was settled then; I was getting my life back on track, and I knew exactly how to do it.

Sometimes it really was as easy as making a list.

16

"CLARA."

The voice was barely a whisper, which meant that I could ignore it and keep sleeping. I'd somehow managed to sleep for a few hours without waking from racing thoughts, but I could tell even in this barely alert moment that my body felt anything but rested. My limbs were heavy and achy, like they had merged with the lumpy old bunk mattress and were now made of rusty coils and ancient foam. The only answer was to keep my eyes closed for the foreseeable future.

"Clara." There it was again, still quiet but more insistent this time. I knew it was Sam, who'd been passed out wrapped around some giant, U-shaped body pillow when I'd tiptoed into Sunrise last night.

She was quiet for what felt a minute, maybe two, and just as my brain powered down and slumber sucked me back in, something soft smacked against my head. I groaned and reached a hand over my face, pulling off a bra as Sam let out a giggle.

With a low whine, I rolled onto my back, pushing my sleeping mask up an inch so I could peer one eye out from underneath. There was my old friend, sitting propped up in her little twin bed by the bathroom, sipping from a giant, sticker-covered water bottle through a smile.

"This is giving me flashbacks," I grumbled, my throat still dry with sleep.

She wiggled her eyebrows at me excitedly. "I've literally been holding off for an hour. It was torture."

"You've been up since…" I dug under my pillow for my glasses, smushing them lopsided onto my face, and willed my eyes to focus on my watch face. "Five-thirty? Did Trey's snoring wake you up?"

She shook her head, her voice still quiet. "Trey didn't make a sound. It's just pregnancy insomnia. It's a fucking bitch."

"Shhh," Trey whisper-hissed at us from above, his head lifted barely an inch off the pillow to shoot us a pissed-off look that was somehow savage despite his eyes being closed.

Sam held back a choked laugh through pressed lips. She pointed toward the door, and I nodded in agreement, sliding out of my sleeping bag and swinging my legs over the edge of the bed. Everything felt stiff, my body tight from the drive up from Boston, and my race against Mack last night.

Mack.

The thought of him took my molasses-slow morning vibe and instantly replaced it with jitters, amping things up to high alert. Now all I wanted to do was hyper-fixate on everything that had happened between us hours ago.

Across from me—and totally oblivious to my current spiral—Sam slipped some Birkenstocks on over her socked feet and shuffled quietly to the front door of the cabin. Anxious to catch up, I tugged my sweatshirt over my head and reached for my flip-flops underneath my bed. My eyes landed on my notebook on the floor next to them, last night's insomnia-fueled list sitting neatly on top, like a present. I stuck the folded piece of paper into my pocket, so I'd have it at the ready.

"Damn, it already feels like fall," I muttered once we were both on the porch, my voice low. The sky was a murky tie-dye of pink and orange, with just a hint of blue around the edges. In front of us, the world seemed to twinkle under the weight of morning dew; even the spiderweb that spread from the edge of the porch to the stair railing was glistening and wet. My eyes adjusted to the light, making out a thin layer of smoke-gray fog rising off the lake, which meant the water was warmer than the air outside, and suddenly my mind went back to what had happened on the dock last night.

"I know, I love it," Sam agreed, still sipping from her massive water jug. "Seriously, my only plan for my maternity leave is to indoctrinate this kid into the cult of leaf-peeping the second they're out of the womb."

I laughed into my hands, blowing on my fingers to keep them warm. Ever since arriving last night, my interactions with Sam had felt downright wonderful, the jokes and silliness returning instantly. But lurking directly underneath was this unspoken strangeness, the tug toward heavier things that needed to be said but hadn't found their way into actual words yet.

There was a pause in our conversation, an opening for me to say something, anything, about Sam's surprise news and what it meant for her life in Vermont, the mess I was in at work, the way I'd been trying to hold my life together but had instead let it all slide through my fingertips.

Do something that scares you. Daily.

Talking to Sam about my feelings felt more terrifying than the high-dive tower.

"Should we go try to find some coffee?" I asked instead.

Coward.

"We could go figure out the ancient coffee maker in the dining hall," Sam said, her free hand wrapped around the base of her belly. "Marla gave me a crash course yesterday in how to run it. My doctor said it was fine to have a cup a day and I've been enjoying every sip."

"Perfect," I agreed, and we took off slowly along the mulch-covered path that led down to the Village. This was the nickname for the trio of buildings that sat at the far east side of camp. The dining hall—with its screened-in, wraparound porch—was the center of everything, a nucleus of frenetic energy.

Just to its left was the infirmary—a place I frequented quite a lot in my time at camp (infected mosquito bites were a real bitch)—and Marla and Steve's tiny year-round cottage. Some Tolkien-obsessed counselor had nicknamed it Bag End decades ago, after the cozy, moss-covered home in *The Hobbit*. Pine Lake's Bag End was shrouded by birch trees and ferns, and I felt a strange sense of relief as we approached that the place looked almost exactly the same as I remembered.

I'd loved Steve and Marla's house as a kid, simply because it looked like it should be made out of gingerbread: a perfectly square house, and a porch that was home to two rocking chairs. Like the cabins, it seemed to glow in its new coat of white paint, the shutters matching the leaves that fluttered above. All it was missing was a gumdrop roof and candy cane fence. It felt so perfectly them, and I wasn't sure what was worse: a stranger moving in or tearing it down.

"Sam," I said, tugging her back gently until we stopped just steps from the dining hall. "I just need to say that I am really, really sorry."

Her hair was down today, and her waves framed her face like a shadow as she looked up, studying me with pitch-black eyes.

"Thanks, bud," she said, never once losing eye contact. "I'm not going to lie, it was a real fucking bummer not to feel like I could tell you my big news. You're my oldest friend."

Her eyes crinkled as she spoke, as if it pained her to say it.

"I know." I fidgeted nervously with the hair tie around my wrist, snapping it against my skin. "I should have been there for you. The last few months have been kinda, you know, hard," I said, offering up what was beginning to feel like the understatement of the year. "But that's no excuse for flaking on you."

"I don't ever want to be an obligation for you," she said as she made her way up the stairs, past the creaky wooden rocking chairs that lined the porch. "Our friendship isn't like a pile of laundry that needs to get washed."

"Sam. You're not dirty clothes," I insisted, following behind her into the giant industrial kitchen. I'd meant it as a joke, but the image took hold in my mind and I couldn't shake it: all my mess-ups and lapses hung out on a line to dry. "I promise, I would take our friend-ship to get dry-cleaned."

Sam laughed at this, and the sound felt promising, like maybe, just maybe, I could fix things.

"Seriously, though." I scooted onto the giant, metal island in the middle of the room, scrubbed within an inch of its life. "I want to know everything. I have a list."

Jesus, I really did have a list for everything.

"All right." Her face was open, inviting. "Ask me anything."

I mimed unraveling a scroll as she watched me with an amused look on her face. It was one I recognized from our youth, her lips almost smiling, eyes squinting, as she decided whether or not to go along with whatever ridiculous idea I'd thrown her way.

I pretended to lick my finger, bringing it down the imaginary page in front of me.

"Okay, number one. Does Regan know?" The actual list of things Sam and I hadn't discussed was longer than just her pregnancy and my current existential crisis. I knew she and her ex-wife had ended things on good terms, but beyond that, I was clueless.

"Yeah, that was one of our harder conversations post-divorce, I think because we'd talked so much about having kids when we were together," she said with a grimace as she tugged open a fresh container of coffee. "But she's supportive. She even bought the car seat off my baby registry."

A baby registry. Another thing I'd missed during Sam's pregnancy, another opportunity to show up, when instead I'd stayed away. The realization left me uneasy once again.

"Are you excited? Scared? Nervous?" I asked.

"Hmm," she said, her eyes shifting in serious thought as she began puttering around the room, opening and closing cabinets. "I'm all of it. Sometimes I feel just one thing—happy, terrified, totally chill about it. And other times I feel, like, every one of those emotions all at once."

"Totally," I said with a nod of my head, urging her to continue. Sam had the mind and heart of a writer, and she always chose her words carefully, even when she was just talking.

She stopped in front of a cabinet, turning to look at me. "I'll be at work, or out to dinner with friends, and then realize my entire life is about to change. And I'm like, 'What the fuck have I done?'"

"I can't even imagine," I said, eyes wide. "I would be shitting my pants."

Sam chortled at this, before growing quiet. "I know it's super cli-chéd, but I think the thing I am most freaked out about is the actual pain of labor. It's like the one thing out of all of this that I truly have zero control over. I just have this fear that I won't be able to handle it."

"I read something once about visualization during labor," I said. "You do this deep breathing thing, and imagine your body opening up like a flower or something like that."

"Hypnotherapy," she said, already a step ahead of me. "My mom got me, like, five books on it. I'm not sure it's my thing."

"Well, you just haven't done it with me," I said confidently. "Screw flowers, I'd have you visualizing good stuff."

I sat up a little straighter, hands nestled on my thighs, and closed my eyes. "Like this. Inhale: bagels."

I sucked a deep breath into my belly, my chest expanding before letting the air go. "And now, exhale: cashmere sweatpants."

I peeled my eyes open, expecting her to be laughing at me. But instead, she stood there with her hands on her belly, eyes shut, focused.

The sight of her sent my heart spinning with love.

"Well done, Mom," I said as she blinked her eyes open, her smile relaxed. "See? You're gonna be great."

"You're a good labor partner," she said as she turned and teetered on her tiptoes for a moment, arms deep in some shelf as an idea took shape in my head. She let out a proud "aha!" as she turned back around and placed two white ceramic mugs on the counter.

"I could be there," I blurted out. "Like, for real."

"Oh, Clara." Sam's face was kind, like a teacher handing you a test back with an F at the top. "You're so sweet. But I'm sure you've got stuff going on. And I have a doula. I'll be fine, it's just nerves."

"Well, the offer stands," I said firmly, even though I hadn't given much thought to how I'd actually hightail it to Vermont, much less explain it to Amaya. And frankly, I didn't care. If Sam needed me there, I'd go.

"Anyway," she continued, bustling around the island, mugs in hand, "when I'm not panicking about contractions, I feel very certain about becoming a mom."

"That all makes sense," I agreed, hopping down off my perch to follow her across the kitchen. "You've always been someone who knows exactly what they want to do."

"I don't know if that's true," she said with a shrug, scooping heaps of ground coffee into the giant, restaurant-style coffee maker. "I went back and forth on it for so long. And then I realized that at some point you just have to decide, you know?"

I nodded as Sam pressed some buttons and the coffee maker switched on with a chugging sound, like a train begrudgingly leaving the station.

"Your turn," she said as she leaned against the counter directly across from me. "Tell me the hard stuff. Give me all the post–breakup ugly details."

"Um, well." I took a deep breath, and then let it all out tumble out. "We sold our place, and I moved into this shitty corporate apartment with no soul, which is awful but also maybe appropriate because—if I'm really being honest—that is kind of how I feel these days."

I ran a hand through my hair, scratching nervously at the nape of my neck. Sam didn't say anything, only watched, giving me the space to keep going.

"I don't know, I've just felt…hollow."

Sam made a sympathetic face as she listened, the coffee bubbling behind her.

"I guess I thought I could just channel all my sad breakup feelings into work. I'm long overdue for a promotion, so why not focus on that? But I'm a mess there, too, so much so that we're, like, two weeks out from the biggest pitch of my life, and my boss forced me to take a vacation because she thinks I'm burnt out."

My chest ached as I talked, almost like I could physically feel it cracking open the more I shared.

"Forced you how?" Sam asked as she slid the mugs across the counter and reached for the coffeepot.

"Literally stood up in front of our entire office the other night and announced it in the middle of a party. On her assistant's desk."

Sam froze for a moment, mid-pour, and then turned to look at me, jaw dropped open in shock. "Are you serious?"

"Yeah," I said, "I know."

"Oh, Clara, that is awful," she said softly as she finished filling our cups.

"It definitely wasn't the best Friday night of my life," I said with a tight smile, before walking over to the fridge to find some cream.

"So what do you think?" Sam asked as she dumped sugar into her cup and swirled it around with a spoon. "*Are* you burnt out?"

"I don't know," I said, my mind racing back to the article I'd scanned last night. "I think I'm scared that if I slow down, or really stop to think about it, I'll find out. And maybe I don't want to know."

It was an admission that left me feeling raw and exposed, and I lifted the coffee to my lips, almost as if I could block more painful thoughts from leaving my mouth.

"Come on." Sam tucked her free arm through mine, and the gesture comforted me more than any words could. We headed back out into the main room of the dining hall, stopping to pause in front of one of the giant plaques that hung along the wooden beams of the ceiling. Each year's Color Week captains were listed underneath the Pine Lake logo, and I followed her gaze up until my eyes bumped into my own name, which sat squarely next to Mack's.

"I'm bummed you never got your letter." She swiveled to glance at me, an apologetic pout on her lips. "I would have loved to hear what fifteen-year-old you had to say."

She wanted me to live a completely different life than I have so far, I thought. But I was still smarting from discussing my dismissal from work. Revealing that I had failed to live up to fifteen-year-old Clara's lofty life goals was even more painful, embarrassing even.

So I took another route.

"I kissed Mack," I blurted out as I slid a chair out at one of the tables, plopping down to sit. "Last night, out on the diving dock."

"Oh my god!" she squealed, dragging out the chair across from me and slowly steadying herself into the seat. "You need to describe every second of what happened, in detail."

Propping her elbows on the table, she looked up at me with an expectant, gossip-hungry grin.

"Okay." I fiddled nervously with the rim of my mug, tapping it like a drum. "It was hot. Like, volcano exploding after one thousand years, lava destroying every village kinda hot."

Sam cackled. "That is very specific imagery, Clara." With her mug clutched between both hands, and her shoulders clenched up by her ears with anticipation, she looked downright giddy. "So how did this village-destroying kiss happen?"

"You know I've always kind of liked Mack." I blew on my coffee, taking a tentative, small sip. "When we were kids."

Sam gave me a knowing look, head cocked. "I literally had a front-row seat to that crush, remember?"

"Right," I agreed, nodding. "But I think that's also why I'm so…"

My heart rattled, an animal trying to break out of its cage.

She leaned forward, eyes narrowing. "So attracted to him? Desperate to jump his bones? Climb on board the Mack train and ride it shotgun?"

She pumped a hand in the air, mimicking a train conductor pulling the horn, and I let out a loud guffaw.

"I was going to say 'constantly annoyed by him,' but your version works too. He made this whole big to-do about giving me the wireless password, and do you know what it is?"

"Clara." She leveled a look at me. "Of course I do. It's pinelake1933."

"Oh my god, so I could have just asked you," I groaned, dragging a hand across my face.

"Yeah, but, you didn't." Sam bit her bottom lip, her expression downright gleeful. "Probably because you knew, deep down, that you wanted Mack…to give it to you."

"Nope," I said with a firm shake of my head. "Don't think I don't know what you're doing. You are setting me up to say, 'That's what she said,' and I will not take that bait. Even I'm not that corny."

"Yeah, you totally are," she said.

"Fuck I am, aren't I?" I said, laughing into my mug.

"You haven't changed, Clara." From the smile on her face I could tell she thought that was a good thing.

I leaned back in my chair, relishing a long sip of coffee. If last night with Mack had been a storm, this morning with Sam was a clear sky, bright and beautiful.

"Anyway," I said, "we both agreed it was something we shouldn't do. So we stopped. And we're not going to do it again. The end."

Sam let out a frustrated groan. "Are you fucking kidding me?"

"What!" I protested, giving her an innocent face. "We're old friends. We mostly just drive each other nuts. I told him it was a bad idea, and he agreed."

"Okay, first of all, romantic flings are always a good idea," she said, waving me off when I opened my mouth to disagree. "But, seriously, Clara, you and Mack kinda make sense. This could be, like, a thing."

"On what planet?" I snarked back, even though it had crossed my mind that there was something about being with him yesterday that just clicked. Although it was probably just my very neglected libido making her opinion known.

"This one," she said, tapping her index finger on the table, like a high school kid on a debate team. "You're both intense and passionate. You have the same sense of humor. You both love to make dumb jokes."

"Excuse me." I clutched a hand to my chest, pretending to be hurt. "My jokes are amazing."

"You're both single," she said.

"We're also on totally different life plans, about to live on different coasts, and drive each other crazy," I countered diplomatically. "Even if Mack wasn't a total chaos agent placed on the planet to annoy me, I'm in no place to pursue anything with anyone right now."

Last night I'd let that untamable, animal side of me take the lead. But now, in the light of day, reality reigned. Land Alewife, run the account, and prove to Amaya that she had no choice but to promote me. That was the path I needed to be on.

"And," I added, "I'm not sure you can solve burnout with boning."

Sam snorted a laugh, and then grew serious. "So what *is* the plan then? Because I know you have one."

"I think," I said, "I just need to remember what it feels like to have fun again."

A shitload of fun, if I was going to be specific.

"Sex," she deadpanned, before winking at me as she shimmied excitedly in her seat.

"No." I gave her a stern look. "Just camp stuff."

"Boo," she jeered, waving her downturned thumb at me.

"Sam!" I laughed. "I swear. It was just something we both needed to get out of our systems."

She narrowed her eyes at me, unconvinced.

"You know no one who says that bullshit line about getting things out of their system really means it, right? Because I can guarantee you both have a lot more things in your systems that you're going to want to get out with each other."

"Oh my god, you're relentless!" I said. "I promise, I'm already over it."

"Sure," she said in a tone that told me she wasn't buying a word of what I was saying. "And I'm not a hundred weeks pregnant."

17

"YOU LOOK LIKE my dad circa 1995."

I gestured at the vintage neon-green Oakleys that hugged Nick's face, the mirrored lenses reflecting the sun like a laser beam.

"I'm going to choose to receive that as a compliment, thank you very much," he said with a quirked smile.

I glanced down at Sam, who was seated in a camping chair, a giant straw sunhat covering her curls. "Are you good, ref?" I asked.

"I have this, what more do I need?" she said, proudly showing off the rusty silver whistle that hung around her neck.

I instinctively dug my hand around my shorts pocket as I stood there, looking for my phone. I'd made the decision to leave it in Sunrise, an attempt to give myself over to the present moment. An excellent plan, in theory. But now, in the actual present, it felt uncomfortable and awkward, like when I'd worn slightly stretched-out underpants to work that constantly shifted around all day. Not having my phone was giving my brain a wedgie.

In its place was the Color Week medal (best to have it on me at all times so I could toss it back at Mack when he least expected it), and my new checklist. It was starting to feel like some sort of talisman, a reminder of why I was here, of the things I wanted to accomplish. And right now, I was here to play this Capture the Flag game and experience some joy, goddamnit.

Just then, Mack sauntered up next to me, decked out in a worn maroon USC Trojans shirt and ancient-looking navy running shorts. Such a casual outfit, but it somehow moved with his body, showing off every bit of tanned skin and tight muscle.

"Hey," he said, running a hand through his bedhead, the pieces of golden-brown hair shooting every which way. Mack looked refreshed and rested, and not like someone who just hours ago had his mouth all over mine.

"Hi!" I chirped, flashing a too-wide, toothy smile. I fingered the folded paper in my pocket, wishing desperately it had a screen that I could flick on to distract myself and avert my gaze. Instead, I just kept staring at Mack with my forced grin.

"Sleep okay?" he asked nonchalantly, stretching an arm overhead and leaning toward one side. I analyzed his tone for any hint of sarcasm or teasing. Surely it was in there; he must be referencing our make-out session in *some* way. But he was giving me no clues this morning, so I just kept playing along.

"Amazing," I lied, nodding agreeably. "Out like a rock. Must have been the swim."

"Clara!" Nick shouted, ending whatever the hell this weird back-and-forth was between Mack and me. "You ready?"

"You know it!" I said, tightening the ponytail at the base of my neck.

"Real Color Week captain energy you've got this week, Millen," Mack said, looking me up and down as he kicked a foot back and grabbed it, balancing on one leg as he stretched. Show-off. "Your shirt's tucked and everything."

"Just getting in the spirit of things!" I said before turning toward the group.

"Okay! Listen up!" I said loudly, waving everyone to order. "Nick's going to review the rules, because we have a very special guest with us today who is new to Capture the Flag." I golf-clapped my hands in Linus's direction, and the rest of the group joined in with whoops and applause.

He was snuggled in behind Eloise, his chin nestled on her shoulder, arms wrapped around her waist, their hands clasped. I turned away, not liking the ugly feeling of jealousy that rose in me at the sight of my friend so clearly in love.

"All right, everyone!" Nick shouted like he was in charge of hundreds of people, even though there were just seven of us.

"Dude, we hear you," Mack said, cupping his ears as he took a step back.

Nick slid his glasses down his nose to give Mack a pointed glare before continuing, just a little bit louder.

"Okay, here we go. Teams are determined at random by drawing names out of a hat, to ensure fairness."

Nick looked up from the clipboard in his hand and eyed the group sternly to make sure we were all listening. "Except we didn't have a hat, so we're using this salad bowl Clara stole from the dining hall this morning."

I did a tiny curtsy as Sam leaned forward and picked up a familiar-looking, dinged-up brown plastic container off the ground, passing it to Nick. "Your bowl, sir."

"Thank you, esteemed referee." He held it out to us like an offering and then plucked a small folded piece of paper out of the bowl before passing it on to Trey.

"Green team!" he announced gleefully.

"Same," Trey said, giving Nick a quick smile. He then handed the bowl to Eloise, who had to unravel her arm from Linus in order to take it.

"Green team too," she said. I swallowed nervously, my fingers toying with my hair, braiding the strands of my ponytail just to have something to do. There was no need to keep drawing out of the bowl—the process of elimination meant that Mack and I were on the same team.

Somehow when I had pitched this idea last night, the thought of us being together on a team never crossed my mind.

Eloise turned toward us. "I expect you two to take good care of Linus."

"Oh, don't worry, El; Millen and I are going to show him how the game's played."

If Mack was also frazzled by our new role as teammates, he didn't let on. Instead, he grinned with competitive delight at Eloise's disappointed face. I recognized this look; he was sniffing out a weakness, plotting how to use this against her in the game.

I'd always liked this shark-like part of Mack that mixed so easily with his mellow, laid-back nature. We'd been kindred spirits in this sense; two very different people who both loved to win.

"And of course," Nick said with a sweep of his hand, "losers buy lunch."

"Well done, Nick," I said.

Sam grabbed the two handkerchiefs, blue and green, from her lap, and tossed them at Nick.

"Questions? Comments? Inside jokes?" he asked.

"No pantsing," Sam said, smirking, directing her gaze at Trey.

"It was an accident!" Trey exclaimed defensively, and everyone but me laughed. I turned slightly to Mack, tilting my head in his direction, but not so near that he'd assume I was trying to get closer to him. I didn't want him to think I was still playing last night over in my mind.

Because I wasn't.

At least, not right this very second.

"I don't remember anyone getting pantsed," I murmured, drifting just close enough to his shoulder to catch a whiff of sunscreen, that industrial-strength camp laundry detergent, and a hint of musky sweat. Eau de Mack.

"It was a few summers ago," he explained. "Four years ago, maybe? We were playing a very drunk game of kickball. Trey accidentally grabbed Regan's shorts while trying to get her out at home plate. It did not go well."

"Sounds like my kind of game." I plastered a smile on my face like a shield, so he wouldn't know that my brain was doing equations of how many summer reunions I'd missed, grieving the memories I'd lost out on making.

Mack nudged me with his shoulder. "Don't worry, Millen. We'll make new inside jokes this week."

I turned to catch his eye, waiting for the wisecrack. Instead, he offered me a kind, knowing smile. This was the most unnerving thing about him, what had unraveled me so intensely last night. He didn't just know where the door was to all the soft, vulnerable truths I rarely revealed to people; he held the key in the palm of his hand.

"All right, Greenies." Nick waved Trey and Eloise toward him as he jogged backward like a soccer pro. "You're with me down by the far goal!"

Eloise paused in front of Linus, planting a hard and fast kiss on his lips before running off after her teammates. He cleared his throat awkwardly and gave us a sheepish look, taking his glasses off and wiping the kiss-created smudges off with his T-shirt.

Mack stood next to him, sunglasses crooked on the top of his head, and looked directly at me, running the edge of his tongue along his bottom lip that had felt like witchcraft when pressed against my neck. He said nothing, but his eyes narrowed as they caught mine, as if to say,

Remember how we did this last night? Remember how good it felt? We could do it again, if you wanted to.

It was enough to send my stomach scrambling with nerves, to weaken all my best intentions. Then I remembered how fast he'd switched from hot to cold, the stupid game with the wireless password. It had been just another one of our silly, antagonistic disagreements, and if it had been anyone else, I would have laughed it off. But every interaction with Mack stayed with me, and stung, lodged under my skin like a splinter.

I turned my gaze back to Linus.

"I have no idea what I'm doing," he began with a tepid smile on his face. Then his slender brow furrowed ever so slightly. "But I think it would be fun to beat my girlfriend."

"Yeah, man," Mack encouraged with a light punch to his shoulder. "That's the spirit."

"She kicked my ass in Bananagrams last week." Linus peered over his shoulder to where Eloise was huddled in a tight circle with Trey and Nick, and his lips unfolded into a smile before turning back to face us. "So she has it coming."

"I like you," I said. "Anyone who loves Eloise but also loves to win is my kind of person."

Linus's face perked up, a blush creeping across his skin.

"And Millen doesn't like anybody that easily, man," Mack chimed in, the teasing dripping from every syllable. "So you should really take that as a compliment."

"Aw, that's not true for everybody." I reached out and patted Mack on the top of his head, trying to ignore the softness of his hair, bouncing like delicate wisps of cotton against my skin. "It's just that you make it so hard."

Linus's eyes darted between us as Mack ducked away from my touch and jogged a few steps away.

"Uh, so how do we play?" he asked.

"The plan is all defense with teams this small," I said matter-of-factly as that familiar competitive fire sizzled up deep inside me, the one that lived for challenges like this. The adrenaline felt like an old friend, sparking up a fire I'd not lit in such a long time.

"Uh, no." Mack gave me a skeptical once-over with a shake of his head. "Nick hates running, so he'll probably be guarding the flag. We should charge them. Rush the field, go deep and be aggressive. Linus, you look like you've got a pep to your step."

Mack gave Linus another confidence-boosting thump on the back, and I rolled my eyes at his bro energy. Mack could charm a rock.

"I ran Division Three cross-country in college," Linus replied, his chest puffing up just a bit.

"Perfect. We all charge the front line, then." Mack said this like it was a done deal, and irritation prickled through my body. "We win with chaos. Whoever gets to the flag first grabs it and rushes back to home base."

Linus nodded, squinting in thought as he listened.

"Or," I interjected, my voice clipped, "Linus could be defending our flag. I can guard the middle of the field, and you help with defense. If he's fast, he'll tag anyone who gets close and we can lock them all up in our jail. And then we all run to their side at once, grab the flag, and win."

"That's playing scared, Millen," Mack said, pushing his scratched Wayfarers up on his forehead to narrow his eyes at me.

"Or it's playing strategically and smart." I folded my arms in front of my chest, holding my ground. "Chaos isn't a strategy."

"It's been a few years for you, Millen. I don't think you remember how this game works." He broke out into a smile as he watched me get more frustrated. "But I just coached the juniors to victory this very summer."

"Are you seriously about to mansplain a children's game to me, Mack?" I asked, taking a step closer to him.

Mack let out a choked laugh, shaking his head. "I'd never dream of it."

"That's definitely what it sounds like," I pushed.

"I have no idea what you're talking about." Mack's eyes sparkled. He was clearly relishing this.

Linus looked between the two of us, confused. "Wait, so which plan are we—"

"Fine." Mack threw his hands up, still smiling. "Let's try it your way, Millen. Linus, just do what she says. Defense it is."

"Glad you're finally catching on," I said, offering him the most obnoxiously pleasant smile I could muster. "Linus—guard the flag at the end of the field. Mack and I will defend the front line. We want to draw them into our territory, tag 'em, and then make a run for their flag while they're tied up in jail."

"Whatever you say, Millen. Do you think you can play nice today?" Mack asked, sliding his sunglasses down his face. His stubble was even more pronounced, and he ran a hand across his jaw, my eyes following, admiring the strong lines of his neck, the tiny dimple in his chin that seemed to disappear whenever he smiled or let out a laugh.

"That depends on how much of an asshole you are," I replied.

"Millen—" Mack said, but Sam's referee whistle cut through our tension, and he swallowed whatever comeback was lingering on his lips. I waved him and Linus to their places on the field, more confident than I'd felt in a long time.

Sam's whistle ripped through the air again, and Eloise dashed onto our side of the field instantly, braid shooting behind her like a comet. Mack and I both raced right at her, but she pivoted on her feet, still youthfully athletic, and rushed directly back to the safety of her team's territory. It was all the time Trey needed to bolt past me, a flash of red tank top and tattoos.

"Crap!" I yelled, trying to keep an eye on him as Eloise taunted us by jogging right toward us again, hopping onto our side of the field with a leap. Our plan—*my plan*—was already starting to crack.

"Mack!" I yelled as I bolted away from her this time. "I'm going for the flag!"

"I thought we were playing D?" he hollered back as he trailed Eloise, who was zigzagging back and forth over the dividing line with a ferocious look of glee on her face.

"Change of plans!" I shouted, my brain making a panicked, split-second decision. "You hold the line!"

He snapped something back at me, but I was too far away to hear, sprinting down the far side of the field inside enemy territory. Trey was already lurking dangerously close to where Linus was defending our flag, and Eloise was surely near him, with Mack on her tail. The only person I had to worry about here was Nick, who was pacing back and forth from his position guarding the flag just to the left of the goal, his eyes trained on me.

My body moved like it had just played the game yesterday, even though it had been years, a decade possibly. Hell, I hadn't even worked out in months. The sneakers on my feet had been collecting dust in my apartment's one tiny closet. But in this moment I was electric, unstoppable.

I slowed to a jog, moving along the edge of the field to the right of Nick's peripheral vision. He'd somehow stopped focusing on me and was instead running up the field away from their flag, gesturing frantically to someone in front of him. It was such a novice move—to leave their flag completely unprotected—that I let out a quiet chuckle under my breath. Poor sweet Nick. I was seriously about to steal this flag out from under his nose.

With a grunt, I launched my body forward, cutting across the field until I was just a few feet away from the green team flag. A win was just inches away from me, and the euphoria of it was coursing through my veins.

It felt fucking amazing.

"Agh!" A hand smacked against my shoulder and tugged at the edge of my tank top. I twisted around to find Eloise behind me, pink-faced and breathing heavily.

"Gotcha," she panted, her face lighting up like the Cheshire Cat.

"Goddamnit," I muttered as she nodded her head toward the soccer goal.

"Jail time, baby."

"But Mack was about to get you!" I protested, begrudgingly turning to follow her.

Eloise shook her head. "Mack's your cellmate."

"Are you serious?" I turned to find that he was indeed pacing around the goal as he flicked his eyes toward his watch every few seconds.

"Off you go!" Eloise said with a playful push toward Mack, who glowered at me as I jogged toward him.

"You were supposed to be guarding her," I hissed, wiping my dirty hands on the front of my tank top. "Do you not know how to play this game?"

I inhaled the tangy scent of my body clinging to my sweat-soaked clothes as I caught my breath, and knew without looking in a mirror that my hair—still knotted in a loose ponytail—was a wet, sticky mess. Normally, I would have felt self-conscious about appearing all disheveled, especially in front of someone I'd kissed the night before. But today was different; all I wanted to do right now was lean into this untamed side of me, and reclaim it as my own.

"It was your idea for us to all be on defense, and then you changed your mind and decided to run across the field!" He waved a hand in the air, toddler tantrum-esque. "What were you thinking?"

"It's called thinking on your feet," I snapped back, looking down at my own watch. Ninety seconds left in jail. We still had a shot to win this. "Changing course. Reworking the plan. You know, like, deciding to do one thing, and then switching and doing another? You're good at that."

I narrowed my eyes as the image of him shooting off the diving dock last night flashed through my mind.

"All I did was follow *your* plan for the game, Millen," he said, once again gesturing around us. "I did exactly what *you* wanted."

His damp, threadbare T-shirt was clinging to his chest, and my eyes—which I swear were only on him to glare—drifted just a bit, and settled right on that one spot along his collarbone that I could still almost feel under my fingertips, hard and smooth.

Goddamnit.

Off to our left, Nick turned around, gawking at us. "Are you two seriously fighting over Capture the Flag?"

"Yes!" we both yelled back, a little too loud.

Just then a shout went up on the other side of the field. Trey was on the move again, arms pumping furiously as a blue flag whipped wildly in his hand.

"Crap," I grumbled under my breath. Trey crossed the midline with a leap, the air punctured by Sam's whistle blaring from the side-line. He collapsed dramatically on the grass, Eloise running over to join him, hands triumphant in the air.

"That's the game. We lost."

"We're going with my plan next time, Millen." Mack's eyes bore down on me as he raked a hand through sweat-soaked hair, looking utterly furious.

"There's not going to *be* a next time, *Sullivan*," I replied, taking off with a jog. I didn't want to give him the satisfaction of "I told you so." He could wallow without me as far as I cared.

Not that I did care about what Mack thought. Not about me, or my Capture the Flag game strategy, or anything, really.

Which is why it didn't matter that I glanced behind me, just to see if he was watching me go, and why I didn't care at all that he wasn't.

Not one bit.

18

"YOU HAVE GOT to be fucking kidding me." The words came out garbled, fighting with my turkey sandwich for room in my mouth.

"What's wrong?" Sam asked from the porch swing, her purple sundress billowing around her feet.

We were spread out across the Sunrise deck, feasting on sandwiches that Mack and Linus had picked up from the General Store deli counter. It was late afternoon now, closer to dinner than lunchtime. I had one hand shoved inside a bag of salt-and-vinegar potato chips. The other was tapping furiously at my phone screen.

"My assistant," I said, passing it over to Sam so she could see for herself. "Lydia."

"You mean, my new best friend," she clarified.

"Yes, that one. She removed every meeting from my calendar!"

"And filled it in with..." Sam used her fingers to zoom in on the screen, her mouth falling open as she read. "Oh my god."

"I know!"

"What?!" Eloise's braid whipped like a tail as she looked back and forth between us.

Next to her Linus painstakingly divided up a sandwich and bag of chips between the two of them. "I want to know too."

"She's filled Clara's calendar with one appointment for the week called, 'Nice try, boss, you're on vacation,'" Sam cackled.

"Wow. I hope she's paid well," Eloise cracked as she reached for her half of the shared sandwich, planting a kiss on Linus's cheek as a thank-you.

Phone back in hand, I swiped over to my email, which luckily had not been shut down.

"You're addicted to that thing." Mack's voice was light, but I could still hear the judgment lingering in his tone.

He'd finished his food in one graceful inhale and was now leaning against the wall that ran around the perimeter of the wooden porch. He was so tall he could perch on the edge of it and still stretch his legs out long in front of him. At some point, after the game, he'd lost his shirt, and it had been hard not to notice how his shorts precariously perched on the edge of his hips.

"So?" It was not my best comeback, and I could tell by the way his brows twitched upward that he was reveling in my rhetorical failure.

"So, I thought you were here to chill out, Millen. Isn't that what Nick said yesterday?" He shifted, crossing his legs as his hands steadied him. He'd always oozed confidence, which still, apparently, irked me. It was also undeniably sexy, and my checklist and letter—which were now both tucked safely inside of my notebook—seemed to whisper "take a lover" in my ear.

"Knowing what's coming up on my work calendar helps me focus," I said, steering all my attention to a hard-to-reach chip in the bottom of my bag, which was suddenly way more interesting than the smattering of dark hair dotting his sun-kissed chest. "I know it's hard to imagine me out in the real world, but I have clients and a team who depend on me. Responsibilities. A job."

"I have a job, and you don't see my phone superglued to my hand," he said, that sensuous smile still lingering.

"I mean an actual job. Not just floating around on a lake during the summer, and then sitting around keeping an eye on an empty camp all winter." I lobbed the words at him like a joke, but they came out as anything but playful.

"Oh, boy," Sam muttered under her breath, and next to me, Linus shot Eloise a confused look, his eyes magnified in his glasses.

"Damn, Millen, if I didn't know better, I'd think you were trying to hurt my feelings." Mack's jaw tightened ever so slightly. "Was that also on your schedule of traditions you wanted to relive this week?"

"I didn't mean it like that," I said, analyzing a chunk of tomato that had fallen out of my sandwich, anything to avoid eye contact with him now. I hadn't intended to insult him, but an angry edge had taken over, one I couldn't quite put a finger on but could feel pulsing through me.

"Eh, you're right. I do float around on the lake a lot." He pushed himself off the railing to stand, and I flashed back to the other night, when he'd pulled that leaf out of my hair and almost knocked the wind out of me. "It'll be good for me to rejoin the real world."

Mack jogged down the stairs and gave us a wave over his shoulder, and I concentrated on chewing my food instead of watching him go or looking back up at my friends, who I could feel staring at me.

Behind us, the door creaked open, and Nick emerged from inside the bunk, sunglasses inexplicably still on, Trey behind him. They had been hovering on a bed, deep in conversation, when I'd wandered into the bunk to change after the game, and I hadn't seen either of them since, until now.

"Where'd Mack go?" Nick asked, studying our group before sitting down in our half-assed circle, reaching for a sandwich.

"Lovers' quarrel," Sam said as she ran a hand through her curls. I shot her a look, but she just shrugged me off in response. "He knows."

My eyes widened an inch, and I swiveled to face Nick, who nodded back. "He didn't tell me, but I figured it out this morning. He was, as my students like to say, acting extremely 'sus' when I asked him about your little swim last night."

"Oh, come on," I said, certain that Mack must have said something—and at once relieved and livid that he might have done so.

"Even if I hadn't figured it out, it was extremely obvious the second I heard the two of you bitching at each other about Capture the Flag strategies," he said, plopping down next to me. "It was like something out of a Hallmark movie."

"It was one kiss," I clarified, my voice firm. "We are just friends."

"Two, if you count the one from the last year of camp," Sam said diplomatically.

"Oh, right!" Nick said. "That one he did tell me about."

"Clara and Mack, sitting in a tree," Trey started to sing. "K-I-S-S-I—"

"Okay, and that was like, one hundred years ago!" I interrupted, voice rising slightly.

"So that's why you were just such an asshole about his job? Because you kissed?" Eloise said, picking a chip out of Linus's stack and giving it a crunch. "That seems like something someone does when they're try-ing to convince themselves they want to be friends with someone who they definitely want to keep making out with."

I opened my mouth to protest but was cut off by Linus.

"Yeah, I realize I only met you twenty-four hours ago, Clara, but I agree with Eloise," he said matter-of-factly, reaching over to pat Eloise on the knee affectionately. "She's almost always right about everything."

"Mill-en, hey, come on, look at me take my shirt off and do a swim race with me." Nick lowered his voice with a slight SoCal twang, puff-ing his chest up in what was the worst Mack impression I'd ever seen.

"Ew, Mack, no, I'm too busy doing very important smart things," Eloise crooned, flipping the tail of her braid with her hand. "You work at a stupid little camp and I do important, fancy marketing things."

"Branding," I interjected, but no one was listening to me now. They were too focused on their impromptu theater production unfolding on the porch.

"Let's make out," Nick said, wagging his tongue back at her as Sam cackled from the swing in the corner.

"Jesus, guys," I said, crunching up my lunch trash in between my hands, channeling my nervous energy into balling up the wrappers as small as I could get them. "I think you're reading too much into things. We got into some dumb argument over Capture the Flag. So what."

"Excuse you, that was an extremely passionate argument over how to play a game where you literally just run around and find a square piece of cloth." Nick pushed his sunglasses up, revealing tired, blood-shot eyes.

"Oh, come on, it's nostalgia!" I said.

"Sexual tension," Linus agreed solemnly, before biting into a chip. "I could feel it the whole game."

"It's probably why you lost," Trey added with a chuckle.

"Okay, that's enough, thanks." I hopped up off the floor, antsy, my skin suddenly feeling as tight and claustrophobic as a wetsuit. "I have a therapist I actually pay to talk to about this stuff."

"Where are you going?" Sam asked, reaching her arms out toward me for a hug. I bonked her gently on the head with my crumpled-up paper bag and then smushed myself next to her on the swing, inhaling the cinnamon-y warmth of her skin as she wrapped an arm around me. Thank god at least one of my friends wasn't giving me crap about kissing Mack.

"That wasn't cool, what I said just now to Mack." I sighed, giving her a quick squeeze back. "I'm going to run down to the boathouse and apologize."

"With your mouth?" she asked, breaking into a grin.

"Oh my god, not you too!" I shrieked at Sam. "I'm leaving now."

"Break a leg, honey," Nick said with a chuckle.

I gave them all one final hearty eye roll before heading inside to toss my trash. It was hard to know exactly what I'd meant by "experience real joy" at fifteen, but now, as my friends' voices drifted in through the screen windows, peals of laughter peppering their conversation, I knew.

It was the comfort of that laughter outside, the tenderness of old friendships, and the way they changed shape through the years but never truly lost their original form. It was the thrill of competition—not of winning, but of believing wholeheartedly that you could.

It was leaping headfirst without thinking of what came next.

19

"HELLO?" I CUPPED my hands against the screen door of the boat-house, peering inside. It was dark, but Mack's old Jeep was parked nearby, so he was clearly around somewhere. I decided to wait, pacing the edge of the beach, walking that fine line where the water lapped against the sand.

The air was heavy underneath the afternoon sun, trees casting amorphous shadows on the water that shook any time a ripple passed through them. Dragonflies whizzed by, dipping down to kiss the lake before launching themselves back to the sky. I dug a knuckle into my jawbone, massaging it aggressively. Lately, I'd been grinding my teeth at night, which left me with a constant, dull ache that throbbed just below my ears during the day.

There was still no sight of Mack, and the humidity in the air was just oppressive enough that I'd been inching my body farther and farther into the water while I waited for him. I was now in all the way to my knees, bending every few seconds to dig around in the sand for rocks to skip as I planned my apology in my head.

I definitely owed him one. Because he wasn't wrong, I *had* been trying to hurt his feelings. Not because I thought his job lacked meaning, or value, or worse—that he did. But because there was a part of me that was worried—very worried—that *my* life, *my* work, did, and in the moment, it had been easier to direct all that anxiety at him than admit it to myself.

"Fuck it," I said out loud, and took a couple of hopping steps back out of the water, kicking off my shorts once I hit the shore, and adding my tank top to the pile before stepping back into the water in my underwear. I was beginning to wonder why I'd even bothered to pack a bathing suit.

Last night I'd forced myself into the water and willed my body to thrash its way to victory. Today I just dropped in, sinking into the cool arms of the lake, paddling out far enough to where I could no longer touch the bottom before flipping onto my back to float. I stretched my arms and legs out wide, a star searching for its light. Overhead was only sky, the evening sun holding on against pale blue, with cloud strokes dotting its canvas.

"Sabatikos," I said quietly, remembering the word Lydia had read to me off her phone the other night. Today was Sunday, the Sabbath. A day of rest. Did this count? I could still feel the tightness across my face, the stiffness in my neck, and a gnawing sensation of fatigue, the ever-present bookend to countless sleepless nights.

But there was something else happening too. The constant barrage of thoughts that normally funneled through my head had slowed. My limbs relaxed in the water, softening like butter left out all day on the kitchen counter. I said the word again, and then filled my chest with air, breathing it out slowly as my body dipped slightly with the gentle current of the water.

Just when I decided I could stay out on the water forever, there was a splash nearby, and it jolted me out of my meditative state into a heart-racing panic, as if a great white shark had magically willed its way into a fresh body of water, or the Loch Ness monster decided to give up Scotland for the slightly less damp wilds of New Hampshire.

I flipped around to tread frantically, legs kicking under me, and there, only about ten feet in front of me, was a loon. Loons and lakes went hand in hand in New Hampshire, and I'd seen plenty in my lifetime. Their melancholy wails were so common throughout the summer nights here that lulls of quiet felt downright odd after the sun fell.

But I'd never seen one this close, so near I could see the way the bird's long neck, ringed in black and white feathers, seemed to pull the rest of its body through the water. It was mesmerizing. She twisted her head in my direction, beady red eyes staring at me, through me, past me.

"Hi," I croaked, my voice a hoarse whisper. "You're so beautiful."

She dipped her head toward the water and shot all the way underneath, so fast it was like she'd almost never existed at all.

"Bye," I said, because I was a person who talked out loud to birds now. I didn't even care if it couldn't understand me. I felt elated, high on the magic of nature.

"Goodbye," a voice said, and for the second time in minutes, I jolted my body around in a panic.

"Jesus Christ, Mack." Of course he was there, floating high and mighty in a bright orange kayak like a knight who'd just strode into town on some massive horse.

"Making new friends?" he asked, and goddamnit, he was still shirtless.

"Yes, I finally found someone who understands me." I sucked in a breath and let my body drop below the surface, escaping the weight of his gaze before popping back up to find him hovering over the edge of the kayak, watching me.

"I'm so happy for you," he said, dipping his paddle into the water to steady himself.

"Actually, I came down here to find you," I said, treading in place. "But you weren't in the boathouse."

Mack shrugged. "I had some things to check out."

"On your kayak?" I asked.

He just nodded. "What'd you need?"

"I don't *need* anything." Suddenly self-conscious, I reached a hand up out of the water to smooth out my hair. "I just wanted to apologize. For what I said earlier. About your job."

"It's okay, Millen. It's not going to be my job much longer." I'd never heard Mack sound bitter, but this was close. He pushed the paddle back into the water, sending the kayak forward just a bit. "Besides, it kinda looks like you're jealous, don't you think?"

"Of what, your job?" I kicked faster to catch up with him. "No. I love what I do."

He twisted around, eyeing me with a cocked brow. "It's just that you made a crack about my job and how all it requires is floating around on the lake, and yet, you're out here. Floating. On the lake."

His paddle hit the water with a decisive splash, and off he went ahead of me, as if he was deliberately trying to get me to admire his taut shoulders. It worked, and even as I dove underwater with my eyes closed, all I could see was his body, shifting from side to side.

He was dragging the boat onto the sandy shore by the time I caught up to him.

"Seriously, though," I said, squeezing the excess water out of my hair, "I'm sorry."

Mack hoisted the kayak up onto the wooden rack that sat beside the lake, yet another opportunity for me to ogle his muscles as they flexed. He nodded, flipping a strand of hair onto his forehead as he turned back around, eyeing me with his arms crossed in front of his chest.

"Okay, Millen, I accept your apology."

His phone dinged in his pocket—which made me remember I'd left mine up at Sunrise—but he didn't even reach for it. It beeped again, and the sound caused me to look directly at his shorts, which then set off a whole fireworks show of racy thoughts in my head. *Gooddamnit.*

"Um, okay, good," I said, suddenly very aware of how little clothing we were both wearing. I wrapped my arms tightly around my chest. "Do you have a towel I can borrow? I'd ask for a T-shirt but you're not wearing one."

Did he notice the way I pressed my lips together tightly, trying to stave off the heat pushing its way onto my cheeks? If he did, he didn't let on. That, or he didn't care.

He simply offered a nonchalant shrug and nodded toward the boat-house. "Come on."

I followed him through the grass along the short path, worn down by decades of footsteps. Mack held the screen door open and ushered me inside with a casual wave of his hand, and then wandered over to a built-in shelf along the far wall that I hadn't noticed last night.

"Catch," he said as he tossed a beach towel at me.

It was huge, complete with a giant, exploding football shooting out of a Patriots logo.

"Really?"

Mack chuckled when I flipped it around. "What, I don't seem like the super-masculine, football dude type to you? It was five dollars on sale at the General Store a couple of summers ago."

I folded my clothes as best I could in a stack on the floor, and got to work drying off, wrapping the towel around my shoulders. His phone sounded again, and I made a point of looking anywhere but at him. It was only then that I really noticed things—the warm recessed lighting overhead, the faded dingy walls now repainted creamy ivory, the windows trimmed in forest green.

The once dark and drab boathouse was now homey and filled with light. It was beautiful. Not beautiful like some sort of HGTV renovation, with shimmering fixtures and barn-chic lanterns. Beautiful in a way that felt true to the spirit of this place.

In place of the ancient linoleum work counter that I remembered being cluttered with broken rudders and empty tubes of sunscreen was a smooth plank of butcher block that extended along the outer wall of the building. A once empty wall we'd rested paddles against haphazardly was now home to a bench that wrapped all the way around to the corner of the room. It was covered in green cushions and gingham pillows, with life preservers stacked neatly underneath.

The dingy pulley-operated door that opened out on the water was long gone, replaced by French doors that drew the sunlight inside like a vortex, making the whole place sparkle. Even the ladder up to the loft was new—thick, soft-grain wood and sturdy steps instead of the narrow, teetering death trap I remembered from my youth.

Just above the folded towels, Mack had displayed all the old sailing regatta trophies from years past, posed next to tiny stacks of rocks that almost surely once lived on the bottom of Pine Lake. I examined their craggy shapes as I got closer, then plucked one off the shelf and rolled it in the palm of my hand. It was a pale, milky white, soft and round with a crack on one side.

"Anytime something special happens I like to grab a stone from the lake and put it up here." His voice was low and so very close behind me, his breath skipping softly over my skin.

"What's this one for?" I asked, holding it up to the light.

"Last day of camp this year," he said matter-of-factly, as if it were obvious.

I nestled it back next to its little stone friends, grabbing a small slab of blue glass next.

"You found this in the lake?" I asked skeptically.

"What are you, a detective?" he teased. "Fine, some I get from other places. That's from my last trip back to LA. Zuma Beach in Malibu always has a ton of sea glass."

He slipped it out of my hand as he stepped closer and reached up over my shoulder to grab a large granite chunk off the top shelf. It was the color of dirty rainwater, with flecks of white and silver that came alive in the light. He held it as his body shifted, leaning one shoulder against the bookcase to face me.

"And this one?" I ran a finger along its rough edges, and my voice felt tight in my throat. I'd been dripping wet just moments ago, but now my body pulsed with a feverish heat.

"Ah, this one's special," he said, looking down at the stone in his hands before resting his eyes back on me, two big blinding suns. "I grabbed it the other day, when I heard you were coming back up this summer."

The meaning behind his words hung heavy between us, and I felt suddenly like I couldn't get enough air into my lungs. "It's huge," I finally blurted out in a gasp, and Mack snorted at the double entendre as he handed it to me.

"Yeah, well, you're a lot, Millen. I couldn't give you some puny old pebble."

I pressed my fingertips gently against the craggy stone like I was holding his entire heart in my hands. Our kiss on the diving raft had been spontaneous, two people caught up in a moment. Old friends who did something rash. But every single thing unfolding between us right now felt very, very deliberate, and if I wasn't careful, I knew I'd only want more, of him, and *from* him.

"I said the other night that we shouldn't, you know." I exhaled slowly, trying not to let on that I was suddenly racked with nerves.

He chuckled softly, Adam's apple bobbing. "I know. We're not going to make things weird."

"But what if I…"

The sound of his text alert chirping once again from his pocket interrupted me.

"Do you want to get that?" I asked.

"Nope," was all he said. "You were about to ask me a question."

Was I really going to put myself out there like this, to *Mack*? Every drop of blood in my body raced to my face, which was hot with anticipation. Yes. Yes, I was.

"Um," I cracked. My throat was the entire Mojave Desert, dust storms and all. "I guess I was wondering, like, what if I wanted to. You know. Do that."

"Do *what*, Millen?" I could tell from the way he lowered his chin to watch me, his gaze unrelenting: He was going to make me say it. This was a game to him, just like everything else between us. And now I was desperate to play.

"Make things weird."

"Well, I think you know I can be very, very weird." Mack took a step forward until our bodies had nowhere else to go but together. "And I happen to think weird is good."

My eyes fluttered closed as his mouth pressed against my bare shoulder, teeth grazing my skin along the edge of my bra strap. He moved up my neck, kissing along the edge of my jaw so, so slowly. It was a spot on my body no one had ever paid attention to before, but under his touch it felt like it was made of one million nerve endings.

Sam was right. Mack wasn't out of my system yet. Not even close.

"Mack." His name crested on a moan I didn't know was inside me. Instinctively I leaned into his lips, pressing myself closer to him. How, I wondered, did I make it through all these years, not seeing him, not touching him like this?

"Mack," I said, louder this time. He pulled away, his face unreadable, breath rapid. "I'm still holding your rock."

Silently, he grabbed it out of my hands and placed it back on the shelf next to us. Then, without a word, he locked his arms back around my waist, pulling me against him until I had no choice but to bring my hands to his chest, nipping at his chin with my mouth.

"The reason I didn't talk to you after we kissed that summer," he said, planting a single kiss down my neck in between each word, "is because I was scared out of my mind."

"That's not like you," I whispered, my voice hoarse. "You're not scared of anything."

My fingers inched up the curve of his neck to the tight line of his jaw, which was covered in rough stubble. I toyed with a strand of his hair, wrapping it around my index finger.

"Oh, I'm scared of a lot of shit, Millen," he mumbled. "Especially letting people down."

"Well, you're not letting me down right now." I exhaled with a shiver, and a soft "Oh" escaped my lips as his hands pressed firmly into my hips. He pulled away for a beat, a ravenous, feral look on his face, as if he couldn't decide if he was going to devour me or take his sweet time.

And then his phone rang.

"Fuck!" he hissed, pulling me closer as if the sound might somehow break our bodies apart.

"I really think you should get that." The words came out garbled, my mouth flush against his collarbone, wanting so badly to stay there.

He fumbled around for his phone, but by the time it was in his hand the ringing had stopped. His eyes scanned the screen, and I watched as his face went from flustered, to confused, to terrified in the span of a single heartbeat.

"Shit," he said finally, digging a hand through his hair as he handed off his phone to me.

"What is it?" I asked, watching as he jogged over to a drawer and yanked out a T-shirt, putting it on so quickly he didn't notice it was backward.

"We have to go," he said, tossing me a sweatshirt that landed at my feet. "It's Sam."

I glanced down, and on the screen was an endless stream of messages from Nick, the most recent one catching my eye immediately.

Just got to the hospital where are you??????

20

"MILLEN." IT WAS the first time Mack had spoken since he'd rushed me into the passenger seat of his ancient, wood-paneled Jeep Wagoneer with a gruff, "Come on." It was a tone I'd initially read as grumpy and then, after watching him drive the twenty minutes to the community hospital with a scowl, I realized that he, like me, was nervous.

We hadn't said a word to each other in the car, driving in tense silence as James Taylor crooned about flying machines thanks to a cassette tape I'd found at my feet.

"Yeah?"

Nick had assured us that Sam was okay, even if she was possibly in labor, but my anxiety still clung to me like an oil spill.

"You okay?" Mack asked as the car sputtered to a stop in the hospital parking lot with one final crank of the gear shift, and he tilted his head to get a good look at me, hair flopping in his face.

His voice was softer now, reassuring even.

I swallowed and finally said out loud the worry that had been plaguing my thoughts for the entire ride. "What if something's wrong with her, or the baby?"

"Didn't Nick say the doctors' initial reaction was 'very chill'?"

"Yes, but—" I was interrupted by the clank of the passenger door as I opened it, the sound sending Mack bolting out of his seat and around the car to meet me, shoving the door closed behind me with a heft of his shoulder.

"Sorry," he said sheepishly. "Gotta add that to my fix-it list. You were saying?"

Streetlights illuminated the pathway to the hospital even though it wasn't quite dark yet, moths darting in and out of the shadows, getting ready for their night's work. Somewhere in the quiet, Mack's fingers laced through mine with a reassuring squeeze that felt intimate in a completely new way. There was nothing sexual about it; it was a gesture entirely intended to be comforting.

"I should have been there to help," I said finally as we neared the entrance, slowing to a stop underneath the flickering red EMERGENCY sign.

I couldn't stop thinking about what Sam had said earlier, over coffee. I didn't want her to be scared—or worse, in pain—and alone.

"Millen, I know you have, like, seventy different superpowers," he said, chuckling when he caught my eye roll at this. "But I'm pretty sure you're not a doctor. I know some folks who work here. She's in good hands."

I opened my mouth to let the words tumble out—I'd let Sam down by flaking on her, flaking on our friendship, and now what if I'd unintentionally done it all over again?

"Okay," I said instead, nodding.

Our friends had claimed a corner of the ER waiting room, and were splayed out in dingy, purple armchairs. Nick paced in front of a TV that hung from the ceiling at a precarious angle, showing some sort of home renovation show with the volume off.

"It's the dream team," Nick said, forsaking a greeting. "I thought about running down to the boathouse, but I didn't want to—"

"He was ready to barge in on you naked." Eloise mustered a tired smile, head nestled on Linus's shoulder. Her eyes glanced down to where my hand was still locked in Mack's, before offering up a knowing twitch of her brow at me as I tugged my fingers loose. "We saw you run inside in your underwear."

"I'd been swimming!" I protested.

"Purely G-rated," Mack added. He looked down at me, eyes glinting, irises the color of cut grass in the fall. I gave the slightest shake of my head back. An unspoken acknowledgment that things had been much closer to PG-13.

"How is she doing?" I asked, desperate for info about Sam, and also eager to get this conversation away from the topic of Mack and me.

"We were brushing our teeth and talking when all of a sudden she was, like, doubled over," Trey said matter-of-factly, as even-keeled as ever. "She called her doula, who said she should get checked out by a doctor, just to be safe."

"So it could be nothing," I said. I waited for relief to wash over me, but all I felt was nervous tension.

Nick nodded. "Or the baby could be coming tonight. We won't know anything until she's been monitored for a bit. So go get some coffee, it's going to be a long night."

"You want?" Mack turned to face me, his hand gently coming up to squeeze my forearm. "I'll go grab some."

"Yeah, thanks," I said, folding my body onto one of the stiff, vinyl chairs next to Eloise with an exhausted sigh.

My mind was too focused on Sam to think about much else, but the sensation of Mack's calloused finger brushing up against my skin just now was a heated reminder of what we'd just been doing.

Eloise patted me on the arm reassuringly. "She's going to be okay," she said.

"I know," I replied, trying to will the words into reality. "But let's talk about something lighter for a minute. I need to take my mind off of things."

She shifted like a cat waking from a nap, stretching an arm in the air as she eyed Mack—now deep in conversation with Nick—speculatively, before turning back to me. "Must have been some swim you guys had. Can we talk about that?"

The digital clock on the wall ticked past 11:59 p.m., and I welcomed Monday with a nervous sigh.

I was the only one in our group still awake, going on my third hour of very intense solitaire gaming on my phone. Mack had lasted alongside me until around eleven, fueled by the late-night caffeine boost, but even he had tapped out and was now slumped over next to me with a sweatshirt on top of his head.

His knee was nestled against mine, a shift in his sleeping body made without intention, but it felt achingly familiar, and something deep inside me wanted him to stay like this forever, close by and casual, touching without thinking.

"Who's here with Samantha Cohen?"

A masked nurse in pink scrubs shuffled out from around a corner, clipboard in hand, looking around the waiting room.

"Me!" I jumped up, shaking off the stiffness in my bones as I rushed over. "How's she doing?"

"She's resting now." The nurse waved me along behind her, clogs clipping on the linoleum floor with purpose. "The doctor just wants to keep her under observation, but she's doing just fine."

"So it was what, a false alarm then? Can that happen?" The relief I'd been hoping for swept through me, like sinking into a hot bath. Sam was fine. *Fine.*

"Braxton-Hicks," she said matter-of-factly without looking back at me.

"Who?" I asked, racking my exhausted brain for some mention of a person with that name. Maybe I should have tried to sleep; my eyes felt like they were coated with rubber cement. The nurse stopped in front of a cracked door and pulled down her face mask, revealing a kind smile. "That's just the name of the contractions. They're more or less harmless and pretty common. Think of them as like the body giving the pregnant person a preview of the real thing."

I'd long ago made the choice not to have kids, but I still understood how my reproductive system worked, pregnancy included. However, this whole idea of a baby being like, "Here I come. Wait, never mind!" was new to me, and sounded incredibly stressful.

"Oh." I nodded, grimacing. "God, being pregnant seems fucking awful."

I smacked a hand over my mouth.

"Sorry," I added. "My brain is operating at, like, five percent right now."

She laughed, a hearty, all-knowing guffaw. "I have three kids, and you're not wrong. But I wouldn't share that opinion with your friend tonight."

"Good advice," I said, and then peered through the cracked door, hoping to catch a glimpse of Sam.

"She's getting some more fluids. We'll start her discharge paperwork in the morning, but she won't be out of here until after lunchtime, probably. She's asked for company."

The nurse gave the door a little nudge and ushered me in with a nod of her head. Sam sat propped up on a giant stack of pillows, remote in hand as she clicked it aggressively, trying to get the TV bolted to the wall to do her bidding.

"Careful, you might break that thing," I said.

"Clara!" she said with a happy shriek as she tossed the remote and opened her arms for a hug. I leaned in gingerly, careful not to bump into her hand that was connected to an IV, a bag of fluids dangling overhead. "It would serve that fucking thing right, making me watch *Shark Week* in the middle of the night."

I settled in on the chair angled next to her bed. "You feeling okay?"

She nodded, curls bobbing, but her brows crinkled with worry. "I seriously thought I was about to have a baby in the back seat of Eloise's car. The pain was *so* intense."

"Did you close your eyes and visualize bagels?" I asked, sliding the chair closer so I could lace her fingers through mine. I hated that I could hear the fear in her voice, no matter how brave she was clearly trying to be.

"Honestly I would have, but it happened so fast." She paused, fiddled with the buttons on the remote. "Clara?"

"Mmm-hmm?" I said casually, expecting some sort of crack to come out of her mouth. Instead, she looked pained with worry. "Sam, what is it?"

"What if I can't do this?" She turned her face toward me, eyes glassy. "I could barely handle *false* labor pains. What if I can't have this baby? What if I'm not ready to be a mom?"

"Sam." I scooted as close to her as I could without climbing into bed next to her. "When we were kids, you not only knew that we were supposed to wash our sheets every week, but you made the rest of us do it. I would have happily slept in a stew of sweat and dirt every summer if it wasn't for you."

She let out a small laugh as she wiped an errant tear away with the back of her hand. "So you think I'm ready to change this baby's sheets."

She'd always been the most self-sufficient person I'd ever known, never homesick or lonely, always so certain in every choice she made. Seeing her so unsure of herself now unnerved me.

"I think you're going to do great," I reassured her. "At all of it. And right now, I'm at your service. What do you need? Vending machine run? Pillow fluffing?"

I picked up a small empty can of cranberry juice off her bedside table. "Let me get you another one of these."

"Clara." She gave me a hard look. "I don't need you to wait on me. I just like having you here."

"Okay, well, that I can do."

"Tell me what happened with Mack," she said. "That'll be a good distraction."

Of all the things I was prepared to do to try to help, this was not one of them. I kicked off my flip-flops and tucked my knees into my chest, wrapping my arms around my legs. "Mack thinks I'm like a big, sparkly rock."

His name set off something inside me, like emotional carbonation, every feeling bubbling to the surface.

"Okay, I am not here to kink-shame, but I'm going to need more info." Sam took a sip from a beige plastic cup, crunching the ice between her teeth.

I cackled at her eloquence, and she gave me a pleased look; I'd forgotten how wicked her sense of humor could be, how well she balanced her steady, serious side with biting wit. It hit me then, like a wave crashing over me, just how very much I'd missed her.

And so I did as she'd requested, and started from the moment I'd last seen her, when I'd bounded off the steps of Sunrise earlier in the afternoon and marched down toward the boathouse to find Mack.

By the time I caught her up to the moment outside the hospital when he grabbed my hand, she'd tucked the blanket up under her chin and was giving me an easy, relaxed smile.

"Can I tell you something?" she asked, and I nodded.

"My mom tried to talk me out of coming this weekend. Long drive, the baby almost being here, blah blah blah. Typical overprotective mom shit. But this is just what I needed."

"Being in the hospital?" I joked.

"No, though she's going to have a field day with that." She gave an exasperated sigh as she waved a hand around the hospital room. "I mean being up here. At camp. Gossiping about crushes and doing stupid shit and laughing to the point of peeing my pants."

"I haven't ever seen you pee your pants before." I jabbed a finger toward her stomach. "It might just be because you're extremely pregnant. Doesn't that happen?"

"Oh, I definitely peed my pants laughing before I got pregnant," she said. "I'm just an under-the-radar pants-peer. Incognito."

"Don't you mean 'incog-pee-to'?" I countered.

"Piss-cognito," she clarified. And with this, we were both laughing, that kind of stomachache-inducing, chest-clasping laugh that felt like an electric charge running through your body.

It had become familiar by now, this feeling of pure happiness that filled me when I least expected it, with zero planning or force from me to help it along. Nick and I locking pinkies in the car, that loon floating by in the lake, Mack's face as he watched me, teetering between amused and awestruck.

I wished more than anything that I could bottle this feeling, tuck it into a tote bag, and carry it with me when it came time to leave Pine Lake. I couldn't take my friends back home to Boston with me, but I could take this: *real joy*.

Just then something clicked, way back in the dark, dusty corners of my brain. This was what we'd been trying—and failing—to capture for our Alewife pitch.

Bottle the feeling.

The creative angle for their Summer Ale appeared fully formed in an instant, a vision of old friends, gatherings around picnic tables that stretched on from day until night, light cast on lake water, and the rich scent of dew-covered grass. It bowled me over so intensely that I had to give my head a shake, not noticing that Sam had gone quiet and was watching me through drooping eyelids, her lips curled just so.

"I think I need to sleep," she said through a huge yawn, and I signaled my agreement with a pat of her hand. There would be no sleep for me, though, not right now. Because it was as if the idea had exploded in my head: Alewife Summer Ale wasn't about the beer, it was about the people you shared it with, the memories you made together.

And that magic was born in the summer: with endless days by the water that stretch on so long it's as if the sun will never set, and laughter that has no clear beginning and no end in sight. Barbecues that turn into legendary all-night celebrations. If you could bottle that feeling, it would be Alewife's Summer Ale.

I was so impressed with myself that I let out an actual laugh under my breath. I think I just solved all our problems with the Alewife pitch. I texted Lydia. Going to write it all out and then send it off to Amaya.

It was time to get to work.

21

I WAS NAKED and kneeling, my shins aching against the floor.

"Millen." Mack brushed his hand through my hair, his voice shooting straight to my core, driving heat in between my legs.

"You're a good girl, aren't you?" I nodded as he pressed his index finger under my chin, tilting my gaze up at him. "I've always wanted this."

He was sitting on Abe's desk in the middle of the Four Points office, a glass of champagne in his other hand. "I want you to—"

"Sorry, honey, but we've gotta check vitals." A voice yanked me out of sleep, followed by the scraping sound of a curtain being abruptly dragged open.

I was not naked and on my knees, ready and willing to do whatever Mack asked. No, I was a sweaty mess, my head lodged against the hospital chair's wooden arm, my back knotted like a tangled necklace from my awkward sleeping position. I flopped myself up to sit, heart still pounding from my dream, and found Sam scraping lime green Jell-O out of a plastic cup, chatting with a very tall nurse who stood next to her, studying the blood pressure machine that was attached to her arm.

"Hello, sunshine," Sam said from her bed.

"I've been out for a while, huh." I gingerly patted my hair; it crunched in my fingers like a pile of twigs and dead leaves. This was now my third day in New Hampshire, and I hadn't even cracked open my little container of travel shampoo yet, much less stepped into the shower. At this point I wasn't sure when I'd last brushed my teeth.

Sam nodded. "Nick and Trey came in a little while ago and you didn't even budge."

"Jesus." I stretched my arms overhead, letting out a huge yawn. "I'm surprised they didn't try to draw on me with a permanent marker."

"Oh, believe me, Nick considered it. But I sent them home."

The nurse shuffled around Sam, making little notes on his clipboard.

"They left?" I asked, blinking a few more times as the clock on the wall slowly came into focus; it was just after nine in the morning.

She nodded. "Everyone headed back to shower and get some food. Don't worry, your ride is waiting for you."

"My ride?" I asked, though I knew she meant Mack, the thought of him cranking my eyes open just a bit more.

"Oh, come on, Clare-bear, don't play dumb. You know who I mean."

"I'll stay," I said quickly, but Sam just leveled a no-bullshit look back at me in response.

"I'm fine now, I swear," she insisted. "Eloise is heading back here in a bit, and she left me with that monster romance book she just finished. I'm dying to find out what it's like to sleep with a werewolf."

Sam waved a thick paperback in my face, a ripped, hairy torso greeting me on the cover.

"I feel like the claws would get in the way of things," I pondered.

"Lots of scratching," Sam agreed, poking her tongue at me.

The nurse's eyes darted up from his clipboard at this, brows cocked, and then quickly returned to his notes.

"I want you to text me immediately if anything even feels remotely off," I said. "Promise?"

She sent me off with an air kiss, and I stumbled out into the fluorescent-lit hallway. With little sleep and no coffee, I only felt half alive, and I dragged myself toward the lobby like a zombie on the hunt for brains, reading my texts through crusty, tired eyes.

There were a bunch of messages on our Pine Lake group chat about Sam, and a frantic need for coffee. Then one from Lydia that just read Stop working—you're on a playcation!

But her text only amped me back up, reminding me of that new idea excitement that had buzzed through me just hours earlier.

I'd drafted an entire proposal on my phone, complete with anecdotes of my own time at Pine Lake to really sell the creative angle. All I needed to do now was get it formatted and sent off to Amaya. I hadn't felt this sensation in so long—the giddiness, that pure love for the work that I did. The thrill of it quickly switched me from exhausted to wide awake as I rounded the corner into the emergency room lobby.

My body noticed Mack before my brain did, my skin prickling with awareness at the sight of him. He was now wearing the faded gray sweatshirt he'd been using as a sleeping mask, and his hair was utter chaos. But he stood with a serious look on his face, arms crossed, listening intently as a boy in a wheelchair waved his hands excitedly, mid-story.

"Hey!" I called, and he glanced up as the doors clicked behind me, his face registering me with a flicker of a smile.

"Millen," he said, waving me closer. "I want you to meet someone."

"Good morning," I said as I gave the kid in front of him an awkward wave.

"This is Travis." He bumped the kid's shoulder affectionately with a rap of his knuckles. "Pine Lake Camp waterskiing all-star. And his dad, Bruce."

Travis was grinning up at Mack with the eyes of someone gazing at his idol. Bruce waved hello with a weary shake of his hand. Both he and his son were splattered with dried mud.

"Travis was just telling me about falling off his mountain bike this morning," Mack said.

"I hit a tree root and flew over the handlebars!" he exclaimed like it was a massive accomplishment. "I thought I could walk it off, but my ankle's broken."

"We're waiting to hear from the doctor if he needs surgery," Bruce added, his voice much less enthusiastic. "This kid nearly gave me a heart attack this morning."

Travis shrugged, still beaming. "I thought it was awesome."

Mack bit back a laugh, pressing his fist against his mouth.

"Bruce here has handled all the exterior painting at Pine Lake for the last few years," Mack explained. "He's the reason everything looks so nice every summer."

"Ah, he's just blowing smoke up my ass." Bruce dismissed him with another wave of his hand, but I could tell by the smile that flickered across his face that he appreciated the compliment.

"He's good at that," I quipped.

Mack's mouth fell open in exaggerated offense. "Hey!"

"It's nice to meet you both," I said. "I hope you heal up fast so you can waterski next summer."

Travis's face fell, and Bruce glanced at his son and then shot a look up at Mack.

"We drove by this morning on our way to the trail," he explained, clearly choosing his words carefully. "I texted my friend who's in real estate and got the dirt."

"Oh," I said as realization hit—they'd seen the SOLD sign in front of camp.

"Don't worry, buddy. We're going to figure something out." Mack's voice was upbeat, but his jaw shifted slightly, a hint of tension. Travis nodded, and his smile returned; clearly, Mack's word was gold to him.

"Let me know what the surgeon says?" Mack asked, and Bruce nodded before offering him a fist bump.

"Will do, man. Appreciate it."

"Travis." Mack reached a hand toward him as if he was about to share a high five, but what followed was some sort of secret handshake, a series of slaps and gestures that ended with Mack and Travis both miming playing the trumpet.

"That was impressive," I said as we waved our goodbyes and walked toward the exit.

"They're shockingly easy to remember after you've done them, like, fifty times," he said nonchalantly. "I can make one up with you if you want, Millen. You know, if you're jealous."

"What, do you have a secret handshake with every camper?" I asked, half joking.

But Mack simply shrugged, a wistful look on his face as he slid into the driver's seat. "Just about."

He smiled as he said this, because—I realized—Mack smiled at everything. His lips curled up slightly more on the right side when he teased me, and they grew to a huge grin when he was genuinely laughing. They parted slightly when he looked at me like he wanted to tear my clothes off, his teeth grazing the edge of his bottom lip. And when he was sad, truly crestfallen like he was now, the edges of his mouth tugged tight across his face, in a thin, flat line.

I loved Mack's smiles. But this one, I couldn't stand. It ate at me as we drove in silence again, Mack fiddling with the radio until some sports talk channel came in through the static. I looked down at the

Alewife notes I'd typed out on my phone hours ago, trying to get my mind back on work, but I couldn't shake the thought of Mack's face, the way he lit up like a sunbeam at Travis.

We were alone again, and the heat of last night—the way his lips had melted against my skin—came rushing back to me in a wave of fizzy nerves. It didn't help that my subconscious had been colluding with my libido, telegraphing Mack make-out sessions as I'd slept. Part of me wanted to demand he pull over on the side of the road, wrap my arms around his neck, and yank him on top of me, right here in the passenger seat. But the sadness that had settled around him since talking with Travis called to another part of me entirely.

"You should buy Pine Lake," I blurted out.

"Huh?" He shot me a confused glance before turning back to the road.

"You should try to buy Pine Lake," I said adamantly. "Fuck this glamping developer. You'd be the perfect person to run the camp and keep it as it is, as it *should* be. Talk to Steve and Marla about it. I bet they'd say yes."

I studied him, searching for some sort of hint of a reaction. Finally, he reached across the console, pulling at my sleeve until my hand was free and wrapped in his own, warm and secure.

"It's complicated, Millen. Also, the guy is offering all cash. And I've already promised my parents I'd start training with them this fall. It just doesn't make sense."

"Stop being so goddamn practical," I teased, curling my knees up onto the seat as he let out a satisfied chuckle. "That sounds frighteningly similar to something I would say."

"What's wrong with that?" His voice was low and sultry, and it hit me like oil on a hot pan. "I like the things that come out of your mouth. Especially the stuff you were saying to me last night."

I cleared my throat. "Maybe we can find a time to, you know."

"Keep making things weird?" He drummed his fingers on the steering wheel, eyes firmly on the road in front of him. If I didn't know better, I'd assume he was nervous. But this was Mack; nothing *ever* fazed him. But the more his fingers tapped against the worn leather, the more I wondered.

"I'll check my calendar," I said finally, attempting a joke as my breath hitched, my body remembering what it had felt like to have his lips on my skin. "See if I have the time."

"I'm pretty sure your assistant cleared it, remember?" His eyes didn't budge, but the corners of his mouth twitched. "I'll have to make sure she pencils me in. I'll need at least a day."

Oh god. We weren't just talking about kissing again, we were planning on it. And maybe—no, definitely—hinting at more.

My brain started scrambling, searching for some way out of this conversation. "First you have to accept this."

I dug around my pocket and sighed with relief when I found what I was looking for. "Here. A vote of confidence."

I dangled the medal in front of him and then draped it over his rearview mirror.

"Oh, I see what you're doing, Millen." He chuckled. "This is all just part of your long con. You're trying to woo me, and then when my guard is down—bam!—you pass the medal back to me."

"Nope." I swiped my palms together with a smack. "No more passing this thing back and forth just to bug each other. This medal has a new meaning."

"Huh," he said, his skepticism exaggerated for comedic effect, brows raised. "Okay, so what does it stand for now? Sexiest Camp Waterfront Director? Longest Running Crush of Clara Millen's Life?"

"I'm trying to be serious right now, Mackenzie Sullivan," I scolded, giving him a cross look.

"I'm sorry, I'm sorry, I'm listening," he said with a pat on my leg.

"What I'm saying is that I think you're great," I continued. "And I'm rooting for you. Just, in general. In *life*. For your happiness and success and all the things you want to do."

The words came out sappier than I intended, and I sat there quietly as they lingered between us. Normally I'd try to deflect, or self-deprecate, anything to try to lighten the conversation, steer it away from this serious, heavy place. But I didn't feel like changing the subject right now. I wanted Mack to know that whatever was happening between us, there was something deeper occurring, too, something that had always been there, since the day we met.

I cared about him.

Mack's cheeks flushed as he glanced at me for a moment. "Thanks, Millen," he said finally, his hand sliding up my thigh until it found mine with a squeeze. "I'm rooting for you too."

22

MACK HAD HOPPED out of the car and raced off to "take care of something" the second we pulled back into Pine Lake. I'd found the rest of the gang in the dining hall, pillaging the fridge to slap together a smorgasbord that included a salad made up predominantly of iceberg lettuce, tater tots, and mini pizza bagels.

Now we were sitting around a table covered in our empty plates, like a pride of lions exhausted after a kill.

"So we're postponing the relay then?" Nick asked as Mack sauntered in through the front doors. "It's late now. It would take forever to set up."

My body temperature seemed to rise every time I laid eyes on Mack, and a feverish sweat took up residency at the base of my neck. If we postponed the relay, it meant that I could spend the afternoon with him, alone. I was still trying to determine if our vague, flirty conversation earlier in his car had been a genuine confirmation of our feelings for each other or just another round of our old Clara versus Mack teasing game.

"I think that makes sense," I said, trying not to hover too long on his face. "And we should wait for Sam."

"She'd be mad if she missed it," Eloise agreed, picking at a leftover piece of lettuce on her plate. "Even if she is only able to watch."

Mack didn't say a word, his eyes shifting to whoever was talking. He seemed completely unaffected, and meanwhile, I was a nervous, desperate mess, fidgeting in my chair.

All I could think about was getting Mack alone again, and I tried to communicate that with my intense stare as his eyes passed over my face, his lips twitching when he caught my eye.

"Nick and I wanted to go for a walk, anyway," Trey said. "So we're fine holding off."

"I'm driving back to the hospital," Eloise said, checking her watch. "She's supposed to text me to pick her up."

"I have to ask Marla about getting back into the office to get stuff for the relay, anyway," I said, rushing to stand. I needed to move my body and shake off this fiery electric feeling. The only thing more overwhelming than being alone with Mack was being close enough to touch him and not being able to do anything about it. "Apparently, there's a whole stash in there."

"I can take you right now," Mack volunteered quickly, finally opening his mouth. "I know where all the best sack race gear is. And I have a key. Unless it would be *weird* to go with me to get it."

His face was utterly nonchalant, but there was no denying the emphasis in his voice.

We were very much on the same page.

"Not weird at all," I said, pushing in my chair and grabbing my trash in one swift movement. "Let's do it!"

"Cool," he said, dragging his hand through his hair as he nodded toward the door, an unmistakable twinkle in his eye.

"'Kay, bye, guys!" I said to our friends, who were still mid-lunch. Normally I'd be self-conscious about their perplexed, amused looks, but I was too wired right now to care, too hopped up on lack of sleep and thoughts of Alewife and Dream Mack calling me "good girl."

"Follow me," he said, his hand on the small of my back. "I know a secret way."

We rushed out through the back door of the kitchen, cutting behind Bag End and down along the water to get to the office.

Mack dug his keys out of his pocket, his hands working quickly as he twisted the lock. He pushed the door open with a grunt. Inside, the office was musty and hot, with that stale, lingering smell that sets in when the windows haven't been opened in a few days.

Dust particles danced in the sunlight, and stacks of manila folders covered both desks that were wedged next to each other in the corner. It was exactly as I remembered, and I knew I'd want to marvel at its frozen-in-time vibe later. But right now, all I cared about was the person in front of me.

"Stuff's in here."

He moved quickly into the next room; walls and walls of shelves, stacked with giant gray bins labeled in thick white packing tape and black pen. Suddenly every inch of my skin was clammy, and I was acutely aware of how small this room was. Here, alone again in this tiny, windowless, glorified closet, my heart drummed steady and loud in my ears. All I could think about was the way his neck had actual, visible muscles, and how badly I wanted to run my teeth against them.

"Nick and Trey are acting weird, don't you think? Why go for a walk?" My mouth was running a mile a minute, because being in a tight space with Mack ignited my adrenaline like a cigarette dropped at a gas station. "That just seems random, right? And they're sleeping in separate beds."

"Millen. I think you're the one acting weird." He took a step toward me, and the room was suddenly void of all oxygen as his fingers tugged at the waist of my shorts, urging me closer.

"Sorry," I whispered, my ability to breathe long gone.

"I think you're forgetting what I told you." His lips grazed my cheek, his breath tickling my ear, and I closed my eyes as the room started to spin around us. "I *like* weird."

And then he was kissing me again. It was both familiar and brand-new, the feeling of his mouth, soft and wanting against mine, short-circuiting my nervous system until all that was left in my brain was a jumble of sounds and feelings, all sensation and no words, except for one that seemed to pulse through my entire body, beating in time with my racing heart: *More. More. More.*

Suddenly we were moving, and then my back smacked up against the shelf behind me, my leg desperately trying to hitch around his hip. He slid one hand up my waist and wrapped the other around the crook of my knee, pinning us closer together. I was grabbing on to anything that could hold me up, his shoulder, the edge of the shelf behind me. I did not care about Amaya, or Alewife, or if the world ceased to exist around us. All I cared about was how his body felt against mine.

The only feeling I wanted to bottle right now was *this*.

"Oh! Oh, I'm sorry." I didn't need to open my eyes to recognize the voice that cut through the chaos of our bodies together.

"Oh my god," I said as Mack pulled away from me, running both his hands through his hair as I tugged down my shirt, which Mack had somehow gotten half over one shoulder.

"Marla," Mack started, his face flushed, from both lust and embarrassment, presumably. "I'm sorry, I—"

"Nope, no need to apologize. I just came here to grab some tax returns, and saw this door was open." She shielded her eyes, but there was no hiding the smile that snuck out underneath. "You two enjoy the storage room."

We stood there, frozen, until we heard the door to the office slam shut, and then Mack turned to me, a hand still on his forehead. "Wow."

"That was awkward," I said, trying to form coherent thoughts as my body tingled.

"Marla has known me since I was ten years old, and I don't think I've ever so much as introduced her to anyone I've dated, much less made out with someone in front of her," he said, his face still stunned.

"Well, it's not like she can fire you," I said with a dazed laugh.

But Mack was distracted. He was looking at the bins on the shelf, which we were technically here to get, and then back up at me.

"Let's get these out of here," he suggested with a shake of his head toward the door. "We can store them in the boathouse."

"Okay," I said, agreeing quickly. He pointed at a box labeled RELAY, and I'd never hoisted something into my arms so fast in my life. It could have weighed fifty pounds or been packed full of feathers. I had no idea. I'd carry a car over my shoulder if it meant getting to finally see Mack naked.

We hustled out of the back room and into the main office, and then out the door. Mack paused to lock up and then took off with a jog, speeding by me, giant bin balanced in his arms.

"Are we racing?" I shouted, a couple of feet behind him.

He whipped his head around, lips parted, eyes narrow in thought, as if he was trying to decide if he should kiss me right here. "I mean, I think we're both about to be winners here, don't you?"

"I'm trying really hard not to make a joke about someone finishing first," I cracked, breathless, working overtime to catch up with him.

Mack stopped abruptly, hunched over the bin in his arms, and let out a belly laugh that didn't seem to have an end. When he finally caught his breath, he cocked his head toward me, teeth grazing his upper lip as he studied my face.

"Don't worry, Millen," he said. "I'll happily take second place if it means you finish first."

23

WE BOTH DROPPED the giant boxes of relay stuff on the floor the second we were inside the boathouse. I stood there, panting, as Mack reached around me and hooked the rudimentary lock closed. The second I heard it clink shut, I reached for him, desperate to remember what it felt like to kiss him.

"Millen." His voice was rough like sandpaper, and then his teeth were skating down the edge of my jaw, his tongue teasing the soft, sensitive skin at the nape of my neck. "I know it's corny to say this, but I've been dying to be alone with you."

"Since when, last night?" I said, running my thumb across his chin, tilting his mouth back against mine.

He chuckled, his breath warm on my skin. "Since last night, since last year, since forever."

Since forever. His words sent my mind spinning wildly, spiraling through a sea of what-ifs and maybes.

But then I caught that mischievous glint in his eye, and it dumped an ice-cold bucket of reality on my head. This was Charming Mack talking, and nothing more. There was no point in reading into what he said, no need to make more of this than what it was: pure, white-hot lust.

"We've wasted a lot of time not doing this," I teased, and I was relieved—disappointed?—to see he was just as eager as I was to get back to our regularly scheduled banter. My hands skated greedily up under his T-shirt, squeezing his ribs. "We really need to catch up."

"Before I start ripping your clothes off," he said, pulling away so that his eyes were flush with mine, "I want to make sure I know your boundaries here. Because we don't have to do anything you don't want to do. Or if you ever want to stop, that's always okay with me."

"Mack, all my boundaries involve you ripping my clothes off, and then some."

He chuckled, that slightly arrogant laugh that was still so familiar, and brought his lips back down to my shoulder, where they bloomed into a smile against my skin.

"I'd like that very much." His voice vibrated against my skin as he continued to slowly tease my neck with his mouth, stopping only to let me yank his shirt off over his head.

Suddenly he spun us around and walked our bodies forward until I was pressed against the counter. Smiling at my involuntary yelp as my ass hit up against the edge of the smooth-as-stone wooden surface, he slid his palms down my body, pausing at the hem of my shorts. He tugged them low until I could kick them off my ankles and then hooked a finger into my cotton briefs, peeling them off me slowly, effortlessly, just like he did everything else.

And then in a move that felt like magic, he stood and lifted me up, setting me on top of the counter. I leaned back, and my head bumped up against something hard, the edge of a paddle board or a rudder or something. I didn't care. If it meant having Mack's mouth on my body, I'd spend the rest of my life wedged up against a canoe if I had to.

My brain jolted back to reality for a second. This is ridiculous, I thought. We are two grown adults who haven't seen each other in years, and we're making out in an old boathouse on top of a slab of wood, and not on, like, I dunno, a king-size bed in the middle of a luxury suite at the Four Seasons.

But the rational part of my mind sputtered to a halt the second I felt his teeth trace the edge of my nipple through my bra, and his hands under my thighs, bringing my legs to wrap around his waist.

Then I remembered: I'd had sex with Charles in a Four Seasons in Hawaii; utterly predictable, formulaic, hump-vibrator-moan-the-end sex. It wasn't the place that made things electric, it was the person there with you. And right now, that person was hooking his fingers under my bra straps, his mouth learning my body, my neck, my breasts, my ribs, the dot of a scar above my hip bone where I had my appendix removed when I was nineteen.

Mack shifted my legs again, bringing them over his shoulders, and then he ran a finger from my belly button to the pubic hair I'd neglected to shave in months, to the most sensitive part of my body. My hands slid into his hair, soft like corn silk through my fingers. I closed my eyes and let myself fall through the darkness.

All his attention was on me, my body, my pleasure, and when my orgasm hit, it felt like diving into the moon-soaked lake, the moment of impact when warm meets cold, those long seconds of swimming through underwater darkness, and then coming up for that first gasp of air.

"Do you have condoms?" The words were choked and desperate coming out of my mouth, my voice raspy and wanting, my heart desperately trying to pound its way out of my chest.

I opened my eyes, and the world came back into focus above me.

Mack rested his cheek on my stomach, his hands lightly tracing lines up and down the backs of my thighs, which were still locked over his shoulders.

"I do," he said, gently unhooking my legs from around him as he stood. "But please know it's been a while."

He gave me a puppy-dog face, all pouty lips and exaggerated sad eyes, as if I was supposed to believe that Mack had ever even uttered the words "dry spell," much less even knew what it was.

"Oh *please*," I scoffed, and he yanked a basket off of the highest shelf at the far end of the counter and pulled out a giant box of condoms. He held it close to his face, squinting to read the package.

"Not expired!" he shouted triumphantly, lifting it overhead like a trophy in what was a typical Mack move.

"Really? It's been a while?" I repeated his words back to him, letting him know I wasn't buying it. "You have a Costco-size box of condoms."

"Millen, god, these aren't for me. Do you know how many counselors get sucked into summer romances up here? I like to look out for them. I'm happy to give you the phone number of the woman I dated last fall if you want to check my references. And no, there hasn't been anyone since."

His eyes stayed on me, wide, and he cleared his throat, giving me a sheepish look that was unbearably sweet. It triggered a recurring thought I'd had over the last few days: Maybe he wasn't as full of it as I thought. Perhaps the always collected, perpetually unflappable man I knew was just very, very good at hiding his nerves. Because for someone who excelled at getting the last word in, he didn't seem to know what to say next.

"Should we go up to the loft?" I asked, sliding off the counter until my feet hit the wooden floor. I reached down and fiddled with my clothes for a quick second, his gaze locked on me as he nodded.

I yanked my bra off over my head and tossed it at him. He caught it, of course, still graceful and athletic even when having a rare awkward moment.

"Yeah, as much as I'd love to do all sorts of things to you up there," he said as he chucked my bra over his shoulder and nodded toward the counter, "I think it might go against the logic of physics."

I laughed out a big, loud "Ha!" that filled up the nervous space between us. I could have sworn there was a slight blush under those tanned cheeks, and he looked like his teenage self again, for just a split second.

The moment my hands gripped the edges of the ladder I froze, suddenly panicked by the realization of this. What the fuck was I doing here, contemplating sex with Mack? I should pick my clothes up off the floor and run right back to Sunrise. Rewind time and press play on the Clara I was just a few days ago.

But that Clara hadn't been working for me. I wasn't just stale at work; my whole life had turned into this crumbling, brittle thing that I could barely hold together anymore.

And so I kept climbing.

I'd never been in the loft before, and it was surprisingly spacious, with a giant screened window that looked out on the lake, showcasing a view of the sunset, the dusky pink sky reflecting off the dark water below. So what if the ceiling was dangerously close to the top of my head. Mack's bed was big and white, with two stacks of pillows and a crisp, light comforter. There was even a tiny bedside table next to it that looked handmade.

I shifted onto the bed and tucked myself in. Just as I felt myself about to get trapped in my head again, he was there to pull me out, his hand sliding down the length of my thigh, to my calf. As if motivated purely by instinct, I responded by shifting my leg closer, draping it over his hip bone.

I had him exactly where I wanted him, and his breath hitched as he traced a finger up my thigh.

"This still okay?" he asked in a gravelly voice, and I kissed him yes.

"Mmm-hmm," I mumbled, and he broke away from me for a second to grab the box of condoms that he'd placed near us. Then there was that sound: the rip, and the shuffling that always followed, and then he sighed, and my entire body ached in response. When he pushed inside me, slower than I'd ever seen him do anything in my entire lifetime, I cried out, uninhibited.

The few times I'd let myself imagine what it would be like if Mack and I ever slept together, I pictured it quick and dirty, a "just get it over with" kind of experience where we'd both dust off our hands when we finished and walk away. Instead, he was slow and patient, as if he was trying to memorize every inch of my body, like he didn't want this to end.

I wrapped my legs around Mack and pulled him closer, shifting my hips higher to meet him as he gripped my hands in his, bringing them to rest alongside my face. Slow kisses morphed into something more frantic, searching, the promise of so much more left to discover.

Finally, for the first time in so long, I felt completely in the moment. I wasn't anxiously anticipating emails from Amaya, or rehashing my failed relationship, or shame-spiraling over the friendships I'd let lapse without realizing it.

I was, simply, *here*.

24

AT SOME POINT, it had become nighttime, and the moon announced itself through the window above us, casting shadows across Mack's back. My hand slipped in and out of the darkness as I scratched my fingers along his spine, my heart leaping a bit when I saw the sated smile on his face. I racked my brain for some sort of quip to dial down the tension still swirling in me and came up empty.

Finally, when I couldn't take the silence one second longer, I blurted out, "So is randomly sleeping with someone at these friend reunions one of the traditions I missed?"

When I accepted my award for Worst Post-Sex Conversation Starter of All Time, I would thank this line for making it all possible. Luckily, Mack just played along.

"I mean there was that time Nick, Eloise, and I—"

Despite his nerves earlier, he now seemed completely unruffled by what had just happened between us.

"Ew, don't even joke about that," I squealed.

He leveled a look at me, his eyes soft like half moons. "I solemnly swear I have not hooked up with any of our friends. Now, Steve and Marla, however—"

"Oh my god, Mack, I'm going to go down there and get a canoe paddle and smack you in the head with it."

"I'm sorry, I'm sorry." He rolled onto his back with a laugh, and pulled me close to him, tucking me into his shoulder, that same spot I'd been drooling over just hours before. "This can be a new tradition. For our last summer at Pine Lake."

I exhaled slowly, letting the warmth of his touch ground me. Mack and I were naked, in his bed, post-sex and cuddling like it was the most normal thing we could be doing right now. And maybe it was, I reasoned. Sex could be low stakes and fun, and we could each go back to our lives in a few days with some solid orgasms under our belts. It was no big deal. And it had been good. Like, really good. Great even?

Great.

It had been great.

I had taken a lover.

Passionately.

Check.

"I shouldn't joke about Marla and Steve like that," he continued, the solemn tone of his voice dragging me into the present. "They're basically family at this point. Honestly, sometimes I like them better than my actual family."

The sadness in his voice as he said this set off an ache in me, and a sudden desire to soothe away the hurt. "Well, don't worry, it's not like you're going to go work for them or anything."

Mack let out a sound that was a cross between a laugh and a groan, pressing a hand against his forehead. "I sound like I'm not grateful for them, and I am. I just always feel slightly out of place with my family, like I'm the one who doesn't quite fit into the Sullivan puzzle. You know, there's a real expectation of what success looks like to my parents, and sadly for them, I am not it."

"And you fit in perfectly here," I said, twisting around to face him. He nodded slowly. "Yeah, I think that's safe to say."

I snuggled in closer and dragged my index finger across his chest, tracing the outline of a heart on his skin, because in this moment it was so obvious to me that this was what drove his every decision. I lived perpetually in my head, but Mack was all heart.

My mind circled back to the renovated boathouse, and the overflowing vegetable garden, the swings on every porch. Pine Lake had always seemed like Steve and Marla's baby, but now that I was here, it was easy to see that it was Mack's magic that sparkled on every surface of this place.

"I haven't really asked you how you feel about Marla and Steve selling this place," I said. "This has got to be hard for you."

Mack sighed, a low sound escaping his lips. "Yeah, it is. I love it here. I love getting to work with the kids every summer. It legitimately makes me happy, even after all this time. Though admittedly I am somewhat relieved when they leave."

He smiled as he said this, a lazy, lopsided twist of his mouth, sliding his arm out from underneath me so he could shift onto his side, our faces inches apart.

"Eight weeks is a long-ass time," I agreed with a laugh, remembering how annoying and intense we'd been as campers. "Even longer with a bunch of hormonal kids in your face twenty-four-seven."

"Ha," he chuckled. "That is a very accurate description of my job. And it is," he agreed with a nod. "But then it's also somehow never long enough. I can't believe I won't be seeing them again."

He paused, a wistful look on his face that gutted me. I reached up and brushed his hair off his forehead.

"I'm sure they appreciate you more than you realize," I said, remembering how stabilizing it felt for me to get to be at Pine Lake every year. "This was my happy place when I was a kid. The time at home, between summers, felt so damn long. I just wanted to be back here, at camp."

"Same." He nodded, nuzzling up against my hand, which was still lingering in his hair. "But I always thought it was just me. I never totally got how many kids truly need this place, as a break from whatever is going on at home."

"I was one of those kids," I said, a vision of Marla wrapping her arms around me outside of the dining hall after a phone call with my mom clear in my mind.

"What do you mean?" he asked, tilting up his head to meet my gaze.

"You know my parents are divorced, right?" I said, and he nodded.

"Yeah, I remember. When we were in high school."

"Right." I snuggled in closer, nestling into his side as I trailed my hand down to his chest. "But my mom thought it would be a good idea to tell me they were splitting up in a letter, which I got in the middle of my last summer here."

"Jesus Christ, Millen." Mack's arm wrapped around my back protectively. "I'm so sorry. I had no idea That's an awful way to find out."

"Yeah, I have PTSD every time I go to get the mail." I tried to pass it off as a joke, but Mack just tugged me closer, like he could tell that hiding beneath my attempts at humor lived the painful, raw truth. "Anyway. Marla always looked out for me. I'm sure it was obvious to her that stuff at home was never great. And that summer especially, she was just always there. I've never forgotten her kindness, how she just seemed to know I needed a little extra attention."

"She's pretty special," he said.

"Yeah, she is," I said, giving him a gentle poke in the ribs. "But you are, too, and I bet you help so many kids without even knowing."

Mack had long exuded a warm, protective big-brother energy that he willingly extended to anyone in his path. Even as a kid, he was unguarded and open, and it dawned on me that this quality probably made him especially good at his job.

"You wanna see something cool?" he asked.

"Obviously," I said as he leaned over the side of the bed, shuffling around for a moment.

He turned back toward me with a small basket in his hands, tilting it forward so I could look inside.

Letters, a big, messy pile of them, all addressed to Mack. "I stay in touch with a bunch of kids all year long."

"Wow." I grabbed one off the top of the stack, holding it in my fingertips. "Andreas Warner. From Worcester."

"Oh, he's a good kid. Picked up sailing in, like, one day, this summer. The way some of these kids just blossom here." He gave his head a small shake, and a look of awe passed across his face. "You wouldn't believe it."

"Actually, I would." My throat tightened, emotion coming on fast. I'd been so earnest, so hopeful, in that letter I'd written to myself all those years ago, valiantly trying to avoid the way my world was crumbling around me with my parents' divorce.

It was the same thing I'd done this past year, diving headfirst into work as if that could somehow protect me from the painful, stinging sadness that pumped through my veins.

I didn't want to hide from life anymore, the good parts or the bad.

I wanted to feel it all.

Mack stroked a hand along my shoulder, a quiet acknowledgment that whatever this was roaring through me, he saw it. But he stayed quiet, giving me room to keep talking.

"It feels really good to be back." I leaned into his touch. "I haven't been here for so long, but it feels like no time has passed."

"Imagine how we all felt," Mack said with a laugh, tilting his chin down to look at me. "Waiting for you to come back up here to visit was like waiting for camp to start as a kid."

I could tell by the tone of his voice that his words weren't said to inspire guilt, or as a taunt. It was, well, sweet, and something about

Mack being all laid out and vulnerable like this peeled a layer off my heart, the protective piece I'd secured in place long ago where Mack was concerned. Here, in his bed, I was made up of feelings, soft and raw.

"I missed you, you know." It came out like a confession, an admission blurted out not just to him, but to myself. The amazing sex was clearly acting like a truth serum, nudging words out of my mouth that I might have otherwise kept locked up.

"I've missed you too, Millen," he said, his voice melting me like sugar on the tongue. "This has been the best friend-union by far."

"And now it's the last one," I said, a sinking feeling settling in my stomach. "I didn't realize how much I wanted to be here, and now it almost feels too late."

There's still so much I need to do, I thought, my mind drifting to the piece of paper hidden under my bed in Sunrise. *So much I'm supposed to get done.*

"Well, we might as well knock out some more camp stuff then," he replied, giving my arm a final squeeze before shifting up to sit. "Is there something you've always wanted to do that you've never done at camp before? Or, we could also just stay up here, watch a movie. Although I don't even have Netflix, so maybe that's a bad idea."

"You can use my password," I said. "It's Boobs69 with a capital B, and at signs in place of the letter Os. B, at sign, at sign, b, s, sixty-nine."

"Holy shit," Mack wheezed laughing. "Are you serious?"

"Very," I said matter-of-factly.

"That is amazing, Millen. And way better than pinelake1933."

"I'm glad you appreciate it. Charles didn't even think it was funny," I said flatly, still disappointed in my ex for his refusal to even crack a smile when I'd say it out loud. It was a stupid, corny joke of a password, but it spoke to the part of our relationship that had hurt the most: We never, ever laughed together.

"Yeah, well, I think we've decided that Charles is an idiot," he added. "And I say that respectfully, of course."

I thought for a moment.

"I've always been too scared to jump off the high dive," I admitted.

"Fifteen feet feels farther at night," he said. "Also as the waterfront director, I can't let you dive off the platform in the dark. Safety first."

"Wow, you are good at your job," I teased as I settled in against him. "Actually, there is something else."

"Name it," he said. "And I'll do my best."

25

TWENTY MINUTES LATER, I was tucked onto the passenger seat of the camp waterskiing boat, dressed only in Mack's giant Pine Lake sweatshirt and a pair of worn, flannel boxers that had clearly been retired from everyday use.

Sam had responded to my latest check-in text with: **Back, going to bed, I love you.** I sent off a row of hearts, and then **Going out on the boat with Mack.**

The engine came alive with a quiet purr, and I tucked my phone away in the small side compartment next to me and watched as Mack steered the boat, maneuvering us out onto the lake with the kind of confident ease of someone who did this daily, without thinking about it.

"Anything specific you've always wanted to do on a nighttime boat ride?" he asked. "Besides the obvious, I mean."

He wiggled his brows at me, and I giggled, still giddy and euphoric from the feeling of his body against mine. Sam was truly going to lose her mind when I told her this latest tidbit of news.

"Will you shut up," I said, turning back and smacking a dangling sweatshirt sleeve at him as he chuckled. "I'm trying to enjoy this. I've never gotten to go out on the lake at night before, and I probably won't again."

"Well, then, I have to show you the sights," he said matter-of-factly, and I waited for some crack to follow. But Mack just turned back toward the water in front of us as the boat puttered along. Finally, after what felt like an endless stretch of quiet, I couldn't take it anymore.

"So, what, you're not going to make some joke about skinny-dipping, or the sights actually being your butt, or something like that?" I asked.

"See, I was trying to keep things above the level, Millen," he said, giving me a disappointed look. "But then you and your dirty mind have to go and get fired up again."

"I think you bring it out of me," I said. It was meant as a joke but landed more like a confession, the unbridled truth about how I felt around him. The last year of my life I'd felt like a broken burner on a gas stove, the pilot light lit but still unable to click on. And then Mack had shown up with the flame, and now I was turned to high heat, all the time.

"I can think of no greater compliment," he said as he steered us left, heading toward the north edge of the lake. This time the quiet that settled in between us was easy, matching the stillness of the lake.

I reached my hand over the edge of the boat and grazed the water, enjoying the thrill of it passing through my fingertips like silk. In the distance, a loon howled just as Mack cut the motor, and we floated toward the edge of the rocky, overgrown shore that jutted out at an angle.

"There," Mack said, pointing to two giant slabs of granite wedged under a canopy of looming pine trees along the shore.

"What exactly am I looking at?" I asked. He was shirtless and dressed only in a pair of jeans, and I stood up and moved next to him, just so that I could feel him against me. He kept one hand on the steering wheel and wrapped the other one around my waist.

"Those two trees mark the spot where the original Pine Lake Camp was built, just behind there," he said, his voice low. "Almost a hundred years ago. It's all overgrown now, but you can still find some original foundations back there. And poison ivy."

"How the hell do you know that?" I whispered. He pulled me down to sit on his lap, tucking his chin on my shoulder.

"When it gets quiet in the winter, I like to go to the library and research the history of this area. Last year I got very into reading about old eighteenth-century farmsteads because I wanted to try to rebuild the art barn porch on my own, using the same structural systems these farmers did a couple of hundred years ago, so I needed to do some research," he explained, wiggling his brows. "Sexy, I know."

I slid my hands over his, lacing our fingers together in my lap. "Honestly, it is kind of sexy."

"One day, I came across the sale documents for Pine Lake, and photos of the original buildings. The camp's only had four owners," he continued, our eyes still locked on those two trees. "Rutherford Gordon bought the land from a farmer in 1918 and built the first cabins himself; then the Finkelstein family bought it from him and opened Pine Lake. Then the Rogerses, who had it for decades, and then on to Steve and Marla. All this land has sat unused for years. I spent last winter imagining what could go up here."

"I'm sure your first idea was a glamping resort," I said sarcastically.

"Oh, obviously," Mack said, playing along. His laugh sent a tickle across my neck. "With a row of tennis courts, right there."

He pointed to a spot along the shore, pristine and untouched. "Then maybe a coffee station? Free lattes."

"Totally," I agreed. "Right next to the yoga studio and infrared sauna."

"Honestly, it doesn't sound bad," he said as he turned us away from the ghosts of Pine Lake Camp past, and toward the center of the lake. "I bet we'd love glamping."

We. *We.*

That small word set off a universe of longing inside of me. But it was pointless to even say this out loud. We were here together for a few more days, living out a fantasy. Soon we'd be separated by thousands of miles.

I stuffed the feeling away.

"You know you're basically proving my point that you should try to buy Pine Lake, right?" I said, admiring the way his hair danced on the wind.

But he didn't respond, and I didn't push it.

Eventually, he stalled the engine, the boat practically still on the water.

"Here," he said, nudging me to stand and then sliding by me to sit on the floor of the boat, his body settling easily against the cushioned bench at the back. "This is the best spot."

I sat down next to him, shoulder to shoulder, knees bent, heads together, our faces tilted upward. He was right; from here, the sky was endless, as if all that was left in the universe were the two of us and a sprinkling of stars.

Mack looped his arm across my lap, tugging me in toward him.

"My boss thinks I'm failing at my job," I blurted out, the words scorching me with humiliation that warmed the back of my neck.

"Millen," he said, giving my thigh a squeeze. "You've been at that job forever, haven't you? Aren't you, like, president of the company by now?"

"According to my boss, Amaya, I have burnout," I said with a defeated sigh. "The pitch I'm supposed to be leading next week is a grade-A shitshow right now. I actually think I've come up with a pretty brilliant fix for it, but still. She basically forced me to take this week off."

Mack nodded. "And what do you think?"

I paused, contemplating his question while he traced circles on my skin with his thumb in a soothing, steady rhythm.

"I think that I've worked so hard because I thought it was the right thing to do. That it would make me happy."

I'd considered these feelings in bits and pieces before, but never quite strung them together like this until now. There was something freeing about finally figuring out a truth like this, but it was equally terrifying. Because if my job wasn't the right thing for me to do, then what was? Trying to answer that felt vast and unknown like the sky spread out before us.

I nuzzled closer into the crook of his arm, his bare skin warm and comforting at this moment, when everything else felt completely up in the air.

"It feels kind of scary," I added, "to even think that I might need a break. Or want one."

"Sometimes the things we want to do are the most terrifying, you know?" he said. "That's never totally made sense to me. But I get it."

I turned to find him looking at me, eyes searching. We were doing it again, talking about one thing while also talking about something else too.

I didn't know what we were to each other, exactly, but we were *something*. It was dawning on me that we always had been, in our own strange way. We'd never just been friends, and I'd been an idiot to even suggest it. Not that I knew a better word. I just knew that we weren't nothing. Not even close. But I had no idea how to even ask about his feelings for me, much less share my own.

"What's terrifying to me right now is not knowing how to get my work mojo back," I said, a half-truth but the only one I knew how to speak to right now. "How do you stop being tired and pissed off? It seems impossible."

"I think the answer is change," he said. "I wouldn't be surprised if that's why Marla and Steve are selling, you know? It's not that they don't love it here. It's just that they're done. It's time for them to move on. But I don't think I'll ever be done with this place."

"I'm having a hard time wrapping my head around some stranger buying it," I murmured, my chest now heavy with the grief that came with the passing of time. It was a sadness I'd felt more of recently, this odd, stabbing sorrow that popped up when I remembered that life truly was beyond my control, no matter how much I wished it wasn't. "You just seem like the obvious person to take over."

Mack was silent next to me, but I could feel the rise and fall of his chest, the kind of exhale that comes with defeat.

"Don't you think?" I pushed. "I mean, it just seems like that would have been your plan."

"*My* plan." His voice was flat, and it landed hard, a rock thrown in the water.

"Yeah, I mean, you didn't ever think about what you'd do after this?" I scooted a little bit closer to him. "Or did you just assume you'd be the waterfront director forever?"

"See, that's the difference between us, Millen," he said. "Planning out my life down to the minute doesn't make me happy. Working with the kids here made me happy. And I was good at it, without having any sort of plan whatsoever."

"I don't plan my life down to the minute," I protested, my fingers jabbing out air quotes as I mimicked him. "I just feel better when I know what's coming next."

"You mean like checking your work calendar while you're on vacation?" he asked.

"Yeah, that's exactly what I mean." The words burned in my chest like a giant paper cut. "There's nothing wrong with being prepared, or knowing what your next step is."

"I'm just trying to understand how you went from telling me you're currently in the shitter at work to somehow instructing me on what to do with my own life?"

His eyes were now slivers of dark green and white, like trees against the clouds, and I could feel the conversation shifting gears, turning on its head, though I wasn't quite sure why.

"I'm not instructing you to do anything," I huffed back at him. "It was just a suggestion."

"Yeah, well, I don't need your suggestions, Millen," he said, his voice clipped and sharp. "Focus on your own life; I can figure out my shit, thank you."

This conversation had unraveled into a tangled mess at my feet, and I had no idea what piece to pull to begin to right it.

"Are you calling me a mess?" I said, voice rising. Everything he said was now hitting like an insult, whether he intended it that way or not.

"No." He raised his hands, frustrated. "But you did just use the word 'failing' to describe yourself."

"So you're saying I'm bad at life." I could feel the reactive side of me going full force, seething, tapping into an angry, familiar hurt that had lingered since I was a teen.

"Didn't you suggest the same thing about me the other day?" he asked. "What was it you said, that all I do is float around on the lake all day?"

"Mack. I said I was sorry for that asinine comment," I said, my voice loud enough to echo off the water.

I felt my throat clench, my voice cracking over the last few words. I wasn't even sure how we got into this conversation, but it felt like riding a bike for the first time with no helmet. Exciting for a moment, but now I was panicking and desperate to pump the brakes.

"Just forget it," I said before he could reply. "And you know what? I *am* focused on my own life. I came up with an amazing idea for my big pitch next week. Wrote it up last night."

"Oh yeah?" he said, somewhere between aloof and mocking.

"Yup. I honestly can't wait to get back home so I can work on it. It's, like, the burnout disappeared the second this thing popped into my brain."

I snapped my fingers, to really prove how easy it had been to fix all my issues overnight. This entire argument felt immature, ridiculous even. Like something from twenty years ago. A race to see who could push the others' buttons harder, and then grin and bear it when they did it back.

"Problem solved, then, huh?" he said, pushing himself back up to sit on the bench.

"Yeah," I said. "Crisis averted. Everything'll be great and back to normal next week. All according to plan."

"Good." He moved back up to sit in front of the steering wheel. "And I'll follow my own plan. Maybe I'll even send you a postcard from LA."

He raised his eyebrows at me, an invitation to challenge him on this, to bicker more, push back harder.

Instead, I stayed on the bottom of the boat and twisted my gaze away from his, shutting down the conversation with a literal cold shoulder. He was moving across the country. I had a life in Boston. Whatever romantic feelings for Mack that I'd let blossom in my heart and grow as fast as ivy were just weeds, covering up what I was truly supposed to be focusing on. What actually mattered.

"I gotta get back to Sunrise. I need some sleep," I announced. Mack replied by switching on the engine with a swift yank, and it sputtered to life with an angry grunt. This time there was nothing peaceful about the quiet between us; it was tight and tense, a decades-old, frayed rubber band just waiting to snap.

26

I FELL ASLEEP pissed off at Mack.

I woke up pissed off at Mack.

And I dug out my camp to-do list from underneath my pillow, where I'd stored it for safekeeping during the night, still pissed off at Mack.

I burned with anger at myself for getting swept up in the sensation of his body against mine, for letting all his ridiculous talk about rocks, and being weird, get to my head. A lover may have been a part of younger Clara's plan. Passion? Sure, fine. But feelings? Love?

She hadn't mentioned a bit about it, not a word.

With good reason, I thought, steaming.

I leaned over the edge of the bed and searched around my purse for a pen and my notebook. Paper smoothed out, I dug the tip of the pen into the center of the box labeled "Take a lot of lovers. Or at least have one passionate love affair," and checked it off.

I pressed down so hard that the paper split, a little tear ripping through the box. I let out a bitter, frustrated growl and flung my notebook to the floor, where it landed with a sharp slap.

"Clara?" Sam's concerned face appeared through the screen door. "Are you finally awake? Are you okay?"

"Yeah," I said, squinting at her through the bright-white sunlight. "Are *you* okay? How are you feeling?"

The sun wasn't shy about taking up every inch of window space around the cabin; it beamed into even the dustiest corner with its arrogant, high-noon energy.

Wait, what time was it, exactly?

I yanked my phone from its charging cord and squinted at the numbers on the screen: 11:24 a.m.

Oh, fuck.

"I literally just took a nap in one of the chairs by the waterfront," she said as she shuffled inside, and I could tell by her tone that she was annoyed I'd even asked. "The doctor said to take it easy, not hole up on bed rest. I'm fine."

"Why didn't anyone wake me up?" I shrieked, shimmying out of my sleeping bag to stand.

"Did you have big plans today? Were you supposed to run a marathon or something?" She was beside me now, massaging the small of her back with the heel of her hand as she watched me, perplexed.

"Wait, are you having contractions again?" I studied her closely, like an archaeologist in front of a newly discovered dinosaur bone.

"Jesus Christ, Clara, I will tell you if I don't feel well, okay?" She let out an exasperated laugh. "Besides you're the one acting like you're going into labor, not me."

"I really wanted us all to make friendship bracelets this morning," I explained, rummaging around my duffel bag for clean clothes. "And then do the relay this afternoon. We put it off yesterday because we didn't want you to miss it."

Hopping into a pair of shorts, I yanked them up to my waist with one hand while somehow wrangling a tank top over my head with the other. I moved into the bathroom still struggling to get my arms through and was just shoving my toothbrush into my mouth when Sam caught up to me.

"Oh, honey," she said, and I could tell she was preparing to say something she knew would disappoint me. "Everyone's already kind of gone off and done their own thing."

I paused, mid-brush, a tiny blob of toothpaste foam dribbling off my bottom lip.

"Seriously?"

Sam nodded, watching as I spat and spooned water into my mouth with my cupped hand.

"Eloise and Linus went to go 'check out a van,'" she said with air quotes. "Nick and Trey have been on some long walk since breakfast and aren't back yet."

"But they went on a walk yesterday," I said, dabbing the water off my chin with the edge of my shirt. "How many walks can a practically married couple go on? They're acting like my grandparents."

"I don't think it's that weird." Sam shrugged, her curls bobbing as she moved. "Regan and I went on a lot of walks. We're in our mid-thirties, Clara. We're practically boomers."

I slumped back down on my bed, defeated.

"I just had this whole plan about how today was supposed to go," I said. "Mack even helped me get all the relay stuff out of the office yesterday."

Just saying his name out loud left me feeling frazzled and confused.

"I know you did," she said sympathetically. "And it's very cute how excited you are to do all this camp stuff. You're like a little kid."

"A very tall little kid," I corrected.

"You were basically this tall when you were eleven," she said. "Look, I think this week just means completely different things for everyone, especially since it's our last time here. We're all in very different places, you know?"

I nodded. I did know.

"It's okay." I tried not to sound too defeated. "I need to finish up this document to send to my boss anyway."

I paused, debating for a moment if I even wanted to ask about Mack. It didn't take long for me to decide that I really, really did.

"Have you seen Mack?" I asked, trying to keep my voice casual, inconspicuous. "Is he around?"

"I ran into him at the dining hall this morning," she said. "He had just had a meeting with Steve and Marla and then said he was heading into town for something."

"Oh. Cool." My attempt at acting chill and aloof faltered as my face fell, remembering his stony gaze last night, our blistering argument in the middle of the lake.

"'*Cool?*'" she repeated back to me, her tone skeptical. "Okay, what happened?"

She shuffled past and sat down gingerly on the edge of her bed, staring at me expectantly, almost like she knew exactly what had gone down with Mack, even without me saying a word.

It took me a minute to recognize exactly what it was: the sixth sense that came along with friendship, knowing everything without knowing anything at all. The realization made my heart swell with gratitude for her.

"We slept together last night, and then immediately got into some stupid fight," I blurted out, unable to contain the words and feelings bubbling up inside of me. "It was amazing, I hate him again, the end."

I tucked my hands under my chin and gave her the toothiest, most deranged smile I could muster, doing my best pageant queen pose.

"Oh, Clara," she said sympathetically, drawing out every letter of my name so that it landed like a slow-moving bomb. "I want to be a good friend and ask if you want to talk about your fight, but I also really, really want to know how the sex was."

I let out a loud laugh, and then dropped my head in my hands with a groan. "It was incredible. He's ruined all future sex for me. Do you want details?"

"Are you kidding me right now?" she said, pressing a hand to her chest like I'd offended her. "I want *explicit* details. Drawings. Maybe a diorama of all the different positions? I have all day."

"Well, we could go hang out in the art barn," I said, peering up at her through my fingers. "I could build you a 3D model of our bodies out of Popsicle sticks."

"Oh my god, *yes*," Sam said with an ecstatic moan as she pushed herself up to stand slowly. "Can we meet in, like, half an hour? I need to call my mom first, and you definitely don't need to overhear that conversation. She's just going to lecture me about how I should come home immediately."

"Your mom doesn't want to hear about Mack going down on me on top of the counter in the boathouse? I could sit in on the call, give her all the deets."

"No he didn't!" Sam's mouth dropped open into a Joker-like grin.

"Oh yeah." I nodded, feeling better with every second that passed. "The Popsicle sticks won't be able to do it justice, but I'll try."

"Okay, thirty minutes!" she said, twiddling her fingers together with childlike glee. "I'll meet you in the art barn, where we're going to play the entire Indigo Girls catalog on my phone—*in order*—and dig up all the finger paint and get weird and crafty."

Weird. The word landed in my stomach like a punch, and I blinked back a reaction, forcing Mack out of my thoughts.

Sam clapped her hands together and bowed her head, clearly pleased with her plan.

"Honestly, that sounds just like old times," I said, marveling at the way Sam seemed to glow, shining in the bright morning light. It hit me—deeper than it had any other time this week—just how much I'd missed her.

"I know," she said, beaming back at me. "Aren't you glad you came?"

"More than you know," I said, suddenly overwhelmed with the urge to cry, even though I felt the exact opposite of sadness right now.

"Mom time." She waved her phone at me, grimacing. "Wish me luck."

"Remind her that you are a grown-up and you can make decisions for yourself!" I shouted behind her as she headed back out through the door, stopping to look at me with a cocked brow.

"Tell your boss the same thing when you email her!" she said as she disappeared back into the sunlight.

I plopped back down onto my bed and grabbed my phone. After a solid twenty minutes of polishing up the document, I cracked open my email.

Amaya, I wrote. I know I'm on my micro-sabbatical, but I had a bit of an epiphany for the Alewife creative and am sending over a detailed outline. Can't wait to hear what you think.

And then I hit send.

27

IT WAS DARK outside when the reply landed in my inbox, short and to the point.

Clara—No work emails on micro-sabbatical. Amaya says you two can discuss next week.—Abe

Abe.

She'd had her assistant respond as if she couldn't even be bothered to answer herself. My fists clenched with actual rage, fingers cracking as they dug into my palms.

Over my thirteen years working for her, I'd become masterful at deciphering Amaya's moods simply based on her email sign-offs. Most of the time it was simply "Amaya," but occasionally on a good day, or a weekend, I'd get a random "xx." I always assumed those came after some sort of bottomless mimosa brunch. Ones signed with "—A" were sent when she was short on patience, on time, on giving a shit.

It was never good to get the "—A." But for her to not even bother to reply herself felt like an incomparable insult. She was clearly trying to send some sort of message, and if her goal was to leave me seething, then she'd accomplished it.

"You have got to be fucking kidding me," I huffed under my breath, pacing next to a paint-covered wooden table.

It was almost nine o'clock; Sam had headed off to bed an hour ago, not long after we'd scarfed down a large pepperoni pizza an awkward teenage boy had delivered to us. I'd wandered down to meet him at the entrance of camp, my hands covered in glue and glitter from the poster I'd been crafting all afternoon. It was part vision board, part unbridled release of tension. Feathers glued together in one corner, torn-out magazine spreads of hikers and beaches in another. In the middle of it all, I'd painted the word "Discover" in neon pink.

Did I know what any of it meant? Not really. But putting it together as our conversation meandered from topic to topic had felt amazing, exactly like Sam had suggested. Art therapy.

I was still riding that creative high when Sam started yawning after our impromptu dance party to "Take on Me," which crackled on the ancient boom box in the corner. I offered to clean up our mess myself, sending her off to go read in bed.

But now with Amaya's rejection leaving me spiraling, I couldn't focus on anything.

I dragged the metal chair back out from under the table and plopped down, opening up the browser on my phone. With a sigh, I tapped out the words Burnout work signs how can you tell and then scrolled through the results that appeared on my screen.

Irritability

Lack of motivation

Exhaustion

Low self-confidence in ability

My anxiety kicked on with each line that I read, heart-thumping adrenaline that went straight to the negative-thought-churning corner of my brain. The list felt like a mirror for exactly how I'd been feeling for months, and this reflection staring back at me through these words was terrifying. It meant that maybe Amaya was right after all.

I swiped the page closed quickly, glancing back at the sink full of glass jars of murky gray water and dirtied paintbrushes that needed scrubbing. I was too wired to walk out of here just yet. Fuck it, I decided. *I'll make a friendship bracelet, then I'll clean up.*

Sam and I had been so swept up in our collaging that we'd skipped bracelet-making completely. Luckily the bin marked EMBROIDERY STRING was easy to find, labeled clearly on a top shelf, almost as if the ghosts of my past had left it there for me to find.

But for all my gung-ho enthusiasm, I had completely forgotten how to actually weave the string together into something resembling a bracelet. I had foolishly assumed this—an activity I had done so frequently as a camper I could quite literally do it with my eyes closed—would come back to me, but other than cutting the string and knotting it, I was completely lost.

Just as I opened YouTube to search for bracelet-making tutorials, a voice came out of nowhere from behind me, causing my heart to try to eject itself from my body.

"Hey."

I spun around, and it only took me a second to make out the shape of Mack, looming tall in the shadow of the door frame.

"Jesus Christ, you scared the crap out of me," I hissed, clutching my phone to my chest. Mack made a sympathetic face as I scowled at him, heart still racing.

"Making friendship bracelets?" He shoved his hands in his jean pockets and sauntered over next to me, peering at the knotted mess of green, white, and blue string I'd Scotch-taped to the table.

"No," I said, scrambling to yank it loose, tossing it in the nearby trash can. I wasn't making it for him. But I wasn't not making it for him, either.

"So sneaky, my Millen." His use of the word *my* pinged something warm and affectionate inside me, but I shoved it aside and willed myself to instead remember how cold he'd been last night in the boat. That was the Mack I needed to focus on right now.

"What's up?" I asked, crossing my arms across my chest as if that could somehow protect my heart from him. As if he hadn't already wrecked it.

"I stopped by Sunrise." Mack leveled a look at me, those forest-colored eyes narrowing, like he was figuring out the fastest route to get inside my head. "Sam said you were still down here."

"Well, you found me." I was determined not to let him back in.

He cleared his throat. "I came here to apologize for how I acted last night."

I watched as he fidgeted with the torn hem of his T-shirt.

"And?" I said finally.

"I'm not saying this as an excuse," he started, and it took everything in my power not to roll my eyes. "But I've had some big decisions to make, and by the time I finally figured out what I wanted, things fell through. It's not going to happen. And I really wanted it to happen."

He palmed his brow, frustrated, as if he still couldn't find the right words.

"Sometimes stuff just doesn't work out, you know? Maybe it's fate. I don't know. But I was upset about it, and when we started talking about life plans, I overreacted. I took it out on you. And I'm just really, really sorry I did that."

It was straightforward enough, no teasing or flirting. I thought back to this morning and how I'd angrily reduced him to a checked box on my list and felt a slight pang of guilt for dismissing him so quickly. But I pushed it aside, because I couldn't help but worry about what he wasn't saying.

"You're being really vague," I said. *Is this about us?* I wanted to ask. *Are we "stuff that doesn't work out"?*

But I didn't. I just glared.

He let out a tired sigh as his eyes scoured the room, avoiding mine. "I know. Sorry. It's too much to get into right now."

"Well. I appreciate the apology," I said, my voice curt, arms still tight and protective. *Definitely* about us.

"Can I make it up to you?" he asked, his eyes crinkling at the corners as he finally gazed down at me.

"How?" I questioned, my voice softening. It was so easy to let him back in, too easy. He was like a gin and tonic at happy hour, the perfect mix of sweet and tart.

"I planned something for us tomorrow morning," he said with a shrug, and if the light were better in there, I could have sworn I'd have picked up a faint blush on his cheeks.

"Kind of like a date, as much as it can be, at a camp."

"Okay," I said, softening a bit, as the word *date* spiraled through my thoughts like a hurricane. "What are we doing?"

"It's a surprise," he said, taking a small step closer to me, his hands still in his pockets. "Just be at the soccer field at ten in the morning tomorrow, and wear sneakers."

He wrestled his hands free and dragged them through his hair, the pieces still sticking up waywardly despite his best attempt at taming them.

"And a sports bra?" I flicked my brows up, eyeing him. I was still pissed, prickly and sensitive even with his apology. But I couldn't resist flirting with him; it was like the only things I wanted to say to him were laced with innuendo.

"I guess?" He shrugged, giving me a clueless face.

"You guess?" I explained, half teasing, half serious. "How am I supposed to trust you if you don't know how my boobs will handle whatever it is you have planned?"

"Okay, yes, wear a sports bra. And I promise, you'll love it." He moved closer until he was standing between my legs, hands on my shoulders. "Trust me. I know you."

He did know me, and I couldn't quite understand how he did it. How after years away and time apart, Mack was somehow wired to the workings of my brain, for better or worse. For a moment, I considered unloading it all on him: Abe's terse reply, and the Google search results that hit way too close to home. How I'd been clinging to my old letter like a road map, and the stinging shame I felt at my life being nothing like I'd hoped it would be when I was fifteen. The way something as basic and vital as joy had escaped me for years, and now it was here, standing right in front of me.

But instead, I just ducked out from under his hands, even though every part of me wanted to throw myself against him, wrap my arms around him, and drag him to the floor. Sex felt simpler than parsing all my painful, unfiltered feelings, or asking him what this was between us, what any of this meant, or if it meant anything at all.

"Good night, Mack," I said, pushing the door open behind me.

I waited for a moment, hoping he'd say something; beg me to stay, tease me, dare me to run back with him to the boathouse, escape all the anxiety coursing through me under the sheets of his bed.

But this time Mack, who always had something to say back to me, said nothing at all.

28

THE NEXT MORNING, I spotted Mack first, standing with his hands clutching the back of his head, fingers lost in that mess of hair, chatting with Nick, who was clad in a Hawaiian shirt the color of fruit punch. He had the same ridiculous glasses he'd worn to our Capture the Flag game a few days ago, but now he'd added a full-on captain's hat.

Even though weirdness lingered from last night, the sight of Mack still vaporized my insides, turning every bone and organ into lovesick gas. Twelve hours without him had been too many, but I quickly shoved the mushy feelings aside and reminded myself that in a few days we'd be separated by an entire country's worth of distance.

The mental clock that ticked closer and closer to me leaving Pine Lake was just the protection I needed right now to keep my heart safe. This couldn't be anything, because soon this place—just like my time with Mack—would be finished, closed, gone for good.

But despite all of that, I couldn't help the hopeful excitement that danced across my skin. I'd been looking forward to this ever since Mack had said the word "date" to me last night. And so I'd left my phone behind in Sunrise today; I didn't want to think about Amaya snubbing my email any more than I already had. And I'd tucked my camp checklist next to it; today I wanted to be free of distractions.

Mack's sparkling laugh cut through my thoughts, and my eyes

lingered too long on the length of his neck, the tensed muscles in his arms, the way his shoulders always seemed just a little too broad for his T-shirts.

Well, free of *most* distractions.

"Well, if it isn't the competition," he said as I sidled up next to him, lips curling into the love child of a smile and a smirk.

"I thought this was a date," I said, genuinely confused about what I was about to get myself into.

"Oh boy, this is gonna be fun." Nick rubbed his hands together, and Mack full-on chortled, buckling at the hips in laughter. I shot him an icy glare, suddenly self-conscious that I'd been excited for a "date" he seemed to view as a joke.

"Can one of you please tell me what's going on?" I asked, looking back and forth between them for clues.

"Patience, my dear Clara," Nick said, reaching up to slide his glasses down an inch, a regular millennial James Bond.

"Fine, then can we discuss your outfit?" I eyed him deliberately, and then shot him a devilish grin.

"Yes, please, can we?" Mack snuck a conspiratorial look at me before turning back to Nick. "Because if you ever get married, I want to borrow this whole look to wear at your wedding."

"Fine, then I'll just have to demote you from officiant to regular boring old guest." Nick's brows knit together over his *Miami Vice* shades.

"You wouldn't dare," Mack said, playfully calling his bluff.

"It's the hat that really pulls it all together." I stood back, eyeing Nick up and down like a fashion designer reviewing a dubious frock on a mannequin.

"Eloise and I raided the costume closet in the theater." Nick gave us both the stink-eye. "Now, can we please get started?"

Mack gestured at Nick, an openhanded invitation to spill the beans.

"We're doing the relay," Nick said matter-of-factly. "Well, *you're* doing the relay."

"Our date...*is* the relay?" I repeated back, turning to Mack.

"You're only here for, like, three more days. I wanted us to do something fun together. Something you couldn't do on a date with anyone else." He was bouncing on his feet with excitement, and suddenly all the doubt I had about him—about *us*—just moments ago was spun on its head yet again.

"And then Nick and I were discussing the relay," he continued. "And how we missed it yesterday, and we thought it might be more fun if it was just the two of us."

"So, like, you want me to kick your ass again?" I taunted, pushing my shoulders back confidently.

"Come on, Millen, you didn't think I could really handle you beating me in our little swim race the other night, did you?" he said in that voice that had just a hint of sultriness. "You know my ego can't take it."

He took a step closer to me, clearly enjoying egging me on. The sight of him like this—cocky and confident—ignited something in me, something familiar and nostalgic. I'd always relished every second we spent verbally sparring like this, but when I was younger, I'd assumed it was because I liked driving him nuts. Now I realized it was the opposite; I adored it, because deep down, I adored him.

I always had.

"Well, I'd say, 'May the best person win' but we all know that's going to be me. So."

I yanked a bottle of sunscreen from the back pocket of my shorts and sprayed it down my arms, purposely ignoring him, just to get under his skin.

"There she is." He shot me a pleased look, his voice laced with something that sounded a lot like affection. "Let's do this."

"Excellent!" Nick said with a smack of his hands. "No rules, except that the first person to complete each of the challenges and burn through their rope wins."

"Oh my god, we're doing an actual rope burn?" I squealed, unable to contain my excitement at this news.

Nick nodded eagerly.

"And the winner can obnoxiously gloat about it forever and ever, in perpetuity." Mack leaned over to gently knock my elbow with his, giving me that self-assured smirk.

There was that glimmer in his eye again, the one I'd seen in Capture the Flag the other day. I'd chalked it up to his competitive nature, and I was still almost certain that's all it was.

And so I ignored the whisper in my gut that told me I wanted it to be more. I wanted it to be because of me.

Nick bent down and reached for the giant tote bag resting near his feet, pulling out two dented silver spoons that were surely from the dining hall, and a small container of a half dozen eggs, popping it open and tipping it toward us.

"Egg and spoon race kicks things off. Take your pick."

"I'm assuming," I said as I gingerly picked an egg out of its little cardboard home, "that these are hard-boiled like when we were kids?"

"Uh, hell no." Nick shook his head firmly, "You're grown-ups now. You get the real stuff."

He paced in front of us like a high school gym coach, fiddling with the whistle that hung around his neck. "All right!" he barked. "Dominant hand behind your back after you put your egg in the spoon. Make it to the other side without dropping it. If you do drop it, you come back and start again."

I steadied my breath and closed my eyes for a beat, traveling back in time to the girl I was when I first walked into Pine Lake Camp. There she was, a little shy, taller than everyone else, and overwhelmed by the chaos of the first day of camp. But then, a shift in just eight short weeks, toward confidence, independence, and friendships that fulfilled me.

"Three," Nick counted down. I exhaled.

Another memory, of that same first day. A kid with shaggy hair bounding out of the camp van, like he couldn't contain the energy that lived inside of him.

"Two."

That kid, five years later. My same height, he'd sprout more inches later. The look of wonder on his face—a flash of fear, desire, things I didn't truly understand at the time. And then he kissed me.

Back in the present day, my fingers clenched the handle of the spoon, and I felt the weight of cotton and polyester sticking to my sweaty skin. My muscles already throbbed even though we hadn't even started moving. I was ready to snap like a mouse trap at any second.

"One."

I took off walking the second Nick's whistle cut through the air, taking tiny, delicate steps so as not to throw the upper part of my body off balance. It already felt lopsided with one arm tense and outstretched, and the other tucked behind my back. Surely I looked ridiculous, like a giant trying to tiptoe through a fairy forest. It seemed impossible that half of my body could be so confused and off-kilter, but this, I realized, was the whole point, not just of this dumb egg walk, or Color Week, but of camp.

We may have just been kids, but we had always been encouraged to use the parts of ourselves that were so often left untapped. And some-times that required pushing yourself into some discomfort, forcing you to really examine what you could actually do, discovering what was possible—or not.

"Slow and steady, Clara," I murmured to myself, because aggressive was probably not the best move to make while walking with an egg nested in a spoon. "Slow and steady."

"You talking to yourself back there, Millen?" Mack asked, just a few inches in front of me. "You sound nervous."

"Just making fun of your technique," I teased as we both picked up our pace, heading toward the two red sacks waiting for us on the ground.

I tossed my egg into the grass as Mack haphazardly tried to shove one long leg into the sack while hopping the other one in after it. It was the most awkward I'd seen him all week, and the sight of him struggling triggered every mushy feeling I'd been trying to suppress.

"Come on, champ," I goaded, laying my sack on the ground, the opening facing up at me.

In one swift jump, I leaped both feet into the center of the bag, bending down to lift the sides up to my waist, forcefully yanking it over my body like pair of tight jeans. "You've got this."

"Jesus, how did you do that?" Mack yelled, clearly frustrated. But I ignored him and took off hopping, gripping the sides of the sack with sweaty hands.

"I'm just naturally better than you!" A half-laugh, half-shriek escaped my lips as I imagined how ridiculous we must look. From the distance, I heard someone scream my name, and that was when I realized the rest of our friends were down by the boathouse, watching and cheering us on.

I stumbled as I tried to quicken my pace, my foot getting tangled in the bottom of the bag. That was enough time for Mack to hop by, his messy hair bouncing past me.

"Oh shit, looks like someone's rusty!" Mack shouted as he literally stumbled into the lead.

"Goddamnit," I snapped, and every competitive cell in my body cranked up to a ten. "Stop trying to distract me just so you can win!"

Kate Spencer

"Hey, Millen," he yelled from a few feet ahead of me. "I have a good one then. This will distract you for sure."

"I'm seriously going to kill you," I huffed in between leaps, bringing up the rear.

"You were my number one camp crush." He sounded out of breath but was still able to get the full sentence out—just as he raced down the hill, his feet pounding on the grass. He moved so quickly that it almost felt like I'd imagined his words, and I stood there for a moment, frozen, before I took off after him.

"No fair!" I shouted, kicking the sack off as I crossed the finish line. I had to catch up to him, to tell him the truth that had lingered behind every single one of my sarcastic quips, every feverish kiss.

"I liked you from the moment I saw you get off that van full of kids coming in from the airport!" I said loudly as I moved toward him at warp speed. "Before we even spoke. So beat that."

It was all I could get out with my heart pounding the way it was.

He stopped, pivoting around to look at me for a split second, his face full of adoration. And then he took off again, ahead of me still.

Down at the beach, a brand-new yellow sponge was waiting at the edge of the water. I grabbed it and dunked it into the lake, cupping it gingerly in my hands so as not to lose any water.

On paper, this part of the relay should be easy: Fill a sponge with water, walk a little bit, and then squeeze it out into a bucket. Piece of cake, baby. But it was all a ruse, designed to hide an exquisite, unique kind of torture, the sponge leaking through your fingertips as you ran back and forth.

I crouched down in front of my red pail, right next to Mack, who was on his knees, frantically wringing his own sponge.

"I've liked you literally for forever, you know," I said, the words spilling out faster than the water I squeezed from my sponge. "And

I've thought about that kiss an abnormal amount over the last few years."

"It *was* a good kiss," he said as he leaped back up to his feet, heading down toward the water. "So good I was too terrified to even look in your direction after."

"I'm glad you're making up for lost time then," I said as I jogged behind him.

Mack stood for a moment at the edge of the water, turning to look at me. "You know, for the last five years, I sat around, waiting for you to finally come back up here. And this year, after Marla and Steve told me they were selling this place, I just figured, fuck it. I'm going to call her, ask her to come. And then Sam texted me and said it was already happening. So maybe it's fate that you're here."

We were in the middle of a race, but he didn't move. Instead, he just held my gaze, hands cupped in front of him with that stupid sponge, as if he were holding my whole heart.

"Last night you said that fate was stuff not working out," I said, completely taken aback. "You weren't talking about us?"

"God, no," he said, squinting as he shook his head at me. "Millen, if anything, this thing with us feels like the only thing in my life that's working right now."

"Mack—"

"Hold that thought," he said, and took off sprinting. I didn't need to see him to know he almost certainly had a shit-eating grin plastered across his face.

"Motherfucker!" I squealed, remembering where I was and who I was battling as I took off toward my bucket. "Oh, you're asking for it now, Mack."

"Honestly, Millen, I don't know whether to be pissed off or turned on by that," he said with a breathless laugh.

"Both, I hope," I said as I clenched my brow, willing my hands to squeeze as hard as they could. And then there it was, my water just skimming the fill line at the top of the bucket. Done.

I stumbled over my legs, racing to where our two ropes hung between wooden stakes in the ground like tiny laundry lines. The rope burn was the pivotal moment of Color Week, days of competition culminating in this one dramatic feat.

My team had lost the rope burn in spectacular fashion that last year at camp, only seconds behind Mack's team, resulting in our inevitable tie. I could still remember how crushed I'd felt, devastated by our team's loss, compounded by the hollow ache I'd already carried that whole week, after my kiss with Mack.

Next to me, I could hear Mack's heavy breath like the pull of the ocean. I turned to give him a quick peek, and the sight of him crouching on the ground, intensely staring at his small stack of kindling in front of him on the ground next to me did that thing to my heart that I now just expected every time I saw him.

"Mack," I said, and when he didn't respond, I said his name again louder. "*Mack*."

His head bounced up, brows clenched, so incredibly focused. "What?"

"What is this, between us?" I kept my eyes on my work, trying to balance yet another stick against the pile. "Seriously. Are we a thing?"

I sounded like I was fifteen again—did anyone even use the phrase "a thing"?—but Mack's reply cut through my spiraling thoughts.

"Millen," he said confidently, "we've *always* been a thing."

"Great. So now I've made it weird by asking," I said, and he laughed.

"How many times do I have to tell you how much I like your weirdness?" he asked. "Please keep making things weird."

"And now what?" I asked, my heart now pounding in my chest

as my hands worked until every stick I'd scavenged was propped up against the others. "I'm going home in a few days. You're moving back to California. Camp isn't even going to exist anymore."

"I don't know," he admitted finally. "Can't we just enjoy the rest of this week together? Pretend it's not really going to end?"

A bright light flicked in the corner of my eye, and sure enough, Mack's fire was now sparked and quickly rising faster than mine. I kept my eyes on the flames in front of me, using my breath to push them higher.

"I think some people might call that living in denial," I replied, unable to hide the sadness in my voice.

I shoved my kindling into the heart of the blaze with a steady poke of an extra stick I'd kept on the ground next to me, attempting to keep the embers fed and glowing. And then with what seemed like a flash, the flames hit the bottom of my rope.

This was the hardest part of the rope burn challenge: the moment when you were in control of absolutely nothing. From here on out, I had to just let the fire run its course.

"Clara," Mack said, and his use of my first name caused my head to spin toward him. "I don't know what happens next. I just know I like you, and I want to be with you right now, even if we only have a couple of days left together."

I finally gave in and looked up at him. He was standing and staring directly down at me, and not at the fire in front of him. Even though his arms were across his chest, he didn't look defensive, not one bit. Instead, he looked like he was deeply and truly sure of himself.

"I've been crazy about you since the day we met, but, like, never more than I am right now," he continued. "You know that, right? I'm making myself clear? Because I'm trying to be better about saying what I mean. And I mean it."

"Yes," I said finally, and my entire body flushed. "I know."

It was the heat from the fire, of course, but whatever was burning between Mack and me felt bigger and hotter than the real thing in front of me.

"Good," he said, and then with a nod of his head toward my rope. "Congratulations."

I broke our eye contact and swung my head around, and there it was in front of me: my rope split in half, two pieces dangling now from the wood stakes that held them.

I'd won.

"You know what this means, right?" I pushed myself up off the ground, scrubbing my dirty hands on the front of my shorts.

"Don't do it, Millen," he said as he pulled up the edge of his T-shirt, bringing it to his brow to wipe away sweat. "I told you, my ego can't take it."

"I kicked your ass!" I whooped. "I won our date!"

He held out his hand for a high five, and when I slapped it he gripped me tight, tugging me into a warm, sweaty hug.

"This was a shitload of fun," I said, mentally checking that particular box on my camp list as my cheek pressed against his shoulder, taking in that scent that was so uniquely him; a mix of an ancient bar of soap, sun-touched skin, sunscreen, and sweat. It wasn't fancy, or musky, or out of an expensive bottle, but it was his, and I was becoming addicted to it.

"Almost as fun as living in denial with you," he muttered, his lips soft against my jaw.

I pulled back, clasped my hand against his pout. "Shh," I scolded. "The first rule of living in denial is not talking about it."

He reached up and laced his fingers through mine, pressing a kiss against our clasped hands. "I won't speak of it again."

But that nagging clock was still ticking away in the back of my mind, counting down our time together second by precious second.

29

ELOISE WAS THE first to reach us, enthusiastically waving a can of hard seltzer in the air as she approached in a bright yellow floppy sun-hat, a sequined, silver vest hanging off her shoulders. "That was amazing," she said. "And very ridiculous to watch."

"I can't believe no one broke a leg in that fucking sack race," Sam muttered as she wrapped an arm gingerly around me. "You are a badass."

Trey appeared next to her with a Bloody Mary in hand, complete with a giant celery stalk. "I have never seen two adults work so hard for something so wonderfully meaningless."

"What are you talking about?" I recoiled, giving him my best offended look. "Camp games mean *everything*."

And they had, once, all those years ago. Competitions that felt like battles, where the heartache of loss was learned alongside the magic of winning. But now I could see them for what they really were: life lessons with training wheels, practice for the real ups and downs to come.

"It was glorious." Trey raised his glass in my honor. "You two are fun to watch together."

"That's because Mack's fun to torture." I did my best villain laugh as I grabbed the water bottle Sam passed me and threw back a gulp.

"It sure doesn't look like he finds it torturous," Eloise chirped, lighting up as Linus and Nick approached.

"Should we take the pontoon boat out?" Trey asked the group. "Cocktails on the water?"

"I'm not drinking, so I can drive," Mack volunteered, standing next to him. His shirt dangled from his hand, and my eyes couldn't focus on anything else but him; the slope of his shoulders, that light sprinkling of chest hair, his taut stomach. I blinked hard, trying to reboot my brain by concentrating on something else.

My gaze landed on three figures standing up on the sloped grass, in front of the dining hall. Marla and Steve I recognized immediately, and I waved them over, still riding the high of my win, wanting to celebrate.

Out of the corner of my eye, I caught Mack's face growing cloudy as they approached, a glare focused solely on the man next to them, a stocky, silver-haired white guy who walked with a purpose. His tidy button-down and fitted slacks felt way too formal for the place, even though he'd paired them with some retro-style hiking boots.

Suddenly I knew exactly who this guy was. And judging from the hint of a scowl lurking just below Mack's forced, pleasant smile, so did he.

"Who won?" Marla asked, our circle opening to include them.

"Clara, obviously." Mack pressed his hand ever so lightly against the curve of my back.

"Congrats," Steve said, tipping a salute at me.

Marla, always so soft and easygoing, stood with her hands crossed in front of her chest, stiff and formal.

"Well." She cleared her throat. "Everyone, this is Brad Bradford. He's the chief financial officer of Glamp Camp."

My stomach sank as we muttered polite greetings back.

"These guys are all former campers and counselors who still come up to visit," Steve said, palming Trey's shoulder affectionately before gesturing toward Mack.

"Brad, Mack's run our waterfront for a decade. He knows more about this place than we do," he said kindly as Mack gave a shake of his head.

"He's just being nice," Mack said, reaching his hand forward.

"Very cool, man," Brad Bradford said, and I could tell from his intense, toothy smile that his handshake was a death grip. "I'd love a tour of the lake sometime."

"We were about to go out—" Trey started, but Mack cut him off.

"We're all heading off to grab lunch," he said, flashing Brad that charming, easygoing grin that I could see right through as a front. "But yeah, anytime before I leave for Los Angeles, I'd be happy to do it."

"Why don't we go grab the golf cart, and I can show you the perimeter of the property," Steve said, steering Brad back toward the Village.

"Great to meet you all," Pine Lake's new owner said with a stiff jerk of his hand.

We watched them go in somber silence, until Nick piped up once they were no longer in hearing distance.

"Brad *Bradford*?" he said with a horrified laugh. "What evil parents would do that to their kid?"

"The same ones who name their kids Linus, I bet," Linus said in his perfectly clipped, serious staccato.

There was a pause, and then an explosion of laughter, but it wasn't the joyful, celebratory kind. That mood had disappeared the second Brad arrived. This was pure relief, the kind of cacophony that defused a tense situation.

Brad was here. Pine Lake was ending, for real.

"So I guess no lake time now?" Trey said. "Unless we want Brad to tag along."

"I think I need a shower," Mack said, sounding sullen. "Maybe we regroup in a few hours? Sunset cruise?"

After a few more minutes of chitchat, people dispersed. Sam headed off to take a nap, and the rest followed her back up to Sunrise to figure out lunch.

"Come on, Millen," Mack said once we were alone. "Let's go clean off. I haven't even shown you the outdoor shower I built last year. I think I might even have some soap, if you're lucky."

He tilted his chin as if to say, "Shall we?"

As if he even had to ask.

The sun tailed us through the trees as we followed a mossy path that wrapped around behind the boathouse. Sure enough, there was a square wooden platform jutting off the back wall of the building, tucked behind a giant boulder and shadowed by a canopy of trees. A smooth slab of granite served as a step, leading up to a tiny deck that jutted out around the shower.

"How the hell have you not even mentioned this to me?" I asked, pausing to admire the tidy row of wooden hooks along the wall, dry towels dangling at the ready.

"What did you want me to say, 'Come let me strip you down and show you my shower'?" he asked.

"Yes," I said, marveling as he swung the door open, guiding me inside. "*Obviously.*"

He laughed. "Well, I was just waiting for the perfect time. Which is clearly today."

A showerhead loomed above, one of those wide, round, rainy types, connected to the boathouse by exposed pipes that traveled down the siding toward the planks of wood below. We were completely hidden by walls, but above us, tree branches danced against the sky.

It was private and secluded, but also exposed enough to the outside world that a thrill rushed through me, head to toe. I'd never had sex with anyone outside before; Charles had tried once, on an empty beach in Cape Cod, but it had felt vulnerable in a way that had turned me off.

But the thought of it spun me now, twirled my insides like cotton candy, knowing I was here, with Mack, safe and protected in our own little bubble.

"You okay?" I asked as I reached for him, holding his face in my hands, studying the angles of his eyebrow to detect any hints of sadness.

"Not really." He shook his head slowly, tilting his chin to kiss my palm. "But I really don't want to think about Brad *Bradford* right now."

I understood. Mack didn't need to talk. He needed a distraction.

I slid my hands down to his chest and pushed him back against the wall, tugging his damp shirt over his head and flinging it toward the door as I grabbed his face, pulling him toward me. His lips were urgent and needy, and he anchored his hands on my hips, holding me closer as I slid my fingers along his cheekbones and into his hair, tightening my grip on that beautiful mess on his head.

He dragged his mouth down to just under my ear, grazing his teeth along my neck.

"You look so hot in those dirty clothes," he said in a low voice, and I let out a laugh. I was still fully dressed in my sweaty relay outfit, which was—by any sort of sexy metric—the opposite of "hot."

"I smell like the love child of an onion and an ashtray," I said, pulse thumping under his touch.

"I'm not kidding," he said, his hands moving up to cup my breasts through the damp cotton of my old Chatham 5K Road Race tank top. "I like you like this, all messy."

"You have some strange fetishes," I teased, eyes fluttering half closed as I pressed my entire body into his touch.

"Nah," he said, his voice deep and rumbling, the beginning of an avalanche. "I just like you. *So much.*"

Mack pulled away for a moment to fiddle with the faucet, and suddenly a steady stream of cool water rained down on us from above. The icy shock of it made me gasp, much to his amusement. But then the temperature quickly shifted warmer, and my focus went back to the touch of his fingers on my skin, the press of his lips against mine, and the water rushing over us.

"Millen," he murmured in my ear, the sound of my name curling inside me like a deep kiss.

"Mmm-hmm?" I said, distracted by the feeling of his chest gently rumbling underneath my palms.

He wasn't just a lover, despite what I'd checked off on that silly list. He wasn't someone to be collected and tossed when I was done with him. Mack was someone I wanted to keep.

"Why did we ever think we shouldn't do this?" He pulled away for a moment, and the look on his face, so steady and sure, told me that this wasn't a question at all. It was a rebuttal, a declaration of our own stupidity, of letting our hardheadedness get in the way.

"Probably because we knew if we did, we wouldn't want to stop," I admitted. I took a step back, yanking at the buttons of my jean shorts, dragging them down, and kicking them to the ground.

Mack bent closer and ran his fingertips slowly down the length of my bare thighs, and then back up to my waist, where he pressed his thumbs gently into my hips. Then, with the weight of his hands guiding me, he shifted me around until my back was flush against his chest.

I settled in against his body, closing my eyes as I let my other senses lead. There was the electric shock of cool air any time the hot water missed my skin, the gentle melody of the drops hitting the wooden planks below us in a steady rhythm, and now the heady smell of coconut as Mack pressed his fingertips to my scalp, dragging them through my hair in slow, luxurious circles.

Then the light scent of cucumber and eucalyptus, soapy and clean, as Mack's hands traveled down the stretch of my arms, to the dimples of my lower back, lingering on parts of my body that I almost always forgot existed, caressing me with reverence and care.

The thoughts in my head were half-formed, a swirling mix of thrill and caution, as an eager, impatient moan slipped out between my lips.

Mack's laugh was as sensuous as his touch. "Patience, Millen. We've got time."

And even though we both knew it was a lie, I let myself believe it, just for a little bit longer.

30

"MILLEN." FINGERTIPS TICKLED my cheek like raindrops.

"Mmm?" I forced my eyes open to find Mack crouched next to me, fully dressed. I'd passed out last night in his bed after too many Bloody Marys on the boat, and sleep had come hard and fast.

"Rise and shine!" Judging from the fog outside the window, it was overcast today, but his beaming face easily took the sun's place. Even in my half-awake state, the sight of him still melted me. I reached a hand up and stroked the rough edge of his jaw, admiring the light stubble on his chin, the crook in his nose that was only visible from certain angles, and the sunspots that freckled his skin.

What I wouldn't give to wake up to this view every morning; to replace the gray Boston skyline with Mack's warm eyes. The thought of Boston brought back with it my simmering anger at Amaya's total disregard of my Alewife email.

"You are way too chipper for this early in the morning," I croaked, grabbing a pillow and slapping it down over my head. But it wasn't Mack I wanted to drown out as much as the anxiety creeping into my brain at the thought of what awaited me back home.

He responded by digging around until he found my earlobe and tugged on it playfully, proving my point.

"It's already eight o'clock! Don't you have big plans today to put together our dessert party spread?"

"Come back to bed for, like, a minute," I begged. The mattress bounced as he slid in next to me, scooting his head close to mine under the pillow so his chin pressed against my shoulder, his breath sweet on my skin. "I'm not meeting Marla until eleven."

She and Steve had agreed to let me rummage through what was left in the dining hall kitchen to put together a massive ice cream sundae bar and had promised me a box of wish boats for tomorrow night's final camp tradition.

I'd be able to leave here on Saturday morning with all the to-do items on my camp list checked off, but for the first time in so long, nothing about completing it left me feeling accomplished. Being here, with Mack and my friends, wasn't something I wanted to be over.

"Well, that gives us two hours to hang out," he said.

"I need coffee first," I said, scooting around until we were nose to nose. "And—" I reached a cupped hand up to my mouth, exhaling. "To brush my teeth."

"What are you talking about?" He ran his hand up the side of my stomach, tickling my ribs. "I love the smell of your morning breath."

I grabbed the pillow behind our heads and smushed it against his face, squinting at the light splattered across the wall.

"Well, I like the smell of your body odor, so I guess we're even," I said, sliding over to the side of the bed and rising with a stretch of my arms.

"Wait, you do?" he asked, propping himself up on his elbow. "I think we need to dig into this, Millen."

"Can we analyze it over coffee?" I asked, pulling on a pair of borrowed sweats.

"Absolutely." Mack nodded toward the ladder. "I have coffee and bagels waiting for you. Also, I bought some heavy cream. That's how you like your coffee, right?"

It was this that woke me up. Not the promise of coffee, though I was freaking psyched to pump my body full of caffeine. It was this vision of Mack waking up early and running out to buy me something as simple as heavy cream, because he knew it would make my life exponentially better. I'd never even mentioned that this was how I liked my coffee, but somehow, he'd noticed.

Once downstairs, I shuffled toward the French doors, swinging them open to take in the outside world. The sunshine was working its way through the sheet of gray covering the sky, and a few scattered rays bounced off the water, glimmering like crystals in the morning light. I took a deep inhale of the crisp morning and turned back into the boathouse to see Mack studying me from the kitchen sink.

If all I did today was stare at the water—and his face—it would be enough.

"Earth to Clara Millen!" Mack's voice was low and insistent, and he beckoned me toward him with a wave, butter knife in hand. "Your bagel's ready."

"Sorry," I said, sidling up next to him at the counter. "I think I forgot what I was supposed to be doing."

"Running the world? Making fun of me? Taking your clothes off?" He slid a steaming mug toward me before reaching up to tug gently on a strand of my hair, twisting it like a ribbon before tucking it behind my ear. "I have more ideas, if you want them."

"Not to insult your genius, but right now I just want to eat," I said as I reached for a bagel.

"Eat. Then nakedness?" He scrunched his face in deep thought, like he was considering the idea. "It's not like we have anything else to do today."

"Um, excuse me, I have a dessert party to organize," I mumbled through a mouthful of soft, doughy deliciousness. "I need to make sure we have enough ice cream and chocolate sauce for seven people."

"Fine, I guess I have no choice but to go run errands then. I need to buy boxes so I can start packing." He reached out a hand, pulling me up to stand. "Come on, let's go eat on the deck."

"This is so freaking good." I waved the bagel in his face as he led me outside. "We have bagels every Friday morning at work from what's supposed to be the best bagel shop in Boston, and these are a billion times better."

"Side hustle of one of the dining hall cooks," Mack explained as he bent down and grabbed a faded sailing rope off the dock, absentmindedly twisting it into a knot. "Kai. She sells them at the farmer's market in town too."

"Well, if this Brad knows what's good for his new resort, he'll hire her," I muttered. I waited for a moment, expecting Mack to chime in, but he stayed quiet, curling the cloud-colored, braided rope around and around, knotting and unknotting, a puzzle he could solve in his sleep.

"You're feisty today," he said finally, turning in his chair to face me. "Did something set you off? Besides, you know. Brad."

He cocked his head in my direction, eyes widening, daring me to reminisce about the way I'd pushed him up against the ladder in the boathouse last night, yanking his boxers down as I slid onto my knees in front of him.

"I know what you're trying to get me to say, Mackenzie Sullivan," I said, reaching down to grab my mug of coffee off the deck. I picked a tiny fly out of it before taking a slow, deliberate sip. His eyes never left my face.

"Wow, Millen, you really do know me well," he said, chuckling.

"And also yes, something did set me off, but not what you're getting at."

He tilted his mug toward me with a nod, giving me room to vent. His face was so open, inviting. I was amazed at how willing he was simply to listen. He didn't seem to fear my vulnerability, and this realization unleashed an overwhelming sense of relief inside of me.

I felt safe with him.

I didn't want Saturday to be the end of this, of *us*.

"So," I said finally. "I sent my boss—"

"Burnout boss?" he interrupted.

"Yes." I chuckled, taking another sip. "That one. Her name's Amaya."

"One sec," he said, gesturing at me to pause as he stood and positioned his chair precisely, so that he faced me instead of the lake.

"Okay, I'm ready." He crossed his legs and brought the mug to his mouth, watching me with his full attention like a late-night TV show host.

"We have this huge pitch next Friday, and it's been a total bust so far," I explained, my voice speeding up into a fast, clipped staccato, like it always did when I was frustrated by something and couldn't fix it. "But I had this epiphany the other night."

"Right. You told me about it on the boat." Mack leaned in a little closer so that our knees kissed and then wrapped his free hand around my calves, urging my feet up into his lap.

"I sent her—Burnout Boss—this creative idea that I had, that would totally ace this pitch. Outlined it in way too much detail. But that's how excited I was about it! It just seems like something this client would love. In my opinion, anyway."

"You're brilliant. I'm sure they would love it." He said this like it was the most obvious thing in the world, and his unconditional vote of confidence left me feeling warm and fuzzy.

"Well, you've never seen me at work, but thank you. Anyway, she blew me off. Had her assistant respond to my message and said she won't talk about it until I'm back in the office next week. Which, honestly, feels too late. We normally float our general ideas by clients before our big meeting. This is just putting us on a terribly shitty deadline."

Mack rubbed the back of his neck in thought. "Okay."

"She's tossing me a roadblock, just to prove her point."

"Which is?" he asked.

"That I should be on vacation, and not working this week."

Mack chuckled as he pressed his thumb into the arch of my foot, gently massaging it. "I agree with her, but I also know you."

"What does that mean?" I asked. "And before you answer, please remember that my foot is dangerously close to your groin right now, so tread carefully."

Mack lifted his hands in self-defense with a laugh. "What I mean is, you're the person who showed up here for the first time in five years and then immediately kicked my ass in a swim race."

"But my Capture the Flag plan was a bust," I countered.

"Oh yeah, your *plan* was terrible," he agreed, sliding his hand down my ankle as I pretended to jerk my foot at him. "But we wouldn't have even played if it wasn't for you making us do it."

"Hmm." I tapped my lip thoughtfully. "I'm still debating whether or not I should kick you in the—"

"What I'm saying is," he interjected, "just send it to the client. You're in charge of the account, right?"

"Technically, I will be, if we land it. And if I don't fuck up at work anymore."

Amaya's words echoed in my mind. *In order for the pitch to be better, I need you to be better.*

"So what do you have to lose?" he asked, softly tracing a figure eight around my ankle bone. "Screw your boss. If you believe in it, send it. Be brave."

He said this matter-of-factly, as if going behind Amaya's back was the logical answer to my problem. And maybe it was. This was the kind of risky, slightly idiotic but also sort of brilliant kind of thing I used to do at Pine Lake as a kid, before I started living life like it was something I was terrified of breaking.

"That would probably piss her off," I surmised.

"Which is maybe what she wants you to do? Wouldn't that signal some sort of new fire in your belly? And prove that her little break idea worked?" he said, giving my foot a squeeze before tucking it back down on the deck.

He bent down and grabbed our two empty coffee cups, heading toward the open doors that led into the boathouse. "Think about it."

Amaya had said no work emails, but she hadn't specified with whom. We always emailed with clients as we prepped for pitches, and I had Gabbie Pereira's contact info on my phone. She'd been one of the most hands-on CEOs we'd ever worked with—even sending us the request for the proposal doc herself. She was probably the kind of client who loved out-of-the-box moves like this, I reasoned.

Do something that scares you. Daily. I'd written. *Take risks, damnit!* I'm sure I'd imagined myself bungee jumping and skydiving on the regular, things that probably seemed terrifying to a clueless fifteen-year-old. What would younger me say about this version of herself, too nervous to send an email?

Fuck it. I reached for my phone.

Gabbie, hey! I typed. Thought you might like a preview of what we have brewing—pun intended—for your Summer Ale. Looking forward to discussing this in person asap.

I cc'ed Lydia and Amaya, and then, just to shove it in Amaya's face, added Abe's name, too, and hit send before I could give it a second thought. The message blasted through the ether, the sound infusing me with an energizing jolt of confidence.

Tucking my phone down by my feet, I tried to settle my nerves by gazing at the water. It spread out before me like a giant slab of glass, perfectly smooth. A loon warbled somewhere in the distance, almost as if it were calling me to join it.

"Hey." I leaned my head into the boathouse, where Mack was stacking newly clean dishes on the counter. "I'm going to go for a swim before I head up to find Marla."

He nodded. "I wouldn't dream of stopping you, Millen."

Then he cupped a hand to shade his eyes and watched as I turned back away from him and into the bright expanse of sunlight, jumping feet first into the water.

31

"GOOD MORNING, EVERYONE!" I chirped, marching into Sunrise, still damp from the lake.

Sam was on her hands and knees on a yoga mat at the foot of her bed, rounding and stretching her spine, as Nick and Trey sat across from each other on Nick's bottom bunk, both staring at their phones with giant cups of Dunkin coffee in hand.

"Hello, sunshine," Sam said as she curled her chin up toward the sky.

"Everyone okay in here?" I asked hesitantly, giving Nick a questioning look. He replied by shaking his head, which I knew meant I shouldn't ask.

"We're good," he said with a tight smile, though the flat tone of his voice suggested otherwise.

"Good, because I'm about to make you eat your weight in ice cream," I said, giving Nick's shoulder an affectionate squeeze as I brushed past him toward my bed, yanking my duffel bag off the floor. I rummaged around for a change of clothes, pulling out a rumpled but clean white tank top and sliding it over my head before grabbing my notebook out of my bag, eager to glance at my now-filled checklist. "I'm going to head up to the dining hall to meet Marla, if anyone wants to join."

"What's your boyfriend up to?" Nick asked as he shuffled by on his way to the bathroom. I haphazardly shoved my letter and list half under my pillow and gave him the stink eye. His tone was purposefully nonchalant, like he was goading me into responding.

It worked.

"He's not my *boyfriend*," I said pointedly.

"What is he then, your lover?" Sam asked as she slowly pushed herself up off the floor. "We all saw that very Mack and Clara date that took place yesterday."

"I mean, some of us were even *on* it," Nick teased.

Sam's choice of words caused my stomach to drop like an anvil. There was no way she could know what was in my letter, but hearing her say "lover" out loud was like a sudden shot of reality to my lust-clouded brain. My letter. It was sitting here in this very bunk, and I still hadn't told anyone about it.

I pushed aside the guilt I felt over my intentional silence. What good would it do bringing it up now, just when we were about to leave?

"I'm going home on Saturday to Boston, he's moving back to California," I said matter-of-factly, and deliberately shifted all of my focus on neatly rolling my clothes up as tightly as possible to avoid her knowing stare.

"I didn't ask for a geography lesson," she pushed. "And besides, you've known each other practically your entire lives."

I'd been foolish to think she'd drop it that quickly.

"It's just a...thing," I said, flustered, as I hopped off my bed, moving toward the door. "For the week."

I had to find a way to end this conversation, and rushing out of there seemed as good a solution as any. The more I talked about Mack, the more I was forced to confront the unsettling truth: that even if I was leaving him soon, my feelings for him weren't going anywhere.

"You know, being a *thing*," Nick repeated back to me, though his eyes were wistfully directed toward his boyfriend, who was still tuning the whole world out, "could really mean anything."

"Is that some sort of riddle?" I asked.

"I just mean that you guys get to decide what you are to each other," he explained, sounding melancholy. "If you want to be together, that's enough."

"I appreciate the love advice," I said as I headed toward the door.

"I'll walk with you," Sam said, following me out. "The doctor said that the more I moved, the sooner this baby will come out."

When we were far enough along the path to be out of listening distance, I finally opened my mouth. "What the hell is going on with Nick and Trey?"

"Are you trying to avoid talking about Mack?" Sam asked with a small, knowing smile as she tucked her waves back into a claw clip.

"Yes," I said, and she coughed out a laugh. "But seriously, what was that?"

Sam shrugged. "They were fine last night. Then something switched after we got coffee. I haven't pushed it."

"Instead you're just grilling me about Mack."

"Exactly!" she said, throwing her hands up in the air. "It's way more fun."

We meandered down toward the Village, just like we had on my first morning back here, only a few days ago. I'd never understood how quickly life could change in a matter of a few short days, until this week.

"Since you asked," I said, glancing down toward the boathouse in the distance. "This is going to sound like I'm twelve, but I like him. Like a *lot*. I don't know if I've ever felt this way about someone before. Is that crazy?"

Suddenly I was reminded of a specific flash of memory from my childhood, during summers spent off the coast of Rhode Island with my cousins and our parents. The adults would watch us from beach chairs as we dodged the waves in the water, shrieking any time one clipped us.

It had felt wildly exhilarating and euphoric, and even a little bit dangerous, with the threat of the undertow always looming, like it could suck you under at any second. These feelings swirling inside me for Mack felt exactly like those rapturous moments of terrifying joy I'd experienced at that beach.

"That's not crazy, Clara, that's called being in love," she said, pausing to take a sip of water, rubbing circles at the base of her belly. "Have you told him?"

I narrowed my eyes intently as if I could somehow detect some sort of pregnancy problem just by studying her. "Are you sure you're okay?"

"The baby just has the hiccups." Sam's eyes could morph from jewels to daggers in an instant, and she leveled a look at me, part affectionate, part annoyed. "Here."

She grabbed my wrist and tugged me toward her gently, placing my hand flat against the low part of her belly. "Can you feel that?"

For a moment everything was still, and then, there it was, a steady thump I could feel against my palm.

"Holy shit!" I looked up at her, mouth dropped open.

"Hiccups are weird," she explained with a shrug.

"Oh my god, that is *wild*," I sputtered, looking between her face and the spot where my hand rested against her belly. It was so implausible—this little person hiccupping inside my best friend's body—that I almost couldn't believe it.

"It is." Sam laughed, and pulled my hand into her own, releasing it with a squeeze. "And now I need you to stop worrying about me. I'm fine. You know that, right?"

"Yes, I do," I admitted, though I didn't feel completely confident in my answer.

She toddled forward down the path, and I followed.

"Good. You'll know when I really need your help, okay?" she said. "Back to you. Telling Mack you're in love with him. Go."

I will? I wanted to ask. There was still a part of me that felt like my friend radar was broken after all these years, and I didn't entirely trust it to work like I wanted. But I could tell Sam was done with that part of our conversation.

"I told him I *liked* him," I clarified, stopping at the circle of Adirondack chairs that sat together in front of the Village, facing the waterfront. "And I do. *A lot.* But I'm leaving. He's moving. This thing between us literally can't go anywhere."

"Hmm." Sam tapped her lip, eyes flitting in exaggerated thought. "Or you could just say, 'Hey, Mack, I'm falling in love with you' and not worry about all that other stuff?"

Somehow, though it was surely impossible, I felt the actual skin of my throat tighten. "I said *like*," I corrected. "Not love."

Sam shook her head at me as she marched past, heading toward the dining hall. "Oh, I know exactly what you said."

32

MARLA INTERRUPTED MY mental pacing with a bright, "Hey, girls!"

She emerged through the screen door of Bag End waving, decked out in her usual khaki shorts and white Pine Lake T-shirt.

"Good morning!" Sam and I shouted back, practically in unison. The delight in her voice matched my own, as if we both relished the feeling of still being seen as a kid in someone's eyes. No matter how old we got, we'd always be campers to Marla, and there was something deeply comforting in the thought.

Steve stuck his head out behind her, offering up a quick hello as Marla made her way down the stairs.

"Do you still have time to help me find all the ice cream stuff in the kitchen?" I asked.

"Sure do." She nodded, watching me with the studious gaze of a pleased professor.

"I'm also trying to get all the wish boat stuff together for tomorrow night," I added.

"Steve's already on it," she said. "He's going to grab it and meet us in the dining hall."

"You two are amazing," I said as her eyes lingered on my face.

"Camp looks good on you, Clara," she said finally.

"Right?" agreed Sam. She glanced over at me, a devious curl to her lips. "What's your secret, Clara?"

Of course, I knew what she was suggesting.

"I swear to god if you weren't pregnant," I muttered as Marla tried to contain a laugh.

"You'd, what, challenge me to a swim race?" Her brows twitched in amusement.

"Oh my god," I groaned.

"I'm sorry, Clare-bear, I had to," she said, giving my shoulder a squeeze. "All right, I'm gonna get my steps in!"

"Shall we?" Marla asked as Sam kept moving, headed down the mulch-covered path toward the water.

"Take me to the ice cream," I said, pumping my fist.

I followed Marla into the dining hall, walking along the rows of tables with chairs stacked neatly on top. Most of my memories here involved endless singing and camp cheers, some that included extravagant clapping routines performed on the table itself. To walk through this giant room when it was silent felt eerie, almost like being in a cemetery.

Once inside the kitchen, she scanned the shelves slowly. "Okay, so what are we looking for? Toppings? How about cookies?"

"We could use all of it," I added, opening the giant freezer chest in the corner. "And ice cream, obviously."

"Well, I know we have plenty of that left over," she said. "We overbought for the ice cream social, so you guys'll be doing us a favor getting rid of it."

"Sure, let us eat your problems for you," I joked as I counted up the containers inside. Four chocolate, four vanilla, three strawberry. More than enough for our group to gorge ourselves on sundaes.

"How did you become the ringleader for all these festivities?" she asked, grabbing the reading glasses that dangled from her collar and sliding them onto her face as she examined a stock list that hung from a clipboard nailed to the wall.

"I guess when I heard you guys were selling, it just really made me want to tap into my old self, and all the things I loved about being up here."

"And how is she doing?" Marla crouched down, tugging at a bin on a lower shelf. "Your old self, I mean."

"I'm not sure," I said, considering the question for a moment. From anyone else, it would have seemed judgmental, asked with the purpose of making a point. But Marla was inquisitive and open, someone who genuinely wanted to know.

"I guess she's happy my current self is here, out of my comfort zone," I said finally. "I haven't really let that side out in a long time."

"Yeah?" she said, cracking open a bin's lid and examining the contents inside. "Why do you think that is?"

"Well," I said, "I've spent my entire life—or I guess, since my parents got divorced—trying to do everything the right way, you know? No surprises. But I'm starting to think all this overplanning and thinking has just led me in circles."

Marla began unloading jars of chocolate sauce onto the industrial-size island in the center of the kitchen.

"I remember how hard that summer was for you," she said, pausing to glance up at me. "It makes sense that you've tried to carve out a life that feels good to you."

"I'm working on it," I said.

"I think it's great you're making the most out of this week," she continued, "and I'm not just talking about *you know who.*"

"Oh my god, Marla." My face flushed, unable to hide my mortification, and I briefly pondered jumping into the freezer to avoid her beaming smile.

"I'm sorry, I'm not trying to embarrass you," she said sweetly. "But I've just known Mack for so long. And I know he's always pined for you."

"That is an amazingly appropriate pun," I said, still blushing as I arranged the glass containers of chocolate sauce in a perfect line in front of me, just to do something with my fidgety hands.

"I know, and I don't get to use it all that often." She chuckled before pointing at a giant cupboard. "Plates and bowls stored in there."

I wandered over in that direction and swung open the wooden doors. "Reconnecting with Mack this week has really been nice." This was the understatement of the century, but it was as far as I was going to go with someone who had second mom status in my life.

"He's a good egg, that one," she said as I dug around a crate of plastic bowls. "Mack's really made this place into something extra special, over the last few years especially."

My skin prickled at the mention of his name, and suddenly I could feel every drop of sweat on my skin. She swung open a cabinet door. "Jackpot. Did you want cones?"

"Uh, sure, we could use cones." I opened up a drawer in my search for spoons and then paused. "Marla, I hope it's okay to say this, but, if he's been so great, why didn't you guys offer to sell Pine Lake to him? It's so obvious that he wants to stay, and we all know he's sitting on a trust fund, so he could afford it, I would assume. I know money is money, and I'm not trying to judge the choice you and Steve made. But, like, *a glamping company*? Over Mack? I just don't get it."

The words spilled out before I could censor myself, and I knew, when her lips formed a straight line, that I'd pricked a sensitive spot, and I immediately regretted asking.

"I'm sorry, it's not even my place to ask that," I said, scrambling to figure out how to back out of this conversation.

"No, it's okay, Clara." She sighed, like someone who so badly wanted to solve a puzzle in front of them but wasn't sure how. "I just assumed you two had talked about this already."

"About what?" I said, an anxious lump growing in my throat. "Did something happen?"

"Oh, no, honey, I'm sorry." She paused in thought for a moment, running her fingertips up the bridge of her nose. "It doesn't quite feel like it's my place to say anything, but we've already opened the door to this conversation, so…"

I pushed the drawer I'd been digging through closed and leaned my elbows on the counter, sliding closer to her, in anxious anticipation over what she was about to tell me.

"See, we actually asked Mack first, right before we listed the place," she continued. "We had hoped he'd say yes. But he had his reasons for saying no, which we respected."

"Wait, I'm not sure I'm following," I said, though the dread thumping through my stomach told me otherwise, that maybe I was following along too well.

"He came back to us a couple of days ago, right after you guys got back from the hospital, and asked us to reconsider, but as you know, we've already moved forward with Glamp Camp." Marla's forehead creased, and it was clear she'd been agonizing over this. "Steve almost cried when he had to turn Mack's offer down, and that man never cries. Not even when the Red Sox finally won the World Series."

I was silent, speeding through my memories of these last few days with Mack, on the boat, in the car, in his bed, the art barn. Our conversations about the shoulds of life, him moving back home, my job. Me, self-righteous and so certain I knew what was best, trying to convince Mack to talk to Marla and Steve, assuming they'd overlooked him somehow. But no—they'd offered it to him first.

This was the big decision he'd mentioned cryptically the other night, the stuff that hadn't worked out. He'd been so pissed off that night on the boat, but as the timeline shifted into place I realized why: He'd just tried to fix his mistake and had been told it was too late.

He could have told me. I'd confided in him about my life's disappointments, laid myself bare about my struggles, because he'd felt safe, and because whatever this was between us had me thinking he felt the same. But he didn't; that much was obvious now.

A flush of foolishness sank through my body; how dumb had I been to read into a few days of sex and whispered feelings? I'd been a distraction for him, a convenient escape from the shit he'd been wallowing in secretly. This really was just a fling, a passionate love affair like I'd once wanted, but nothing more.

At least I'd gotten a check mark out of it.

Marla reached into a box, grabbed two giant containers of caramel syrup, and handed them to me. "Here. My favorite."

I accepted them without thinking; my hand was moving like a robot's as I lined up the containers on the counter. I was both stuck in my own head and floating far out in space.

Why hadn't he told me? Why had he told our group that he'd just found out about Steve and Marla selling when it was clear he'd known for way longer?

And why hadn't he said yes to them, when he so clearly wanted to be here?

"Clara?"

"Mmm?" I said, landing back in the present.

"Your phone's ringing."

"Oh. Oh!"

The name on the screen was my own, which could only mean one thing.

Oh, shit.

"Hello?" I answered.

"It's me." Lydia's voice was low and conspiratorial.

"I figured."

"I'm hiding in your office," she said, her voice hushed. "Amaya got your email to Gabbie and just called an emergency meeting of the creative team. She's been hovering over Delilah's desk for the last twenty minutes."

"Oh, shit." My phone suddenly felt like a rock in my palm, tempting me to run down to the waterfront and toss it into the lake. "Is that good or bad?"

"I don't know, but it's definitely something," she said. "I thought you should know."

"You're the best," I said. "She basically ignored my first message, so I kinda took a leap of faith."

"I mean, your list did tell you to do scary shit," she replied. "Are you still crossing things off?"

"You could say that," I said bitterly, envisioning Mack's name scribbled directly under the words "take a lover." "I don't have a dog yet, but otherwise, I'm feeling pretty accomplished."

"Where on the list did it say 'go rogue at work'?" she asked with a nervous laugh.

"I think it qualifies as 'do something that scares you,'" I guessed, the nerves in my stomach doubling, work anxiety piling on top of what I'd just learned from Marla about Mack.

"Well, you've definitely scared Amaya. I'm proud of you," she said. "Shit. I gotta go, I'll call you back as soon as I know what's going on."

When I finally looked up from my phone screen, Steve was in the doorway to the kitchen, a massive cardboard box cradled in his arms.

"Special delivery for Clara Millen," he said in his deep Maine accent. "A box of wishes."

I let out a tight laugh, a sad sound of disbelief. Just hours ago I'd known exactly what—and *who*—I'd wish for. But now it was clear—no matter how much I wanted something more with Mack, there was no way that would ever come true.

33

I'D AVOIDED EVERYONE all afternoon by lingering in the kitchen of the dining hall, channeling my nervous energy into arranging and rearranging a kitchen cart full of treats. This was supposed to be a celebration, one silly, final hurrah in the form of a sugar rush, before we said goodbye to Pine Lake for the very last time.

My friends were all gathered on the other side of the door, hooting and hollering and ready to get their ice cream party on. Yet here I was, a storm cloud, heavy and dark, my big feelings about to spill all over the place.

Lydia had gone radio silent since her earlier call, but with enough deep breaths, I'd almost been able to convince myself that there was nothing to freak out over. Maybe Amaya hadn't been rage-panicking over my unsolicited email directly to our client.

But Mack not telling me about turning down Steve and Marla's offer was something I couldn't quite square as easily, especially against our last few days together. I'd thought I'd gotten the most authentic side of him, but maybe he'd just charmed me like he did everyone else. Whatever his reason for not telling me, the fact that he'd skated around it stung.

I cracked open the swinging kitchen door and caught sight of him sitting gamely at one of the giant circular dining tables, hands behind his head as he laughed at something Sam was saying. The longer the minutes ticked by, the more the ice cream on the cart in front of me morphed into liquid.

I couldn't avoid him any longer.

"All right, everybody!" I barreled out of the kitchen pushing the massive, industrial-size food cart. The day's heat—and the general lack of air-conditioning in every building at Pine Lake—had left my tank top damp and my hair glued to the back of my neck. I hadn't expected to break a sweat prepping for a dessert party, but then again, I'd also gone overboard.

I'd put together a spread fit for seventy people, as opposed to seven: quarts of Brigham's ice cream and sherbet, plus every topping imaginable—sprinkles, whipped cream, chocolate sauce, caramel sauce, and a giant glass jar overflowing with maraschino cherries. I'd triumphantly dug out an old container of Oreos from the kitchen pantry, and Eloise and Linus had picked up a giant plastic box of cupcakes from the General Store, plus a container of brownies.

"Remember, we're playing truth or dare," Eloise said as she dug into a tub of vanilla, scooping a softball-sized amount into Linus's bowl.

"You go first then," Sam said, reaching for the sherbet as she popped a cherry into her mouth.

"Okay." Eloise looked up, a bottle of chocolate syrup squeezed between her hands. "Clara, truth or dare."

"Dare," I said quickly.

A smile spread across her face. "I dare you to dump this bottle on your head."

"Seriously?" I countered. "You don't want me to try to jump from table to table, or something like that?"

She nodded her head, a wicked grin on her face.

"Fine," I said. "I'll do it." She tossed the bottle at me, and I caught it with two hands, giving it a shake. I held it over my head and squeezed, and a spray of gooey brown spluttered all over my face.

"Oh, shit!" Nick cackled as Sam watched me, mouth in an O. "I'm impressed, Clara."

I wiped a stream of chocolate out of my eye and flung it in his direction, splattering it across his shirt.

It dawned on me that now was my chance to get the truth out of Mack about what Marla had told me.

"Mack—truth or dare."

"Truth," Mack said finally.

"Why didn't you tell us that Steve and Marla wanted you to take over Pine Lake, and you turned them down?"

I tried to keep my voice casual, but I could feel the hurt etching lines across my face. He hadn't told me, and I wanted to know why.

"Whoa," Trey said as Nick opened his mouth, closed it, and opened it again as if he kept finding and losing his words.

"Wait, *seriously*?" Sam asked, dumbfounded, as Eloise smacked her hands down on the table, jolting our bowls.

"I knew it!" she shrieked.

"Oh really, El, you knew?" Trey teased. "You haven't been paying attention to anything but your boyfriend all week."

"Honey, why are you picking on her?" Nick asked, finally discovering his voice again. Across the table, Linus calmly removed his glasses and rubbed them clean with a corner of his T-shirt before setting them back on the bridge of his nose, his expression unmoving as he studied them.

"I'm not picking on anyone. I'm—" Trey was cut off by the slap of vanilla ice cream hitting his face.

Linus's hand was still in the bowl when Trey turned toward him, furious.

"What the fuck, mate?" he spat.

"Wow, Linus," Mack said, sounding both taken aback and impressed. "You starting a food fight, man?"

"Okay, I think we all need to take a pause," Sam said, slowly standing with her hands outstretched, as if she could capture this ferocious energy, shove it back in its cage.

"Are you going to answer, Mack?" I pushed. "Because Marla told me."

Mack shrugged, a cool look on his face shutting me out. "So then what is it you want to know?"

"We talked about it," I said, my voice rising, ice cream scooper whipping through the air as I gestured with my hand. "About you buying this place."

Mack shrugged. "*You* talked about it, Clara. You never actually asked me about buying Pine Lake."

"That's not fair," I said. "I was trying to tell you I believed in you."

"Or maybe you're just nostalgic," he said, rubbing a hand along his chin as if he were a professor spewing some philosophical theory. "For this place, for the past. I mean, isn't that what this is all about? Hanging on to a fantasy that will never be real?" he continued, gesturing around the dining hall.

"I think you're talking about yourself, and why you dragged me into bed," I said, scowling. "You just used me to distract yourself from Pine Lake closing, and your life changing."

"Oh *I* used *you*? Really?" Mack dug into his pocket, pulling out a small folded piece of paper. The edges were frayed, liked it had been torn out of a notebook.

"I finished your friendship bracelet," he said, tossing something small and green at me. "The one you threw out in the art barn the other night. I came by Sunrise to drop it off this morning, and this was on your bed."

He was holding my camp list in his hand.

"You read my private stuff?" My heart was clawing its way out of my chest, and my voice was sharp and rising.

Mack leaned back in his chair like he was preparing to lob another grenade in my direction. "It was right on top of the letter you wrote yourself on the last night of camp, which I'm pretty sure you told us you never got."

I glanced over at Sam, who was watching me with a hard, knowing look on her face.

Fuck.

He pointed his spoon at me angrily. "You've been checking things off like we're just some items on your to-do list. Have fun? Check. Be with your friends? Check!"

"That's not fair," I started.

He scanned the group. "Did you guys know about this? I'm number seven on the list. Take a—"

A mix of hurt and embarrassment roared through me, so deep it felt etched into my bones. My shame over Amaya's mid-party declaration of my burnout was nothing compared to this.

I grabbed the can of whipped cream in front of me before he could finish, and with a sharp press of the nozzle, I unleashed a stream of sticky white froth at his head, until he looked more snowman than human.

"Okay, it's a food fight," Sam groaned, pushing her chair out with a huff. "I'm Switzerland! I'm taking all your phones so they don't get destroyed."

"Sam, wait." I moved to try to stop her, but a blob of something cold smacked my shoulder and slid down my arm.

"Oh, it's a fucking food fight all right!" Nick shrieked with ecstatic abandon, dumping a bowl of cherries in Trey's lap.

Sam grabbed our stuff off the table and made her escape onto the porch, but the rest of us were too far gone, full-grown adults sucked into this vortex of big feelings and personal confessions, with edible weapons within reach. Suddenly, it was mayhem, the kind of chaos that burst forth from your amygdala before the rational side of the brain could kick in and stop the worst from happening.

"Since we're all being honest, why don't you say what you've been wanting to say this entire trip?" Nick challenged Trey as he stood up from the table.

"Fine," Trey said as he tore open the plastic box of cupcakes. "I want a break. From us. There, are you happy?"

He smashed a cupcake onto Nick's shoulder and then turned and lobbed one at Mack, who was now dashing toward the back of the room clutching a bottle of chocolate sauce.

"It's been obvious for months," Nick hissed, reaching for a melting bowl of vanilla. "I keep trying to bring it up! Why can't you ever just say what you feel?"

I was so caught up in the breakup unfolding in front of me that I didn't notice Eloise creeping up behind me until something sticky shot against my neck, dripping right down the back of my shirt.

Swinging around with a gasp, I found her grinning with a bottle of caramel syrup in her hands. Behind her Linus stood staring in shock at his hands, which looked like they'd just been used to murder a family of Hershey Bars.

I charged over to a shelf near the fridge that held all the condiments placed on tables during the summer. A tube of ketchup sang out to me in all its bright red, staining glory, and it felt powerful in my hands, especially when I ran back and squirted it directly on Trey's pristine white sneakers before turning my aim back to Eloise.

"Clara, that is not okay!" Nick protested, and then dug a mound of frosting off his chest and smeared it down my face.

"See, this is why I haven't even said anything to you about our relationship, because you're always telling everyone what they can and can't do," Trey groused, kicking the tomato glop off his shoe.

"Well, it's a good thing we're breaking up, then. You won't have to listen to me talk anymore!" Nick shouted before grabbing the chocolate ice cream and storming off toward Linus, who was currently licking something off Eloise's finger.

Trey watched him, an odd look on his face, before he turned back toward me. Silently, he grabbed the ketchup bottle out of my hand and marched after his now-ex-boyfriend.

There was only one person left for me to find. I swiped the lone box of brownies from the table and took off for Mack.

Following the long route down a row of tables toward the back of the dining hall, I crept up on him slowly, stepping carefully over a slippery patch of melted vanilla.

When I was close, I leveled a brownie in his direction. It landed with a thump in the center of his forehead, chocolate crumbles sticking to his face. Mack froze, coughing out a shocked laugh before stepping toward me, close enough to swipe a finger across my brow, gathering up a chunk of frosting and smearing it against my bottom lip.

He pressed down gently, and as if on instinct my tongue shot out, swiping the sugary sweetness away. Now it was my turn to freeze, heat pooling between my legs, twisting me undone like a cork being yanked out of a champagne bottle.

He took advantage of my moment of weakness and yanked a brownie out of the box in my hands, patting it flat on my head like a pancake.

"Fuck!" I squealed, reaching for another sugary blob and smashing it onto his chest, grinding it into his shirt like I was trying to scrub grease out of a dirty pan. My focus was so intense that it took me a second to notice that Mack's hand had paused, gently cupping my face.

"Give me my list back," I demanded, glaring at him through ice cream-covered lashes.

"You are really pretty when you're fired up, you know that?" He said it with delight like he'd just discovered something wonderful and couldn't wait to share it with the world. *"Lover."*

Everything went silent when Mack touched me, my senses giving up all autonomy, fully under his control. Everything in me that wanted to be angry with him seemed to melt away when his thumb pressed against my bottom teeth, his index finger stroking my chin. I was so focused on the sensation that it barely registered at first when my phone's obnoxiously loud ring sounded from the porch, where Sam had gone to escape the chaos.

"Shit! Shit shit shit," I said, dropping the brownies on the floor and taking off toward the door. Sam was moving through the doorway, holding my phone in her hand.

I skidded to a stop in front of her.

"I answered it," she said, a strange look on her face. Oh no.

Amaya's serene face, perfectly coiffed as always, appeared on my screen.

"Clara, hi. I'm here with the whole team."

Suddenly the faces of my colleagues panned by as she scanned the camera across them, crammed into her office. Lydia was sandwiched on a couch with a laptop on her knees and gave me a small wave.

"I need you back in the—" Her mouth dropped, her sentence left hanging, unfinished. "What the hell happened to you?"

"She started a food fight," Mack yelled a few feet behind me now.

"You started it!" I hissed back. "And please stop, it's my boss."

"Well, take a shower, scrub your face, whatever you need to do. And then I need you to get back here ASAP."

"I'm sorry, *what?*" Her intensity caught me off guard. It shouldn't have—I'd only been gone from work for a few days—but my ability to snap to order whenever Amaya came calling had already dulled. "I can't. I'm in New Hampshire. At my old camp."

"I know, I know, and I am so excited you've been enjoying your micro-sabbatical. But, Clara, the pitch you sent to Gabbie? She loved it."

"She did?" I asked, trying to process what she was telling me.

"*I* did too," she added quickly. "I always knew you were brilliant."

"But you said I was burned out." My fists clenched, fingernails stabbing my sticky palms. She'd forced me out of the office, rebuffed my email, and was now demanding I drop everything and run back to my desk. "You told me I had to take this time off."

"And it worked!" she exclaimed, almost like she was trying to convince me. "Gabbie loved your idea so much that they've moved our pitch to tomorrow morning and won't hear it unless you're the one presenting."

"Seriously?" I asked, dumbfounded. My plan had somehow succeeded, exactly how I'd wanted. I'd done it.

"Yes," Amaya replied, her voice sounding sharp and impatient. "I need you at the Four Points office at ten a.m."

I waited for the rush of excitement, the pleased, relieved warmth I always got from doing a good job. Instead, a sad, empty feeling settled in my stomach as I realized—I'd have to leave right now.

"Listen, Clara, this is huge," Amaya said finally, her voice shifting from irritated to sincere. "You knocked it out of the park, okay? The stuff about sitting around the campfire, the letters you wrote yourselves? Finding yourself in the faces of old friends? Gabbie ate that shit up. And now you need to come back and close the deal."

"Close the deal," I repeated back. I kept waiting for some sort of euphoria to wash over me, but I simply felt numb.

Amaya piped up again. "They're going to cancel if you're not there," she said, and it was then that I heard her anxiety, could sense her fear of losing this huge account, right through whatever satellite in space was connecting this call.

And knowing I could do this, could calm Amaya and prove I wasn't a failure, I shifted back into work mode, like Clark Kent walking into that phone booth and stepping out as Superman.

Land Alewife, run the account, snag a promotion.

"Okay!" I agreed, forcing an upbeat game face. "I can't wait."

My voice was chipper, but anxious sweat pooled in the crooks of my knees, my eyes blinking furiously. Luckily, my panic wasn't registering with Amaya.

Instead, she just shouted a satisfied, "Excellent!" and waved good-bye with a flap of her hand, her tiny video screen fading to black.

This was it. My chance to prove myself. This was what I'd wanted all along, wasn't it?

So why was I crying?

"Clara?" Eloise took a step forward. "Is everything okay?"

I pressed my eyes tight for a second, but there was no holding back the tears that spilled down my sticky, frosting-covered face.

"Um, I should go pack," I said, the words coming out so fast they blended into each other. I took off out the door of the dining hall and down the steps, moving so fast I was breathless in seconds.

Except I didn't run toward Sunrise. Cabins flashed by in my peripheral vision, blotches of white and green, as I sprinted down the hill to the water. I didn't even bother taking off my clothes this time, pausing only to kick off my shoes and toss my phone next to them on the grass.

All I wanted to do was lose myself in the water, as if submerging in the depths of Pine Lake one last time could somehow help me figure out just what the hell I was doing with my life. Normally I stayed close to shore, opting to float off near the diving dock before heading back to the beach. Today I kept going, as if I could swim myself to clarity.

But after a good ten minutes of paddling my frustrations out, I flipped onto my back, my hair spreading out like smoke behind my head. I waited for a sign, a loon to land gracefully beside me or howl mournfully. Something to tell me I was on the right path, to assure me of what happened next.

I'd checked all the boxes and done everything I thought I was supposed to do—in Boston, and here at camp. I was headed back home on the verge of professional rebirth, Amaya all but begging me to come and save the day.

Yet here I was, still drifting and unmoored.

34

I WASN'T SURE what I expected when I finally got back to Sunrise, but it definitely wasn't Sam quietly making herself busy at the foot of my bed. She stood there, in all her tiny, steady, very pregnant glory, running her hand down the length of my sleeping bag, smoothing out the shimmery, wrinkled fabric.

She glanced up and acknowledged me without saying a word, despite me hovering nearby in dripping wet clothes.

"You don't need to help me pack, you know," I finally mumbled, not quite rising to the occasion. "It will take me like two seconds."

"Oh, I know," she said, the sleeping bag now tucked under her armpit. She shook out the bag it came in with a decisive thwack. "But I want to."

"Where is everyone?" I asked, looking around the cabin as I toweled myself off.

"Cleaning up the dining hall."

"I'll go back and help after I pack," I said, mentally calculating the time it would take me to drive home after I'd helped with cleanup.

"Don't you have to get back to Boston?" she said, her voice deliberate and calm. But she wouldn't meet my eyes, and I knew she was disappointed. "Seems like your boss needs you."

"Oh, Sam. Fuck, I'm sorry. I know it's shitty for me to leave early," I said. "But this pitch is a huge deal for me."

"Clara, you're not *shitty* for leaving early," she said firmly, offering up air quotes with her one free hand.

"I feel—" I started, but she cut me off.

"You're shitty for plenty of other reasons, but not that." She smiled, but her voice still didn't sound right. "I know your job is important to you. And I know how much it means to you to fix things there. If you want to go do this pitch, you should."

"I do," I said, though I wasn't quite sure that was the truth anymore. I yanked my duffel bag off the floor and began haphazardly grabbing stuff off the small shelves next to the bed. I didn't have the energy to change out of my damp, food-stained clothes. I'd deal with them when I got back home to Boston, along with the rest of my life.

"Do you want to be my friend?" she asked pointedly, eyes fixed on me. "Because from what it sounds like, you only came back up here to make you feel better about yourself. That's the part that feels shitty."

"Sam," I said, face crumbling. "Of course I want to be your friend. I want that more than anything."

She followed me into the bathroom, that sleeping bag still in her arms, trailing behind her like a tail as she watched me struggle with the cap to my toothpaste.

"So why didn't you tell us that you got your letter?" The hurt in her voice was palpable now. "Because I asked, Clara. And you clearly avoided answering."

All I could do was shrug. I could feel myself shifting back into survival mode, gaze down, steady, focusing intently on making sure my sunscreen lid was locked, bag zipped up tight.

"Fine," she said when I didn't reply, and for the first time, she seemed truly exasperated with me, her patience finally dead-ending. "Here's what I want from you, then. I want you to be honest, even when it's awkward or uncomfortable, and to show up because you want

251

to, not because you feel like you have to. You don't have to prove anything to us—or yourself."

I walked back and tossed my clear plastic bag of toiletries next to my pillow. At the foot of the bed, Sam's forehead wrinkled in frustration as she tried to wrangle my sleeping bag into its pencil-sized carrying bag, a feat for any mortal human, much less one who was nine months pregnant.

"Do you want me to do that?" I asked, fretting once again.

"Clara." Sam leveled a look at me that told me now was seriously not the time to mess with her. "Do you know how annoying it is to go from being a self-sufficient human to everyone suddenly treating you like you might break? I can roll up a fucking sleeping bag."

I exhaled a short laugh as I folded my T-shirt. "You're right, and I'm sorry."

"I'm so excited to be a mom." She sat down on the bed with an exhausted huff. "But it also feels like it's eating away at everything else that I am. No one sees me as Sam, the Frisbee golf captain, or Sam, the librarian. My mom doesn't see me as anything but some sort of helpless creature that needs constant tending."

"I don't think I knew you played Frisbee golf," I said sheepishly, and she chuckled.

"I picked it up when Regan and I moved to Brooklyn, and Burlington has a huge community," she said. "And I don't mind that you don't know. I just don't want to only be Sam, the pregnant person. And then Sam, the mom."

"You aren't," I said softly. "And you won't be. Nothing could ever change who you are at your core."

"*Exactly.*" Sam shot me a purposeful look as she knotted her curls on top of her head and then busied herself with my toiletries.

The intense feeling of misunderstanding—of myself, of my life, of the people in it—bubbled up from inside until I felt it spill out into the tips of my fingers. I tugged at the zipper of my bag so hard that it caught and snapped off in my hand, and suddenly I was crying again.

"Sam." I dragged my now broken duffel bag off the bed, and it hit the floor with a loud thud. "My letter was literally a checklist of what I wanted my life to be. When I opened it and realized I couldn't check off a single box?"

I let out a sour, sad laugh.

"Do you know how awful that felt? I'd let myself down, but, worse, I'd let all of you down. I'm not the Clara you knew anymore. I'm just...I don't even know..." I ended on a sob that morphed into a hiccup and shook my head in shame.

"Oh, Clara," Sam said, her face softening as she took a step closer to me.

"I hadn't shown up for you guys like I wanted to. Like you *deserve*. And I hate that about myself." I dragged the edge of my T-shirt up to my face and tried to wipe the tears away.

"Hey," she said, scooting closer to me on the bed. "Don't forget that I knew you then, and I know you now. And there's no way that girl would be disappointed by who you are. And *I'm* certainly not disappointed."

Sam's gaze was kind now, but it did nothing to quell the well of sorrow that sat at the center of my body.

"The person I wanted myself to be, all adventurous and full of joy and shit? I didn't become that. But then, the person I was trying to be instead—with my steady job and perfect relationship—I didn't become that either." I was rambling, emotions and words tangling together. "And how ridiculous was it to think I could accomplish everything in that stupid letter in one week, when I haven't been able to in twenty years?"

"Not ridiculous at all," she said matter-of-factly as she clutched my pillow in her lap. "You literally showed up here and got us all to do stuff we haven't done in years. When was the last time any of us played Capture the Flag?"

I shrugged, not following where she was going with this.

"That's what I always imagined you guys were doing when I wasn't here," I said. "I had literal FOMO about it."

"We mostly just hung out on the beach and stared at our phones and got drunk," she said. "Which is a lot of fun, I'm not gonna lie."

"Well, I had FOMO about that too," I clarified.

"My point is, like, why do we really want to come back here? Why did you finally come up, after all these years away?"

"To see you," I said slowly, my breath calming in my chest. "And our friends."

She nodded, pleased that I seemed to be getting it. "Why does this place, and all these games and traditions, even mean anything to us at all?"

"Because we do them with each other," I said finally.

"When I say I want you to show up, that's seriously all I want from you. To be with you. To be your friend," she explained. "I'm not here with any other expectations than that. And maybe you don't need to have any either."

She looked down at her phone as I crammed my notebook back into my tote.

"I've got to help Nick with something down at the beach," she said abruptly. "Meet us down there when you finish packing, okay?"

I tilted my head in question.

"Trust me," she said. "I'm pretty sure it was on your list."

35

WHEN MY BAGS were finally packed, I dragged them out to the porch, only to find Mack leaning against the railing, slouched, arms crossed. If this were an eighties movie, he'd be wearing a polo shirt and sweater vest, and synth music would swell as he pushed himself to stand, sauntering toward me in slow motion.

Instead, he golf-clapped as he watched me lug my crap out the door.

"Thanks for the help," I huffed sarcastically.

"I just wanted to see if the city girl could make it on her own," he said as he wrangled my bag out of my hands and brought it down the steps, dropping it onto the grass. "Well done."

"You know you were raised in a metropolis of, like, eight million people?" I asked. "If anything, I should be calling you 'city boy.'"

"Wow, did you Wikipedia Los Angeles, Millen?" Normally, he'd tease me like this with a smile, eyes watching me, eagerly waiting for my next move. Right now, he just seemed sad.

"No. I'm just naturally this smart."

Mack nodded, grazing his teeth against his upper lip in thought.

"We're all meeting up at the waterfront before you go," he said finally. "I thought I could walk you down. And I wanted to give you this."

He reached around to his back pocket and then held up my checklist, and the friendship bracelet, dropping both into my open palm.

"I didn't mean to read it, you know," he apologized. "But it was there on your bed, and I saw my name. I thought maybe it was a letter to me."

I narrowed my eyes at him. "Oh, what, like, 'Dear Mack, stop snooping through my shit, Love, Clara'?" I asked.

He laughed at this.

"I wasn't snooping. I was coming to give you a friendship bracelet, like a fucking lovesick kid."

He said this like he was horrified with himself, his hands pressed against his forehead as he shook his head.

"You weren't supposed to see it," I explained, my heart sinking, the edges of the paper sharp in my hand. "I'm sorry."

"Why, because then I'd know you were sleeping with me just to check off a box?" he said with a wounded laugh. "Though I am flattered that you think of me as your lover."

"Mack, I wrote that list twenty years ago. And I've wanted you even longer than that. You were never just a thing to check off my list." I reached forward and dusted a sprinkling of crumbs off the sleeve of his shirt.

"I just wish you'd been honest with me about it." He swiped a hand across his face, and in the fading light I noticed bits of brownie still in his hair.

"Like you were about buying this place?" I pushed. "Every time I brought up Pine Lake, and Marla and Steve selling it, you just stayed quiet. You should have said something."

"I thought you said shoulds were bullshit," he countered, testing me.

"You know what I mean, Mack." I gesticulated as I talked, enunciating each syllable with a jab of my hands.

"And what did you want me to say, that I feel like a loser who panicked?" He paced along the side of the cabin, kicking the ground with each step. "That I just couldn't get past the idea that maybe I'd fail? Or that I'm terrified I'd screw everything up and ruin this place?"

"I mean, it's a start," I said with a frustrated wave.

"It just felt easier to say no to them. And then I did, and I regretted it immediately, but I couldn't change it. I lost it. I lost this place for me, and for you guys, and for every kid who comes here and loves it more than we ever did. That's fucking embarrassing. I'm *embarrassed*, Clara."

He exhaled, his body softening ever so slightly as if just admitting this out loud was a release.

"It was a lot easier to say yes to my parents," he added. "At least I know I can't mess that up."

He sat down on the steps, and I tucked myself in next to him, finding his hand.

"My ex? Charles?" I said, my voice quieting. "I wasted almost a decade waiting around for him to propose because that's what I thought was supposed to happen when you're with someone for that long. And instead, he dumped me and got engaged to someone else before I even went on an actual date with someone new."

Mack's lips parted slightly and then closed, like there was something he wanted to say but wasn't sure how it would land and changed his mind.

"Okay," he said finally.

"He wears jorts now," I said, like this explained everything. "Jean shorts."

This got a laugh out of him, a low chuckle, then a shake of his head. "What's wrong with jean shorts? You wear them."

I knew he was thinking back to the pair he had peeled off me in the shower, and even in the middle of all this tension I felt heat grow from the center of my body, emanating out through every pore.

"It's not the shorts that are wrong," I said. "It's that I thought I did everything right in that relationship. I played it so fucking safe. And it still failed. *I* failed."

I paused for a moment, steadying my breath in an attempt to slow my pounding heart. "Anyway. I got the letter I wrote myself back on that last night of camp, and it was honestly mortifying. I let my younger self down. So I know what it's like to feel embarrassed. I haven't really done anything that she wanted me to do."

His eyes fluttered across my face, and I knew instinctively what he was doing: checking in, trying to read me, making sure I was okay. This was what I now understood about Mack: Even when he was joking around with people, which was almost all the time, he was always digging a little deeper, taking the temperature, making sure the water was just right.

I rolled my eyes as I ran through younger Clara's list off the top of my head, massaging my fingertips against my throbbing brow. "Experience joy? Do shit that scares me? Have a passionate love affair? I had no idea what life was actually like when I was that age. But it felt like a solution, you know? Some way to get my life back on track now."

There was that look from him again, the one that looked like someone had jabbed a fist in his face, a quick flinch, something adjacent to pain.

"And yes, you did check the lover box for me, okay? And honestly, you deserve it. You are..." I trailed off, suddenly self-conscious. "It's been amazing. Beyond what I've imagined being with someone could be."

He nodded in quiet agreement.

"But you have been everything else on the list too. Joy, and fun, and sometimes scary. I made a list of things I wanted for myself when I was fifteen, and you check every single box."

He pulled his hand from mine and wrapped his arm around my back, hugging me close. I wanted to stay like this forever, my cheek pressed against his chest, solid and steady and warm. He pressed a kiss to the top of my head and let out a ragged sigh.

"I wish you'd come up earlier," he said quietly. "Broken up with your jean-shorts boyfriend years ago."

"I wish you weren't moving back to California," I replied. "And that I didn't have to leave tonight. I wish we had more time."

Around us, the world settled into its usual bedtime routine: colors shifting, water stilling. I loved the simplicity of this evening transformation; beyond just its beauty, it was steady and dependable, even as the seasons marched forward.

"Wow, the leaves are starting to change," I said, noticing a flicker of yellow in the trees behind the dining hall.

"Yeah, it always happens here in late August," he said. "It sneaks up on you."

"I guess it's like you said the other day when we got here. Change is good. I just wish it didn't mean having to say goodbye."

The soft cotton of his T-shirt felt like heaven against my skin, with the heady scent of him lingering just beneath the surface. "Well, let's not then," he said, his hand solid and reassuring against my back.

"How much longer can you stay tonight?"

I looked down at my watch. "An hour?" I guessed. "Ish?"

"That's sixty very long minutes together, Millen," he said. "Let's not waste a single one."

36

"CAN EVERYONE GATHER round please?" Nick said, summoning our group over to him like a cruise director when we got down to the beach. He was still coated in a rainbow of smeared food, and when I looked around, I noticed no one else had changed either. They must have come right from cleaning the dining hall to the beach. "I realize things just got a little out of hand up there."

"That's one way to put it," Eloise muttered, hand wound around Linus's arm.

"But," Nick continued, shooting her a look, "we're going to call a truce for tonight, because we have one final camp tradition to do, and we're going to do it now before Clara has to leave."

I looked at him, confused, until Trey emerged from the boathouse holding a giant container in his arms.

Of course.

"Wish boats?" I exclaimed, hands clasped at my chest.

It was the same box Steve had grabbed for me this morning.

"They *were* part of your plan for the week, right?" Mack said, turning to flash me one of those playful smiles I loved so much.

"Yes," I said with a nod. "But we're supposed to do them tomorrow, on our last night. Like we did as kids. And it's barely dark out."

"Clara, there's no hard and fast rule that says that," Sam said. "Besides, we can do whatever we want."

"Well, you know that's occasionally out of my comfort zone," I replied, thinking of the conversation we'd just had in Sunrise.

"You're learning," was all she said back.

Trey knelt by the box and started digging through, passing out the small white pillar candles, and tiny square pieces of wood, each with a small hole carved in the center.

"Candles?" Linus asked, skeptically examining the slab of cut timber in his hand as Sam passed him a black marker.

"Wish boats, honey," Eloise corrected as she grabbed one for herself. "We write wishes on the bottom of the wooden part. The candles go in the center. If it reaches the other side of the lake without the flame going out, your wish comes true."

"That seems virtually impossible, considering the distance, and the chance that the elements could change at any second," Linus mused, glancing out at the water, as if he could measure the circumference with his eyes.

"Eh, it's all part of the fun, mate," Trey said, offering him a paternal pat on the back. "Sometimes the impossible actually happens."

Trey smiled at me, and I scanned his face for any signs of grief or anger after his blowup with Nick hours earlier in the dining hall. But he seemed at ease, like a weight had been lifted, finally. The only thing on his face was a smear of chocolate sauce.

I wandered over to the edge of the water and plopped myself down in the sand, rubbing my thumb against the unfinished side of my wooden block. Wishes were one of those things that seemed so obvious until you were faced with actually coming up with one. There were endless possibilities, but it had always been impossible to pick just one.

"Hey." I looked up to find Nick standing above me. "Want some company?"

"I'd love it," I said, patting the ground next to me. "Especially if it's you."

He slid in next to me, tucking his knees into his chest.

"So," he said. "Is it too soon to wish for a hot, mysterious man to waltz into my life next week?"

I chuckled, playing with the piece of wood in my hands. "Look, I support whatever you need to do right now."

I leaned closer, nudged him with my shoulder. "Seriously, though. You okay?"

"Honestly? Yeah, I am." He nodded, a relieved look on his face. "I mean, I didn't intend for it to explode like that. We've just been dancing around the topic forever."

"I don't understand. If you knew things weren't good between you guys, why didn't you bring it up with Trey?" I asked as I fiddled with a stone on the ground before tossing it into the water. "I know I haven't seen you in a while, but if there's one thing I know about you, Nick, it's that you're good at talking things through."

"Yeah, that's been, like, the whole problem in our relationship. I'm too good at talking."

He let out a sigh, but nothing about him seemed resigned. He looked content. At peace, even. "I just needed him to own his feelings for once, you know? And speak them out loud. I've been talking for the both of us for way too long."

"Yeah, I got that when you yelled at me about his sneakers," I said, nestling my head against his shoulder for a brief moment.

"In my defense, they are practically brand-new," he said, chuckling. "So in this case, I think my yelling was pretty valid."

"Look," I said, finally managing to eke out a laugh. "The saying goes, 'All's fair in love and food fights.'"

We sat in the quiet for a moment, swatting away mosquitos and deer flies and all the other creatures who came out to drink human blood as night fell.

"I'm sorry I'm leaving you in the lurch," I said. "I said yes to my boss and didn't even think about how you guys are going to get back to the airport."

"Eloise is on it," he said. "She and Linus are going to give us a ride."

"Good." I nodded. "But I'm also sorry for not being around these last few years. For falling out of touch. For being MIA from our friendship."

"Hey," Nick said, reaching out for my arm. "Do you know what my letter said?"

I shrugged, and when his expectant stare didn't leave my face, I gave in with a smile.

"Live laugh love?"

He cackled at this, shaking his head. "Look, the poem was horrible, I'll admit it. But then, at the end, I wrote, 'It's okay if you mess up a lot.' And I remember writing that poem, but I don't remember writing that, or even why I wrote it. But that's the thing that has stuck with me since getting it back."

"Maybe we were all a lot wiser as teens than we gave ourselves credit for," I mused.

"No one expects you to be a perfect friend, Clara," he said gently as he stood with a stretch. "Just a good one. So try to be kind to yourself. You're only human."

Be kind to yourself. Number five on my list. "That is exactly what I told myself to do in my letter," I marveled.

"See?" he said, his face brightening into something big and beautiful, just like his heart. "You were on to something then. You should listen to yourself more often."

We were interrupted by a shriek, and I spun around to find Linus down on one knee in front of Eloise, who was clutching her bright pink face.

"Oh my fucking god!" I gasped, scrambling to stand. "Did you have any idea?" I whispered to Nick, who was now standing next to me, mouth agape.

"Linus may have asked Trey and me when a good time to propose might be," he said. "But he was supposed to do this tomorrow night, so I didn't realize he had changed plans."

"Well, it's a good thing you didn't tell him to do it during the dessert party," I joked.

He choked back a laugh, and then grabbed my hand, squeezing it as we watched Eloise and Linus embrace.

"I'm so happy for them," he said, his voice barely a whisper.

Mack was standing directly behind Linus, and he caught my eye, his mouth in a giant O.

"Holy shit," I mouthed to him, laughing. He shook his head back at me in disbelief, beaming with the kind of shock that only came after moments like this.

Linus was now back on his feet with Eloise wrapped around him, kissing him like it was their last and first time together, all at once.

"There's no ring," he said to her when she finally pulled away. "Because you'd kill me if I picked out something that you hated."

"Oh my god, he's so right," Eloise gushed as Sam immediately embraced her in a hug. "And because we're about to spend all that money on the van."

"What van?" Nick asked, perplexed.

"We just put an offer on a sprinter van we found, near here actually," Linus explained. "We're thinking of quitting our jobs to travel."

"Wait, you're doing hashtag van life?" Mack could barely hold back the look of shock on his face. "You two?"

"Yes, Mack." Eloise stuck her tongue out at him, but the rest of her face was ecstatic, like her freckles might start sparkling at any second. I was so used to her containing her emotions that the sight of her like this still startled me a little. "Weren't you just rattling on about change being necessary the other day? Well, this is me doing that."

Mack acquiesced with a bow of his head, clapping his hands.

"You all need to see what my wish was!" Eloise squealed, still a fountain of utter delight.

Next to her, Linus, so stoic and serious, glowed in a way that seemed beyond human, like all the love he felt was causing him to ignite from the inside out.

She flipped over the small wooden block in her hand, where she'd written "ENGAGED" in all caps.

"You beat me to it," she said, grabbing him for another kiss, and the rest of us *awwww*ed in unison.

Across from me, as everyone else gathered around Linus and Eloise, Mack motioned in my direction. He took off down the beach, away from the boathouse, and I followed, a few steps behind him.

He waited for me at the edge of the water, wish boat in hand.

"What are you wishing for?" he asked, staring at me intently as I laced my fingers through his.

"For you to finally be humble," I teased, glancing up at those bright, kind eyes, that long nose with the little bump, and that hair still sticking up all over the place.

"Too late for that." He chuckled, leaning forward to place a soft kiss on the bridge of my nose as he let go of my hand.

"I know," I said, poking him in the ribs with the corner of my wish boat. "A real waste of my wish."

"Come on in." He beckoned, shuffling slowly into the water, his eyes never leaving my face. "The water's warm!"

I gave one glance back to the shore and then fixed my eyes on Mack's shadowy figure in front of me and followed. Soon the water was just below the edge of my shorts, his body inches from mine.

"Made it," I declared, dipping my free hand into the water and flicking it onto his face. He ducked, but a few drops still landed on his forehead, and on instinct I reached up to wipe them away, tracing my fingers along his creased brow, down the firm line of his cheekbone to those soft lips that were always, always smiling.

"See?" He said it as if running fully dressed into the lake was the most obvious choice we could make. "I knew you could do it."

I didn't need a letter from the past to know how fifteen-year-old Clara would want this goodbye to go. She'd tell me to profess all my feelings to Mack right now, honest and raw and muddled, and demand I throw my car keys into the lake and drag him back to his bed, all my good logic and reasonable life choices be damned.

But I didn't trust that she knew what was right, any more than I trusted myself now, at thirty-five.

And so I did what I knew how to do best: I went along with the plan.

"I should hit the road soon," I said, trying to keep my voice steady, sure.

"Here," he said, flicking a lighter in his hand, the flame appearing like magic as he brought it to the tip of his candle. "Let's make our wishes."

I cupped a hand around my candle as he leaned closer, kissing his candle to mine until the wick sparked and caught fire.

I had written something on the bottom of my wish boat, something that hadn't appeared on any of my previous lists. It was, I realized now, the thing I wanted more than anything.

"Do you think they'll come true?" I asked, knowing full well that mine was impossible, completely out of reach.

"I'm not sure I believe in wishes," he said finally. "I always tell my campers that I think it depends on how badly you want them."

He placed his wish boat onto the water, giving it a small push with his finger as it bobbed out away from us.

One thing. One simple, impossible thing.

More time.

"I'll wish real hard then," I said quietly.

Mack took a step back until he was close behind me, sliding his arms around my waist. I didn't move, taking one last minute to relish the feeling of his body pressed against mine.

Finally, I bent forward, dropping my wish boat into the water.

And then, I let it go.

37

EVERYTHING ABOUT MY apartment felt worse than I remembered. The walls were starker, the color of urine under the dim overhead light. The rooms seemed like they'd shrunk, the furniture drab and dingy. Nothing about this place would ever feel like home.

"Hi, Richard," I said, greeting my sad, deceased plant on the windowsill.

It was a little after midnight, and I promptly got to work unpacking my duffel bag. Then I read over the final pitch document Lydia had forwarded for tomorrow's meeting and washed the wineglasses she and I had left in the sink. When that didn't provoke even as much as a yawn, I wandered into the bathroom and pulled out a clay face mask my mom had sent me as a Christmas gift last year, slathered it on, and crawled into bed for thirty minutes of Tetris on my phone.

I followed it with a sleep meditation, and two melatonin, and still, nothing.

I officially couldn't sleep.

By the time the sun started to creep up around the skyscrapers outside my window, I was showered and dressed, and I still had four hours until I had to be at the Alewife office downtown. If I was in New Hampshire, I'd probably be diving into the lake right now. But I was back in Boston and had to improvise, so I did the next best thing I could think of: I got the largest cup of coffee sold at Starbucks, and I set off walking.

At the end of Charles Street, I crossed into the Public Garden, following a winding pathway past a giant blooming willow on the edge of the park. I said hello to the bronze duckling statues that lived along the cobblestone path and meandered toward the tiny pond in the center of the park.

I wondered what my friends were doing at Pine Lake at that very moment. Sam was probably awake, propped up in bed reading her werewolf romance. Nick and Trey—if they were speaking—were almost certainly asleep. Eloise and Linus were probably, well, not asleep.

Then I imagined Mack, lying in bed with one arm tucked underneath his head, reading a letter from one of his campers. Or maybe he was out on the boat, wind tossing his hair around, watching the dragonflies wake up with the morning light.

I missed him. It was an ache so complete that my body actually throbbed. I considered texting him for a moment, but there was nothing left to rehash, or say, even. Instead, I let my mind play tricks on me as I walked, fantasizing that I could still smell the sweet, dewy grass outside Sunrise, feel the chill of the lake water against my skin, hear the wail of the loons calling in the distance.

I stopped short in the middle of the path, cutting off a runner who cursed at me under his breath. I listened, my ears straining until I caught it again, clearer this time. That sound wasn't just some wish in my head. Somewhere nearby was a loon, in the middle of Boston, no less, warbling like crazy.

I tossed my half-drunk coffee into the nearest garbage can and took off jogging down the winding strip of gray asphalt that led me closer to the water. The pond spread out before me like an oasis, and tucked just under the bridge that bisected its middle was a row of swan boats.

"Am I losing my mind?" I said out loud to a couple of pigeons who pecked at something underneath a bench nearby. But there it was again, the unmistakable high-pitched call of the same birds who had floated alongside me all week in Pine Lake.

I'd never once seen a loon outside of New Hampshire, much less in an actual city, but as I wandered off the path and down the grass, there it was, smack-dab in the middle of the greenish-black water.

I got as close as I could to the edge, close enough that I could see tiny guppies darting along the surface. My eyes trailed the loon as it moved toward the far end of the pond, and then scanned back toward the boats, where I noticed a woman crouched close by. She also seemed to be studying the bird intently, and I took off toward her, as if she might hold all the answers as to how a loon ended up in the middle of the Public Garden.

As her features came into clear view, I realized she was young—no more than seventeen—though the way her brow tensed over her cat-eyed glasses gave her the air of an ancient professor who'd had tenure longer than she'd been alive.

"Hey. Is that…" I pointed, unsure of what I was even asking.

"A loon, yeah," she said as the small black bird disappeared under the water.

"How the hell did it end up in the middle of Boston?" I asked, squinting as I scanned the murky water, willing it to appear again.

"No idea. It just showed up last week." She tucked a strand of short, black hair behind her ear as she looked up at me. "I interned all summer with the Audubon Society so I had to learn a lot about birds. I think it's a female; the male loons are normally bigger."

"Is that why you're here? To take care of the bird?" I asked, and she laughed at this in the particular way only a teenager could, like it was the dumbest question in the world, but they didn't judge you at all for asking it.

"No," she explained, fiddling with the hem of her ruffled, floral dress. "I just did my internship for my community service credit for school. I go to Boston Latin."

"That's a good school," I said, trying to figure out how to make small talk with a teenager. How the hell did Mack do this? I felt like a robot.

"It's fine." The girl shrugged, shifting her scuffed-up black Doc Martens underneath her knees. "I only have one more year, and then I can get out of Boston."

"College?"

"Yeah," she said with a nod. "I'm applying early to Brown."

"Well, I'm actually from Providence originally," I said. "And I couldn't wait to get out of there. So I guess we swapped cities. I'm Clara, by the way."

"Mei," she said with a quick wave. "I live nearby." She pointed at the row of townhouses that ran along the edge of the park. "I come here in the morning sometimes, and a few days ago I noticed the loon."

I scanned the ground near where she sat cross-legged. Beside her were a phone, a notebook, and a small vape pen, and I understood instantly why she was down here by the water at six-thirty in the morning. For a fleeting moment, I recognized everything about her, even though I'd never seen her before in my life.

The need to escape, the itch that came from being this close to the start of adulthood, the childlike wonder that still shared a home alongside her teenage cynicism.

"I like your haircut," I said. "It's cool."

She fingered the choppy edges that stuck out just below her earlobes. "Thanks. I did it myself. My mom hates it."

"Well, that's normally a good thing, right?" I asked.

She laughed. "I guess."

We were quiet for a moment, and in the silence, I noticed the beauty of the gardens around us. Lush greenery, curving, meandering paths, blooming hydrangeas. Even the swan boats, which I'd always written off as cheesy, were lovely up close, delicately carved, and regal in their beauty.

"I haven't been down here since my boyfriend and I broke up," I said. "It's actually kind of pretty."

"You broke up with someone at the swan boats?" she asked with a hint of incredulity in her measured voice.

"Yeah. I don't recommend it."

Then there was a splash in the water, and we both turned to watch the loon, who was craning her sinewy neck as her wings pounded against the water.

My heart thumped with excitement but also worry; it felt like I'd unexpectedly run into an old friend who was now in a very bad place.

"It seems..." I leaned closer to the water, watching its frantic movements. "Like it can't get out."

She nodded. "Yeah, I googled it and texted my boss. I guess loons sometimes get stuck in small bodies of water because they need a lot of space to actually fly away, like a plane on a runway. She's been trying for the last couple of days to take off."

Worry immediately settled itself in my chest. "What if she it doesn't figure it out?"

She shrugged, twisting back around to study the bird. "They'll bring some animal rescue people in to help, move it to a larger lake. But I think it'll get there on its own. Poor thing just needs some time."

We stood there quietly, watching it dip its head underneath the water every now and then in between frustrated attempts at flight. Finally, it stilled and floated, giving up on escape for now. But you could see it in the bird's eyes: She was plotting. She knew it was time to go, now or never.

She just had to figure out how to leave.

38

ALEWIFE'S HEADQUARTERS WERE based out of the second floor of an old mill in the Seaport neighborhood that had—like so many things in this area—been renovated and turned into shiny new offices that still maintained a hint of "character," a nod to Boston's never-ending cycle of new things springing up on top of the very old.

The decor was the cool, corporate version of farmhouse chic: Revived wooden floors glimmered, a sparkling relic of centuries past. Giant iron light fixtures hung from high ceilings, looming like thunder clouds over their open floor plan. The bottom floor of the building housed the Alewife tasting room, which had opened last fall to great acclaim.

I paced in their lobby, sipping an Alewife-branded bottle of water their receptionist had handed me when I walked in, fifteen minutes early. My mind should have been focused on the meeting, but all I could think about was the loon stuck in the pond with those swan boats, Mack puttering around the boathouse, Sam nestled under a giant stack of pillows, all my friends together, sipping coffee on the porch of Sunrise.

"Clara!" Amaya breezed through the door with her arms wide, beelining for me as her salmon-colored silk dress moved with her like a second skin. Behind her, assistant Abe lingered like always, double-fisting giant iced coffees.

"I am *so* sorry I interrupted your time off," she said, grabbing me by the shoulders with a squeeze. "I hope you know I wouldn't have done it if it wasn't an utter emergency."

Her eyes were sincere and regretful, and I knew she hadn't purposely gone out of her way to sabotage this break she'd made me take. But that almost made it worse; despite her speech and her adamant insistence that I log off and focus on myself, Four Points was still expected to come before all of that. Before my own needs. Before me.

"I got a chance to check out the rundown you sent last night, and it looks great," she said with a smack of her lips, freshly glossed in rosy, shimmery pink. "It seems like even just a little break got your creative juices flowing again."

"Yeah, I think the time off definitely helped me figure some stuff out," I agreed with a nod.

"Clara!" Lydia had arrived with the rest of our creative team, clad in a head-to-toe lime-green pantsuit and trendy platform sneakers. She clasped a hand to her mouth when she realized I was having one-on-one time with Amaya and made herself busy with Abe and whatever stack of handouts he'd brought for the meeting.

"Gabbie's beyond excited." Amaya kept chattering away as the receptionist waved for us to follow and then led us farther into the office. "I guess anytime I need you to nail a job, I'll just send you away to the woods for a week. As soon as we're done here, let's talk about your role on the team, okay?"

"Yeah, that sounds great," I agreed, trying to muster up some excitement about my future at Four Points. She was all but announcing that a promotion was in my future, and yet I couldn't bring myself to care.

Thankfully, the sight of the conference room's glass wall set my adrenaline off like a cocktail—shaken, not stirred. The rush of the pitch, the thrill of the sell; these things still drove me. There was nothing quite like knowing an idea you'd created, carved out of thin air and shaped into something special, had the possibility of being brought to life. This was the part of my job I still loved, no matter how burnt out on the rest of it I was.

Getting people excited about the magic of what could possibly be was what I did best. No matter what self-doubt I struggled with, I knew this in my bones. And judging by the confident, beaming smile on Gabbie Pereira's face when we entered, Amaya had been right. This pitch was in the bag.

"Hello, Four Points!" she bellowed, chic silver bangles clanging on her wrist as she waved us in like I'd seen Oprah Winfrey do on old clips of her holiday episodes on YouTube. She had the confident, no-nonsense vibe of someone who grew up dealing with customers in her parents' coffee shop—which was something she touted in almost every interview of hers I'd read. Next to Gabbie were two white dudes with practically identically groomed beards, just trimmed enough to be clean-cut but still long enough to appear rugged, like they could have just been casually chopping wood before walking into this meeting. They nodded their hellos.

"Thanks for having us!" Amaya shuffled around the table to greet Gabbie with a half-hug reserved solely for business acquaintances whom you've gotten drunk with a couple of times.

She slid into a chair directly across from me. "I'll let Clara take it from here, since you're already acquainted with her ideas for your Summer Ale launch."

Amaya's eyebrows knitted together ever so slightly, a flicker of something that looked like annoyance shadowing her face. Maybe the non-stale version of Clara hadn't really been what she'd wanted, after all.

With a nod over to Delilah, who was hunched over her laptop, running the presentation, I stood and pushed my chair in, smoothing the creases in my skirt one last time.

"I've spent the last several days with old friends," I said, delivering the words I'd written in my initial outline, practically word for word. "They're the kind of people everyone deserves to have in their lives, the ones who have cheered me through my best moments and loved me through my worst. Sometimes we don't talk for months or see each other for years, even. But when we're together, the inside jokes come flooding back. The stories and memories we shared and made this last week—sometimes with Alewife beers in hand—had us laughing for hours, often to the point of tears."

I motioned for Delilah to switch to the next slide, the photo I'd taken on our first night back at Pine Lake. My friends were blurry shapes around the campfire, the sun a distant memory behind the pines.

"At one point I thought to myself, 'God, if only I could bottle this feeling.' And that is exactly what Four Points can and will invoke with Alewife's Summer Ale, if you hire our team to launch this exciting new product."

"I absolutely loved that your inspiration came from your own life." Gabbie rolled up the sleeves of her blazer and nodded along eagerly, as Amaya's gaze flicked between the two of us, clearly pleased with how this was going.

"Yes, it all came to me after spending the week with dear friends." I swallowed down the fireball of emotion that was trying to work its way out of my body. I was seated at a pristine table at one of the most influential companies in Boston, facing my dream client. The new account, the promotion—it was all about to become mine. Except I didn't really want any of it. Not anymore.

Maybe I never had.

I just needed to get through the meeting. Then I could figure out my feelings.

One more hour.

I cleared my throat and tried to push forward, focusing on Gabbie's keen face.

"We want to not just tap into that nostalgic summer feeling most of us have, but to offer the promise of new memories to come, with Alewife being the perfect catalyst."

"Love that," Gabbie said as she rested her elbows on the table, leaning in. "The play on friendship as a selling point feels very authentic, which is what we want."

"Yes, it—"

My phone buzzed in my bag, causing me to jump.

"Sorry." I bent down and grabbed my phone, swiping through to the message. "One second, let me just shut this off."

Clara I'm in labor.

My hand shook slightly, head pounding. It was Sam.

For real this time.

"Is everything okay, Clara?" Amaya's voice was soft but pointed, a more delicate and discreet version of, "Hey, pay the fuck attention to our client."

"Yes! Yes. Let me just turn this on do not disturb real quick." I fiddled with my phone as I searched for some way to turn off my alerts. My brain wasn't computing. I'd done this a million times, but for some reason, I couldn't figure out how to stop it from buzzing.

But then again, I didn't want to.

I might not have known what I wanted for my future, but this was certain: I wanted to be there for Sam.

I'm on my way, I typed, before looking up at the room full of confused faces around me.

"You know what? I can't do this." The words came out clear and direct, fearless. Lydia twisted in her chair to look at me, mouth agape.

"Should we take five minutes?" Gabbie gently smacked her hands together, plan settled. "I could definitely use a bathroom break."

I shook my head. "No. I mean, I can't do this pitch, or work on this project. I'm sorry."

"Clara." Amaya's voice was dagger-sharp, swiftly weaponizing my name as a warning.

"I think I'm quitting? Wait, why did I ask that like a question? It's not a question at all. I am. I'm quitting. Amaya, I've loved working for you, but I think it's time for me to move on."

I expected panic, anticipated its acidic rise in my chest. Instead, an eerie calm settled over me. How had I not realized this before?

My work hadn't been stale because I was floundering or bad at my job; it was stale because I didn't want to do it anymore.

"If this is about making you come home early"—Amaya's face was frozen in a smile, which I knew was a cover, her way of staying in control of the nightmare unfolding in front of a client no less—"we can obviously talk about extra vacation time. And I'll expedite your promotion paperwork. I'll have Abe get on that now."

Next to her, Abe was already on his phone, typing away.

"I appreciate that. But I don't want extra vacation time, or a promotion," I said, shoving everything I'd laid out on the table back into my bag. "There's nothing you can give me that will make me stay."

"I am very confused right now," Gabbie said, reaching for her glass and chugging it back in one swift motion. She dragged a hand across her mouth. "Are we not doing this?"

I looked over to Lydia, who offered me an encouraging nod of her head. "Gabbie, I'm so sorry. But this whole idea came to me because of how amazing it felt to be back with my oldest friends, who I hadn't seen in years. Because I'd been so focused on this job, even time away felt like a distraction. But they're not a distraction. They're the people who truly get me, you know? Like even in the moments when I have no idea what the fuck I'm doing with my life. Like right now, maybe. This definitely might be one of those moments."

"Clara." The smile had evaporated from Amaya's face, replaced with steely determination. "I'm counting on you. Gabbie's counting on you. *Lydia's* counting on you."

"I'm actually not counting on you at all," Lydia said, but Amaya didn't even acknowledge her. She kept speaking, slow and deliberate. But a quick glance down revealed her fingers clenching the edge of the table, the tips almost white.

"We're *all* counting on you, Clara," she repeated. "You committed to working on this project. I think we're owed that."

"How about what I owe myself?" I said, my chair squeaking against the wood floor as I shoved it back. "My friend Sam needs me. She's counting on me to be there for her. And that's what I want to do."

I turned back to Gabbie and her bearded henchmen. "I can either stand here and try to sell you on this idea of magical summers and everlasting friendships or go show up for the person in my life who embodies all of those things. Seems like an obvious choice."

Lydia let out a shocked laugh and raised her hands in quiet applause as I stood.

"The plan we've come up with for your Summer Ale is solid, no matter who's in charge," I said to Gabbie. "And we have great people at Four Points. Amaya will set you up with an amazing team. Lydia could probably finish this pitch right now."

"Oh no, not happening," she said, taking one final swig of her water. "I'm going with you. Amaya, this can be my micro-sabbatical, right?"

She jumped up without waiting for Amaya's answer and maneuvered around the table until she was close enough to loop her free hand through my arm, tugging me away from the table as Gabbie and Amaya sat and watched, stunned into a kind of horrified stupor.

"Thank you," I said with one final look at my now ex-boss. "I think the time off really did help me figure some stuff out. But you should call it a 'playcation.' Something fun, if you want people to be excited about it. Micro-sabbatical is so formal and stiff."

I grabbed my bag off of the chair—phone still buzzing inside—and pushed through the conference room door, practically skipping with Lydia down the path of open cubicles that led to reception. My heart pounded out a song inside my chest as we spilled out the front doors, back into the bustling Boston morning.

"You remember how I called you the other day and said you were a genius for going rogue and sending the creative to Gabbie?" Lydia said.

"Yes," I said, still in a daze from what had just happened inside. "Why?"

She looked up at me, glowing. "I was wrong. That? Just now? Was genius. *That* was fucking going rogue."

"Well, I probably should get out of here before I change my mind and go rogue on going rogue," I said, digging into my bag for my phone. My fingers brushed up against something smooth and round and I tugged it loose, holding it up in the morning sunlight.

The medal.

I'd left it with Mack in his Jeep a few days ago; a peace offering, a sign that I believed in him, completely and unconditionally. And somehow he'd slipped it back to me, just like we'd always done. Except this time, I knew it meant something different. Or at least, I hoped it did.

I'm rooting for you.

"Clara?" Lydia asked. "Are you okay?"

"I'm fine," I said slowly, dropping the medal around my neck. "Actually, no, I'm not fine."

"Wait, you're not?" She winced in confusion.

"I'm great. I'm really great, actually. And I need to get to New Hampshire."

"I can split an Uber with you back to your apartment," she said. "Help you pack?"

"Yeah," I said, thinking. "I just need to hurry because, you know, there's a baby coming."

"I can move fast," she agreed, already tapping on the Uber app on her phone. "I'll get us a car."

"Hey, Lydia, let me ask you something," I said, an idea twenty years in the making solidifying in my brain in real-time.

"Sure," she said, glancing up at me expectantly, still in assistant mode even though I was no longer her boss. "What's up?"

"Have you ever cut anyone's hair?"

39

EXACTLY THREE HOURS after I'd hugged Lydia goodbye in front of my building and gunned my Prius through the streets of Boston and onto the highway, I was at the hospital, clomping through the lobby in the heeled sandals that I'd worn to Alewife this morning.

"Can I help you?" The bearded, white-haired man behind the reception desk peered up at me from behind his glasses.

"Oh," I huffed with an anxious exhale, slowing down for the first time today long enough to notice that my heart was bouncing in my chest like a pinball machine, shoulders tight and pinched. Even my butt muscles were, well, clenched. "Yes, please. I have a friend in the maternity ward?"

He pointed a long finger toward the hallway to his left. "Waiting room is thataway," Hospital Santa said and then looked back down at his computer screen.

I hustled off, following the trail of flickering overhead lights down the hallway and around the corner, which emptied out into a waiting room that was decidedly more cheerful than the one we'd crashed in a few nights ago. Cozy couches were positioned around a coffee table, and the walls were a soothing, inoffensive yellow.

And in the middle of the room was Eloise, pacing in a circle as she inhaled a Snickers bar.

"El!" I called, bolting toward her.

"OhmahgodClawa," she said through a full mouth, collapsing against me as I caught her in a hug. "I'm so glad you made it."

"Me too, how is she?" I rushed.

Eloise took a step back, gawking at me. "What. The. Fuck. Did you do to your hair?"

"I had my assistant cut it today." I reached up and felt around the jagged edges where Lydia had attempted her best "French bob," based on pictures she'd pulled up on her phone during the Uber ride to my apartment. "We didn't have much time, so she kinda hacked it off in like, two chops. I might have had a little bit of a midlife crisis this morning. But it's all good. I'm good."

"I like it. I've just never seen you with short hair." She took another bite, pausing to admire Lydia and my kitchen shears' handiwork. "It's, like, crazy uneven, but maybe that's what's cool right now?"

"I think you of all people would know if something was cool," I said, my face breaking out into a massive grin. I was so happy to be back with my friends.

She swatted me away, pretending to be bashful.

"How is she?" I said, refocusing.

"She got the epidural when we got here, so she's been resting, but the doctor thinks she'll be pushing very soon. I'm about to head back in there."

Eloise clenched her teeth together nervously. "I thought labor was supposed to be, like, days long, but this baby is coming fast."

"Her mom must be freaking out," I said.

"Oh, Marla and I have both been on the phone with her all morning," she said. "She's probably getting pulled over for speeding right now."

"And everyone else is—"

"Back at Pine Lake. Mack tried to load everyone into his car, but Sam screamed at them to stay back, and I drove her."

"Oh," I said, suddenly nervous that maybe I'd misread the intention of Sam's texts. "Should I go there, then?"

"Clara," she said, leveling a hard look at me as she licked the chocolate off her thumb. "She literally asked me no less than five times for your ETA."

"Okay, phew," I said, my heart swelling with relief that Sam hadn't just wanted me here, she'd expected me, trusted I'd come. "So should we just wait out here then?"

Eloise let out a laugh as she crumpled up the wrapper, tossing it underhand in the trash can next to us.

"Oh no, my friend. You're about to go help have a baby."

"Me?" I was still in my work clothes, teetering in my uncomfortable heels, and decked out in the light blue suit set that I'd worn this morning, to match the color of our proposed branding palette for Alewife.

"Yes, you," said Eloise finally. "I'm handling music and taking photos."

"Wait. I don't know what to do," I said, my voice pitched with panic. I didn't know the first thing about childbirth, other than every terrible portrayal I'd seen on TV. I was utterly lost, with no plan at all. "I told her I wanted to be here to help, but I didn't mean like, *doing* labor!"

"Clara," Eloise said, her voice firm. "She just wants you in there. You'll figure the rest out."

I nodded, remembering what Sam had said a few days earlier.

You'll know when I really need your help.

I didn't need to know what I was doing. I just needed to be there. To show up.

This, I finally knew how to do.

I lasted all of five minutes in the delivery room in my heels. Soon they were shoved next to the tiny plastic couch where Eloise sat, poised and elegant as if there wasn't a person giving birth a mere two feet away across from her, as she tapped out mood music selections on Sam's phone.

"I had everything planned." It had been the first thing Sam had moaned at me when I walked into the room. She was naked except for a soft, wireless bra, her brow covered in the faintest sheen of sweat, ringlets swept off her face with a headband.

"I know you did," I said, reaching down to stroke her forehead. I knew that feeling all too well.

"Please don't touch me," she grumbled, her eyes glazed over. "I can't handle being touched right now."

"You got it," I said with a firm nod. "I'm here to help however you need me, okay?"

I reached up to tuck my hair behind my ears only to find I barely had anything there anymore. I kept forgetting today's frantic chop in my kitchen, as Lydia hacked my hair off over the trash can. Had it really only been a few hours since I stood by the swan boats, watching a loon flail in the water next to a stranger? It seemed like decades ago, another lifetime, even.

Today had been chaotic and terrifying, reckless and racked with stress. Scary, for sure. But also joyful, and meaningful; and here, right now, full of love.

I didn't need to follow any list to right the course of my life.

It was all here, waiting for me to just live it.

Suddenly, the Spice Girls burst forth from Eloise's phone, and Sam waved a thumbs-up in her direction as she exhaled a low, guttural moan.

I shot Eloise a confused look. "Seriously?" I mouthed.

"It's her labor playlist!" she whispered back as one of the nurses who'd been fluttering in and out of the room appeared to check Sam's dilation, bending over her spread legs.

"If you wanna be my lover, you gotta get with my friends," the Spice Girls warbled from the phone's speaker.

"Clara, this song seems appropriate for your list," Sam said in a husky, exhausted voice as the nurse bent over her. "Maybe you and Mack should dance to this?"

"I cannot believe you're able to make jokes right now," I said, positioning myself next to her head.

"Look, moms really are superheroes," she quipped, closing her eyes. "And the epidural helps."

Sam stilled, quiet, and then winced as she began breathing through another contraction, exhaling out a rumbling "Ahhhhh" as she clenched her hands, gripping the sheet beneath her.

"Honey, you're nine centimeters dilated, and everything looks great," the nurse said matter-of-factly. "The doctor will be right in any minute, okay? It's almost time."

"Time for what?" I asked her.

"Time for her to push," the nurse said, like I should know exactly what was about to happen. "You can help by standing right by her and encouraging her."

I knew what childbirth entailed, obviously. But I also felt completely clueless, desperate to duck out. But there was no leaving. I was here and determined to stay.

"Okay," I said, heart racing. "Sam, is that cool? I'm going to be right here the whole time."

"Give her something to focus on," the nurse said, like it was obvious.

"Oh my god, should we seriously do the hypnotherapy breathing thing?" I asked, my voice rising an octave with panic.

"Just tell me a story," Sam said, cracking a weary smile. "Like when the hell did you cut your hair?"

Another contraction hit before I could even open my mouth, and this time Sam let out a loud "Fuck!" just as the Spice Girls harmonized their final "zigazig-ah."

My life in this moment was nothing like what I would have imagined it to be at fifteen. And yet somehow, I knew in my bones that being here, now, was everything I would have wanted.

40

OLIVE ANNE COHEN was born on a Friday afternoon in August, weighing eight pounds two ounces, and clocking in at twenty inches long. She had a thick mop of black hair, not shocking considering her mom. In the three hours that I'd known her, I'd gathered that her interests included scrunching up her very tiny face, squawk-crying, and pecking at her mom's nipples as she figured out how to nurse.

Sam's mom, Joann, had arrived just as Olive's head was crowning, and now she was holding the tightly swaddled baby against her chest, bobbing side to side in the corner of the tiny recovery room.

"Auntie Clara!" Sam announced when I returned from the vending machine with my red Gatorade and the bag of Doritos I'd inhaled on the walk back. She had a hospital gown half draped over her body, her hair now loose and flowing. The adrenaline of childbirth was still emanating from her; she glowed, rosy and bright, and seemed like she could have leaped out of that bed and polished off one hundred push-ups, no problem.

"Do we need to be quiet?" I whispered, pointing at the watermelon-sized bundle in Joann's arms.

Sam shook her head. "Babies love noise. The womb sounds like a highway at rush hour. They can sleep through anything."

"Speaking of, do you want to try to get some rest?" I asked.

"You know, I thought I would be exhausted, but I feel like I could push a truck across a bridge with my hands," she said, marveling at herself. "Also, my doctor told me I need to try to fart in the next hour, so buckle up."

"Samantha!" her mom scolded with a laugh.

"Mom, why are you acting like we don't talk about farts all the time?" she said before turning back to me with the kind of eye roll only a daughter could give their mom: irritated beyond belief and yet somehow still full of love. "She's trying to impress you."

"I find you very impressive already, Mrs. Cohen," I said, hovering over her shoulder to admire her new granddaughter.

"Thank you, Clara," Sam's mom said, never taking her eyes off Olive.

"She's so beautiful." I couldn't stop marveling at every small detail. Her face was pink and full, eyes shut like little crescent moons. She was everything; a galaxy of stars, a tiny universe. I'd never felt so overwhelmed by limitless love in my life.

"I know," Sam said before taking a sip from a plastic cup full of tiny ice cubes and chomping them in her mouth. "I can't believe I made that."

"Our bodies are seriously amazing," I said, almost like I was just realizing this for the first time.

"Speaking of," Sam continued. "I peed while you were getting food, which, let me tell you, is slightly terrifying after vaginal childbirth. You're lucky you missed it. I scared Eloise away with that adventure."

"Samantha!" her mom said again.

"Mom," Sam huffed. "We all have vulvas here, including Olive. I think it's fine to talk about them."

I pressed my palm to my mouth, suppressing a laugh. I had seen

Eloise on her way out of the hospital before she headed back to Pine Lake, and she did, indeed, mention the drama of Sam shouting with pain from the toilet, trying to pee.

"Do you see why I wanted you here?" she said in a low, conspiratorial voice.

I nodded. "I wouldn't have missed it."

Sam patted a hand on her bed, an order for me to sit on the edge. "You didn't have to come, you know that, right? I really was just texting you because I wanted you to know it was happening."

"Sam." I leveled a look at her. "I really appreciate that you've given me a lot of space to screw up in our friendship. And I also appreciate you giving me the chance to make things right. But yes, I know I didn't have to be here. I wanted to be here."

"Wait, also, your hair," she said as if she had just remembered it was now almost six inches shorter and hacked unevenly to my chin. "You still haven't told me what the hell you did in the last twenty-four hours since I saw you."

"Well, you know, you've been busy," I teased.

"And now I have to sit in this room with a baby and try to pass gas," she said, "so I have literally all the time in the world."

"I quit my job this morning," I said, marveling at how good that felt to say. The entire car ride here I kept waiting for the fear to creep in, for the self-doubt to take over my brain.

I was still waiting.

"Before the pitch?" she asked, sitting up a little straighter as she reached for her cup of ice. "Or after it?"

"In the middle of it," I clarified.

"Holy shit, Clara!" She sucked air through her teeth, flinching at this news. "I thought you loved your job, though?"

"I did," I agreed, shifting a little closer to her. "But I've spent a lot of my time doing everything but letting myself really stop and think about what might make me happy."

"Well, that's always scary to do," she agreed.

"It's terrifying," I said. "Which is what I wrote to myself in my camp letter. I wanted to be doing things that scared me. So thank you for saving it all these years and sending it. I didn't know how much I needed it."

"Somebody's lips are moving again," Joann cooed as she brought Olive back over to Sam, gently resting her in the crook of Sam's arm. Sure enough, Olive's pink lips were puckering, even though her eyes were still closed. Sam pulled down the hospital gown, nestling Olive against her bare skin.

"Can you believe my letter didn't mention having kids at all?" She looked down at Olive, eyes full of wonder, and then back at me. "I wrote that I wanted to live in Rome."

"You still can," I said. "Maybe Olive will be an amazing traveler."

"I'm definitely going to save it for her to read someday," she said. "So when she's fifteen and thinks she has the world figured out, I can remind her that I thought so once too."

I followed her eyes back over to her daughter. "She has so much hair. Like more than Mack, even."

Sam coughed out a laugh. "Please do not tell me my child looks like your boyfriend. To be clear, he is not the sperm donor."

"He's not my boyfriend," I said, though I wasn't sure exactly what we were to each other. "Nothing's changed since I left yesterday. He's still leaving, and now I'm—well, who knows what I'm doing."

"Look. He's definitely your *something*," she said thoughtfully. "Or he's going to be. I tried calling Regan my 'partner' for like, one day, and I hated it."

"Eloise called Linus her partner when she introduced him!" I remembered, and Sam grimaced.

"Well, wife always felt weird too," she said as she focused on guiding Olive's mouth toward her breast. "We used to say 'my person,' which worked. Until, you know, our marriage didn't."

"How do you even know, though?" I asked, and suddenly felt very self-conscious, like I was back in middle school, trying to work out a math equation on the whiteboard in front of the whole class. "I thought Nick and Trey were, like, this perfect couple."

"Well, first of all, perfect is bullshit," Sam said. "Every couple has issues and differences and, honestly, shit they downright hate about the other person."

"Sure," I said. "I guess what I mean is, how do I know if Mack is my person? What if I'm wrong?"

"Clara," she said as she stroked the dark wisps of Olive's hair and then traced a finger lightly across the two perfect arches above her eyes. "There is no way to really know. You just have to trust yourself. And be okay with it, and yourself, if you do end up being wrong."

"There is a part of me that thinks maybe Mack has been my person this whole time," I confessed. "I just never wanted to admit it."

"Aw, look at you!" Sam squealed. "I love that. I love you. I love the two of you together. Why do you think I've been pushing you to get up here every summer?"

"Uh, because I'm your oldest friend?" I guessed. "And you wanted to see me?"

"Okay, fine, that is true," she said with a laugh, just as a nurse breezed in through the door. "But maybe also because you and Mack have been in love with each other forever and so goddamn stubborn about it, so someone had to help you two get there."

"I think that's my cue to go," I said, nodding at the nurse. "But I'll let you know what he says."

"You're going back to camp?" Sam asked.

I nodded, giving her a wink. "I have one more thing to check off my list."

"I hope it's that you're done with lists," Sam teased.

I gave her mom a quick hug before placing a kiss on the top of Sam's head and ogling Olive one last time.

"Hey, Clara?" Sam said as I grabbed my shoes, which were still on the floor next to my bag.

"Yeah?" I asked.

"You're my person, too, you know." I don't think I'd ever seen Sam look more beautiful than right now, and the sight of her melted me, overwhelmed me with all that was good in my world.

I nodded. "You too."

"I've always known that," she said. "I'm glad you finally figured it out."

"Me too," I agreed.

"And I guess if I have to share you," she said, giving me that sly look of hers as she stretched her arm out for the nurse, "I'm okay doing that with Mack."

41

I DEFINITELY DID not need to run from the Pine Lake parking lot directly to the waterfront, but somehow it was the only way my legs would move. I couldn't get there fast enough; I took off the second I parked, barefoot, dashing in the dark past the soccer field and down the rambling field, toward the shores of Pine Lake.

I left everything behind in my car—keys, phone, the shoes I had been wearing this morning. My camp letter, and the revised list I wrote last weekend, remained shoved inside my purse next to the medal I shared with Mack.

All that I had right now was myself. And for once, that felt like enough.

My feet tangled with the hem of my pants as I moved—they were meant to be worn with an extra three inches of heel, but I somehow managed not to trip as I sprinted. Maybe it was the superpower of being in love, or the rush that came from drastically altering your life on a whim. Whatever it was, I was unstoppable. I even managed to yank my suit jacket off my arms, hurling it behind me as I ran.

I had something I needed to do before I found my friends, and Mack, and unfurled the entirety of my heart onto them. This mission involved me ripping at the button of my pants and kicking them off frantically on the beach as if at any moment I might lose my courage. Finally, I waded into the lake in nothing but my camisole and underwear, pushing through the chill of the water and forcing myself to dunk fully underneath.

My breath caught in my chest as the water surrounded me—had it somehow gotten five degrees colder since I left yesterday?—but I forced myself to stay in, taking off with a swift rush of arms and legs, moving straight toward the diving dock. Of all the things I'd listed in that letter years ago, jumping off the high dive had seemed like the easiest thing to complete. All I had to do was swim out, climb up the ladder, and leap.

Simple.

And yet.

Even now, as I clambered up onto the dock, determined, I was utterly terrified. Fifteen feet suddenly felt infinite, a jump into the abyss of nothingness, a place I might never return from.

I gripped the sides of the ladder, the rungs endless above me. But still, I took a step onto the first one and shivered in the cool evening air. I pushed myself up to the next, and then again and again, until I was finally on the high-dive platform, at the top of the world.

All I had to do now was jump.

"Millen!"

Mack was standing on the dock of the boathouse, waving his arms overhead at me. He was a human lighthouse, brightening up the sky, and trying to guide me home through the water.

Adrenaline pulsed up my spine as I lifted an already-pruning hand and waved.

"Hi!" I shouted back.

He dashed inside for a moment, and then ran out through the side door, jogging to the beach. "What the hell are you doing?"

"I told myself I'd jump off the high dive!" I explained. "In my list!"

The boathouse door slammed shut again, and I looked over to find Nick, Trey, Eloise, and Linus gathered on the steps. They were shapeless blobs from all the way out here, especially in the murky, fading light. But Nick seemed to be holding something like a champagne bottle in his hand, and I gave them all a little wave.

Eloise moved toward the beach, hands cupped at her mouth. "I didn't tell them you were coming!"

I gave her a thumbs-up, thanking her for keeping the promise I had asked her to make when we'd said goodbye at the hospital.

Mack's head whipped between her and me as he took a couple steps into the water. He raised both his hands in confusion, and I knew this was it, my first and last chance to finally do the thing I wanted more than anything.

"Mack!" I screamed through the quiet, and somewhere across the lake a dog barked, almost certainly alarmed at the noise I was making. "I love you!"

He stood there, frozen, his hands on his hips, the way he always stood when he was trying to figure things out. Then, without a word, he hopped a few steps deeper into the water and dove in.

He swam faster than when we raced, slicing a straight line through the water, from the shore directly to me.

My chest tightened, terrified, as my hands searched for something to hold on to. But my phone was in the car, and my hair was now too short to be a satisfying distraction. All I could do was stand there and watch as he got closer and closer.

Finally, he was just below me, treading water, staring up at me as he caught his breath.

"Hi," I said again. My voice was peaking, like a microphone too dangerously close to an amp. "I love you."

For once, Mack was speechless. He didn't even crack a smile.

"I'm in love with you. I have been for years," I blathered, peering down at him. "But nothing about it ever made sense to me."

"That sounds bad," he said, the look on his face shifting from blank to skeptical.

"Wait, hold on," I said, resisting the urge to panic, shut down. "Let me figure out how to say this."

I found my breath and steadied myself.

Then I tried again.

"I've been working really hard to follow this path I set up for myself years ago. What I thought I needed to do to live an easy and happy life. I literally tried to check the right boxes, you know? But nothing about any of it actually made me happy."

I was babbling now, almost frantic, the words unstoppable. But with each one, I could feel a lightness settle in across my body. The more I said, the better I felt.

"It turns out, happiness doesn't come from shit being easy. I think—and I may be wrong—it comes from surviving the hard stuff and doing it with people you love. And, I love you. I want to do the hard stuff with you. I don't know how, with you going to California. Also I quit my job this morning, so I have zero plans. I normally think everything out, but I haven't thought this out at all, clearly."

There it was. The truth, in all its messy, humbling glory. Speaking it out loud hadn't been nearly as scary as I'd imagined. It felt complete, like the moment you pressed the final piece into a jigsaw puzzle.

It had taken forever. But suddenly, everything fit.

Mack simply nodded, and then dove underwater, swimming the last few feet until he reached the raft. I peered over the edge of the platform and watched as he scrambled up onto the dock below me and then climbed the rungs of the diving platform ladder, two at a time. He said nothing when he got to the top; all he could do was press a hand to his hip as he caught his breath.

We stood there on the small slab of wood, no more than four feet wide, staring at each other.

Finally, he opened his mouth.

"Millen," he said, "I thought I told you that I can't let you jump off the high dive at night."

I let out a huff. "That's seriously what you—"

He pressed a finger to my lips and then dragged it down to my chin gently. His whole hand cupped my face, the caress of his fingers setting off fireworks along my jaw.

"Because it's not safe. And the idea of anything happening to you, of you getting hurt or losing you, makes me sick to my stomach. I was getting ready to drive down to Boston tomorrow morning to talk to you, but clearly, in true Clara Millen form, you beat me to it."

I laughed, a shallow gasp. It was the sound of pure, sweet relief. "I always beat you."

"I know," he said, nodding. "You do. Just like you beat me to saying 'I love you' first."

His other hand found the curve of my lower back, pulling me a step closer to him. "And I do love you," he said. "A scary amount."

And then he kissed me.

Frantic, like it was the first time.

Tender, like we'd been doing this forever.

Shouts rose up from the shore, a chorus of cheers in the distance.

Our friends were still watching.

"Oh my god," I said as I pressed one final peck to his lips.

"Everyone's in a festive mood," he explained, nuzzling against my neck.

"Because of Sam," I said, assuming they'd dug up a bottle of champagne somewhere for a toast to Olive.

"Yes," he said, and then he took a step back, his eyebrows furrowing into something serious. "But also because Marla and Steve stopped by this afternoon. Turns out the cash offer from our friend Brad the Glamper was dependent on a loan that fell through yesterday. The cash doesn't exist."

"The cash," I repeated back, "*doesn't exist.*"

"That's right," he said with a solemn nod. "That means no tennis courts or yoga studios."

"But what else does it mean, Mack?" I said, not wanting to push him, despite everything I hoped he would say.

"It means I'm going to be spending all day tomorrow filling out a lot of paperwork and hoping that the bank approves my loan," he said.

"Are you..."

He finished my question before I could get the words out.

"What, scared? Yeah, shitless," he said with a shake of his head. "But also, I'm kinda not."

"Yeah." I nodded slowly, reaching down and snaking my fingers through his. "I think I know exactly how you feel."

Our eyes locked on each other, and I knew I was grinning just as hard and foolishly as he was. He pulled me closer, bringing our hands to his chest, and the familiar comfort of his body settled everything inside of me.

"What do we do now?" I asked as I tucked myself against him, his arms protective and warm against my back. We were sixteen feet in the air, in the dark, in the middle of the lake, surrounded by the endless unknown.

"We jump off," he said matter-of-factly. "And swim back to the shore."

"I thought you said I shouldn't do that at night," I countered.

"I said you shouldn't do it alone," he corrected.

When he caught me rolling my eyes playfully at this, he reached up and squeezed my earlobe between his fingertips, giving it a soft tug. "Also, aren't you the one who told me we weren't doing shoulds anymore?"

Before I could reply, we were interrupted by a distinct sound overhead, the steady drumbeat of wings. I looked up to find a loon, stretched out wide above us, gliding through the air toward the surface of the lake. There was nothing graceful about its landing; it skidded to a stop with an awkward flap of its feathers, spraying water in its wake, as it settled with a loud flutter.

But just as quickly, it relaxed and shook out its body. Then it coasted for a moment, nonchalant and at ease, before diving underwater, like it was right back where it needed to be.

"So what are we going to do, then?" I asked him finally, squeezing his hands tightly.

"Millen," he said, smiling at me in that beautiful, familiar way, his teeth grazing his bottom lip, his eyes solely on me. "We're just gonna have to jump. Together."

Epilogue

Dear fifteen-year-old Clara,

Hello from your much older self.

It's currently 12:24 a.m. and I am sitting here on the boathouse deck overlooking Pine Lake. This is still your absolute favorite place in the world. Soon, it's going to be your full-time home. Mack and I have started painting the inside of Bag End, and we'll hopefully be moved in there by late September.

Right now, there is a stack of chairs to deal with, and tables to return to the vendor tomorrow morning. I/you forgot to tip the caterers, too. But we'll worry about all of that later.

Tonight, for some reason, I felt called to sit here in front of the lake and write to you.

Maybe it's because it's been a whole year since I first read your letter to me. Tonight, we just finished up the first wedding here at Pine Lake, and it went off without a hitch. I can still see all the wish boats the guests put in the lake, twinkling off in the distance.

It was beautiful, and magical, and so full of joy. I'm learning on my feet, of course. I don't totally know what I am doing, planning actual events. And I may be doing it all wrong! But that's what I love most about it. The trust people place in me, to do my best for them.

The trust I have to have in myself.

Next month, we're hosting a memorial service for a family in town, whose dad grew up on this lake. I can't think of a more meaningful way to use this place in the off-season.

Right now, all the guests are back in their cabins. Mack just dropped Eloise and Linus off at the Honeymoon Suite via motorboat. He worked on it all year, and it's stunning—a private, romantic one-room cabin, with an outdoor shower and gorgeous views of the water. Most importantly, it's far away from everyone else, right where the original camp buildings used to be.

Cuz, you know. Newlyweds should have some privacy.

Sam's here with Olive—who is about to walk and can already say "hi!"—and Nick brought a date!!! A very sweet guy he met online, and Trey seemed completely fine with it. No drama was detected. Trey hung out with Lydia for most of the night when she wasn't helping me, and last I saw they were on their way to do karaoke in Sunrise. (That's where the after-party is, no surprise there.)

She's been working for me remotely, helping to coordinate our first season of events here, and might come up through the fall. We're still figuring it all out.

But the most important thing is that you're here. *I'm* here.

With the people who mean the world to us.

I think that is what you would have wanted.

No, I know it is.

I still try to listen to your words and follow your advice, but it's funny—I've almost stopped thinking about it. All your hopes, everything you wanted—those things are just a part of me now. Starting my own business is scary every freaking day. But there's joy everywhere.

And Mack has been with me through every single second of it.

I wish I could go back in time and tell you that you got the life you thought you should be living.

It's filled with so much love, laughter, and the occasional disagreement.

(I mean, I am living with Mack, after all.)

You'll just have to trust me—trust us, I guess—we did it. I'm proud of us.

So. I'm signing off because our handsome, very sexy, passionate lover-turned-boyfriend is demanding we deal with storing the chairs tomorrow, and instead go for a late-night swim out to the diving dock. Right now he's pacing around inside the boathouse and making Noodle anxious.

(Noodle is eighty pounds of pit bull and husky and a giant scaredy-cat who occasionally pees when he gets excited, but we love him.)

Mack thinks he's being smooth, but last week I found a small red box tucked inside his box full of his letters from campers.

And if it's what I think it is, and he asks, I'm going to say yes.

Remember—I love you.

XO, Me/You/Clara

AUTHOR'S NOTE

I had the immense privilege of attending sleepaway camp as a kid. Writing *One Last Summer* further reinforced for me how vital camp and the outdoors can be for young people, but also how inaccessible and out of reach these things are for so many. The American Camp Association has an incredible database of accredited camps that serve a variety of populations and needs. It can be found online at https://find.acacamps.org/.

ACKNOWLEDGMENTS

First, my infinite gratitude to anyone who encountered me—even briefly—while I was in the middle of the writing process. Thank you to those who asked, "How are you?" or "How's the writing going?" or "What's new? or "Can I take your order?" and did not cower or run when I launched into a detailed, panicked account of my latest spiral. So many people (Friends! Family! Strangers!) showed up for me with big, open hearts during the writing of this book, and I am so grateful to each and every one of you.

To my editor, Amy Pierpont, thank you for always seeing me, as both a writer and human, and for championing these stories. I've learned so much from you, and every word I write is better for it.

To my agent, Holly Root. I would not be here without your relentless support and wisdom. Thank you for guiding me through every project and for always dropping books off at my house when I need a romance fix. (Which is always, let's be real.)

Much gratitude to Alyssa Maltese and the entire crew at Root Literary, my foreign rights agent Heather Baror-Shapiro, and her team at Baror International, my film agent Mary Pender at UTA, and Kristin Dwyer and the great folks at Leo PR.

Acknowledgments

I am so lucky to work with fantastic people at Forever/Grand Central, including Alex Logan, Grace Fischetti, Sam Brody, and Carolyn Kurek, as well as copy editor Becky Maines. Thank you also to Daniela Medina and Holly Ovenden for the stunning cover design and illustration. You all make this magic happen, and I'm so grateful.

Estelle Hallick and Dana Cuadrado, you are my literal promotional dream team and have my eternal gratitude.

A massive number of generous, wonderful people read various iterations of this book over the years, in all its messy, draft-y forms. Thank you Julia Collard, Jodi Cobb, Ilana Cohn Sullivan, Eirene Donohue, Joy Engel, Maggie Grady Wood, Tanya Doyle Gradet, Erin La Rosa, Gwen Mesco, Jen McCreary, Sarah Monson, Bridget Moloney-Sinclair, Jennifer Pardilla, Katie Reich, Elissa Sussman, Kate Sweeney, Lacie Waldon, and other folks I am almost certainly forgetting. I cannot tell you how much your notes, feedback, and encouragement helped me see the light at the end of the tunnel.

Thank you Jessiline Berry for organizing our Pile writing groups and to the members of the Pile and Write!Write!Write! for your endless support and love. Lori Elberg drew me a diagram of a sexy scene that was eventually cut from the book, but her image will live on in my heart forever.

Kat Lewis, Heather Lazare, and Jeanne DeVito, thank you all for helping me work out how to tell this story.

Sarah Enni, Maurene Goo, Zan Romanoff, Doree Shafrir, and Elissa Sussman—thank you for being my treasured group text and IRL writing safe haven.

And to my ever-growing community of writer friends—what would I do without you?! Getting to know so many of you has been one of the best parts of being an author. Your camaraderie is a lifesaver.

To every person who has picked up a copy of one of my books and read it or shared it in some way, there are no words to properly express my gratitude. I am so thankful for your support.

Eleanor and Lydia, thank you for being the best kids and for sometimes remembering to pick up your wet towels off the floor. There is nothing I love more in this world than being your mom.

Anthony, you are my #1. Thank you for all of it.

Mom, isn't this wild? God, how I wish you were here to see it. It's all for you, but the loon, especially, is for you.

Dad, this book is dedicated to you but really every book I write could be dedicated to you. You are simply the best father, friend, and mentor and put up with more teasing than any reasonable human should; I hope you know how much I love you for it.

I broke my hand very badly in the middle of writing this book, which is truly a hilarious and stupid thing to happen to a writer on a deadline. Thank you to my orthopedic surgeon, Dr. Ray Raven, and the OSS Hand Therapy team for your care and diligence in fixing me back up, and to all the friends who came to my rescue and helped me and my family out during this time.

Hot tip—do not wrap the rope around your hand while playing tug-of-war with a bunch of mom friends. It will almost certainly not go well.

ABOUT THE AUTHOR

Kate Spencer is an author, journalist, and cohost of the podcast *Forever35*. Her memoir, *The Dead Moms Club*, was published by Seal Press in 2017. She lives with her husband and two kids in Los Angeles.

767